T0008079

DIAMOND
CUT

Also by Thomas B. Cavanagh

Murderland

Head Games

Prodigal Son

DIAMOND
CUT

A NOVEL

THOMAS B. CAVANAGH

OCEANVIEW PUBLISHING
SARASOTA, FLORIDA

Copyright © 2024 by Thomas B. Cavanagh

All rights reserved. No part of this book may be reproduced in any form or by any electronic or mechanical means, including information storage and retrieval systems, without permission in writing from the publisher, except by a reviewer who may quote brief passages in a review.

This book is a work of fiction. Names, characters, businesses, organizations, places, and incidents either are the products of the author's imagination or are used fictitiously. Any resemblance to actual events, businesses, locales, or persons living or dead, is entirely coincidental.

ISBN 978-1-60809-595-7

Published in the United States of America by Oceanview Publishing

Sarasota, Florida

www.oceanviewpub.com

10 9 8 7 6 5 4 3 2 1

For Emilie,
who loved to read more than anyone
I have ever known.

We love and miss you, Mom.

*A diamond with a flaw is worth more than
a pebble without imperfections.*

CHINESE PROVERB

DIAMOND
CUT

CHAPTER 1

I USED TO HAVE SEX for a living. Now, on a strictly part-time basis, I get paid not to. The guy I was getting paid to not sleep with tonight was a forty-one-year-old married father of two named Jeremy Knox. Of course, he had no idea he wasn't getting lucky tonight. I had met him once before, two days earlier. I was told that he often liked to spend his lunch hour at a local Hooters knockoff called Cheerleaders. The place was wedged between a Chipotle and a Panera Bread on the restaurant row area of University Blvd. out by the University of Central Florida. So, two days ago, I put on a little too much makeup and slipped into a dark suit with a skirt two inches shorter and heels an inch longer than I would normally wear in polite company and headed out to the east side of town. Not that the clientele of Cheerleaders exactly qualified as polite company.

I had been given his photo and background file by a fellow private investigator who had been hired by Jeremy Knox's wife. It seemed Mrs. Knox suspected Jeremy of fooling around and, if her suspicions were correct, she wanted evidence to take with her into divorce court. I was the bait and Jeremy was the tuna.

At the risk of being immodest, I'm not bad bait. At thirty-one, I'm still plenty young for ol' Jeremy and can still fill out a tight business suit. I keep in shape and the heels did make my calves look good. My shoulder-length hair is styled simply but tastefully, so that it frames my face without making me look like I'm wearing a helmet. I had never colored my hair, instead feeling generally satisfied with my natural sandy-blonde.

The restaurant was filled with basically two types: college boys from nearby University of Central Florida and government contractors from the dozens of training and simulation companies in the adjacent research park. Although I wasn't the only female customer, it wouldn't be an exaggeration to say I was in a minority of no more than ten or fifteen percent. So, while it wasn't completely weird for someone like me to stroll into Cheerleaders at 12:15 on a Tuesday afternoon, I knew I would at least attract a few looks. Fine. That was exactly what I wanted.

I caught a lucky break. Jeremy sat alone at the bar with a menu in his hand. The file said that he often spent his lunch hour here with some buddies from work. But sometimes alone. Fortunately, today the buddies were absent. Sure, if he had been in a group maybe I could have slipped him my number with a "hey, I noticed you, call me" note, but it's always better to fish for tuna alone, one-on-one. So, I sidled up and took an open seat next to him.

I knew that he noticed me. A girl can tell. I crossed my legs. Damn, my calves *did* look good. If these heels weren't such a pain to walk in, I might wear them more often. A buxom coed in a tight black t-shirt and nylon shorts delivered him a burger and fries. She handed over a menu and went off to pour me a diet cola. I saw Jeremy try not to check out the waitress's perky backside. But he just couldn't help himself. Hell, I could barely help myself. It was an impressive derriere.

"So, what's good in here?" I asked, offering Jeremy my best disarming smile.

"Pardon?" he said, quickly blinking his gaze away from the nylon shorts.

I waved the menu. "What's good? Any local specialties?" I had just intentionally established that I was from out of town and that I was extroverted enough to strike up a conversation with a complete stranger. Plus, with the literally dozens of nearby dining options, I was willing to come into this classy place alone for lunch.

"Well," Jeremy said. "It's kind of a wings place. But . . ." He leaned over conspiratorially. "I prefer the burgers."

"Thanks for the tip." I gave him a wink and a smile. "Maybe I'll just stick with a salad." They can say whatever they like about not caring. Most guys still expect women to eat salads. I extended my hand to shake. "Hi. I'm Karen." Of course, my name is not Karen. Not even close.

He took my hand and a smile of unexpected possibility bloomed slowly across his face. "Jeremy."

"And what do you do, *Jeremy*?" I asked and plucked a french fry from his plate. Then I smiled and took a bite.

His smile widened at the boldness of my eating off his plate. "Uh, I'm a program manager for Aeron Sim. We build training and simulation systems. Mostly for the military."

"Well, that sounds pretty cool." I then proceeded to share the lie that the other P.I. and I had concocted. I was posing as an account manager for an educational software company who was trying to get the university to buy one of my company's systems. I was only in town through the weekend. I was based in California—as far away from Florida as possible, offering fewer chances of messy entanglements. I suggested that we move from the bar to a table, to which Jeremy eagerly agreed.

I steered him toward an open seat that offered an unobstructed view from the table where my colleague sat, discreetly recording us with a hidden camera. I noticed that he, too, had ordered a burger.

During the course of the next seventy minutes, I managed to make Jeremy feel like the most interesting guy in Orlando, while simultaneously working my way through a surprisingly large Asian chicken salad. I made sure to touch Jeremy on the arm a few times for the camera, laughing at his somewhat lame attempts to be amusing, getting my flirt on. I knew before it was over that I had my tuna on the hook. We parted with a handshake that I held too meaningfully long and an agreement to meet after work the next day for drinks at my hotel. I could just imagine the story he was going to tell Mrs. Knox about having to work late on a deadline or meet with military clients who were visiting from D.C.

So I now found myself sitting in the bar at the nearby Hilton, nursing a club soda and cranberry, waiting for Prince Charming to show up. My P.I. colleague, a guy named Mike Garrity from a competing but friendly agency, sat across the room, hidden camera pointed at me. This time I was wearing a wire to record our conversation in the likely event that Jeremy elected not to exercise his right to remain silent. I took a sip from my drink and spotted Jeremy entering the lobby.

He located me quickly, perhaps even eagerly, and sat across a low cocktail table. He ordered a gin and tonic from a passing waitress and leaned back in his seat, smirking at me.

"Hello again," I said.

The smirk widened. "This is a nice place. You're staying here?"

"That's right." I sipped from my club soda and cranberry, pretending it was alcoholic. "Are you hungry?"

He smiled wolfishly. "Starving."

I faked an equally wolfish smile, but it felt awkward, like I was contorting my face after biting a lemon. "The restaurant here is pretty good. We could grab a bite."

"Sure . . ."

His drink arrived and he downed half of it on the walk across the lobby to the restaurant. We found a seat and I saw Garrity shift his position in the bar to get a better shot of our dinner.

For the second time in two days, I broke bread with this creep. I suppose he was attractive enough. His hair was mostly still dark brown with a few gray flecks sprinkled in. His smile was confident but with an almost charming boyish quality. His clothes were decent, department store Ralph Lauren, with nice, patterned socks and a pair of Rockport shoes. But despite his respectable looks, the fact that he was a married father sitting here presumably expecting to bed a stranger just made him odious to me.

As the meal wore on, and he drank three more gin and tonics, all pretense regarding why he was here began to vanish. And I, in turn, began to get more and more anxious about the inevitable trip upstairs. You see, I don't do hotel rooms. I've only been on the inside of a hotel room maybe twice in the last six years and never overnight. I won't lie on a hotel bed. Never again.

The mere idea of entering a hotel room made me fidgety and, as the meal wound down, I felt my heart rate start to increase, pounding my temples. When we agreed to the job, Garrity had told me that he needed a shot of us entering the hotel room. As soon as the door shut, I could pop back out and make my escape, but video of the two of us entering the room and closing the door was what Mrs. Knox was paying for. So I knew from the beginning how this gig would end. But I thought I could handle it. I'm a professional, right? *A professional* . . . That was an unfortunate term to occur to me in this context. The more I thought about the elevator ride up and the long walk down the hall to the room Garrity had booked for the night, the more nauseous I felt. I pushed my half-eaten chicken away and realized that Jeremy was saying something. I forced myself to attend to the job.

"You really are hot, you know," he said, not quite slurring, but definitely not entirely sober. "But you know that. Hot women always know they're hot. So, no boyfriend back in California? Really?"

I swallowed the golf ball of nerves that was forming in my throat and forced a smile. "Really. Just me and my cat."

He broke out the devilish grin. "Just you and your cat . . . So . . . what kind of pussy do you have?"

Oh brother. This kind of witty banter couldn't possibly be how he had courted his wife. I looked away so he didn't catch my eye roll. The thought of the hotel room suddenly squeezed me hard in the stomach. I coughed into my hand, trying not to gag. I felt like I had snakes squirming in my gut. I excused myself to the ladies' room where I spent four minutes in a bathroom stall, attempting to calm my breathing, preventing myself from hyper-ventilating. If I blew this gig because of my issue with hotel rooms, I might not get paid. Billy was always threatening to fire me. Brother or not, he might finally go through with it. This was my job. My career now. With my background, my options were limited. Plus, I actually liked being a private investigator. I told myself to pull it together.

I splashed some water on my face—I was sweating at my hairline. I felt a bead trickle through my hair at my temple. Then I dried off and fixed my makeup. I took a deep breath and pushed back out into the hotel lobby. I marched up to the table and, before I lost my nerve—or puked—asked, "Are you ready to come upstairs now?"

Jeremy paused for just a beat before responding. "I've been ready since I met you, baby."

"Good. Let's go."

I turned and started walking. As Jeremy hastily threw some cash on the table for the drinks and dinner, I saw Mike Garrity slide out of his seat in the lobby and head up the stairwell. He had booked a room on the second floor so he could get up there and into position while we waited for the elevator. I hadn't given him any warning and he was now having to hustle. But I had no choice. I was losing my resolve and had to get this over with before it was completely gone.

Jeremy and I stepped into the elevator and found ourselves alone. He immediately pushed himself up against me and kissed my neck and ear. I let him. I could take his touch for one floor. I have endured much worse for much longer. I sent my mind to the blank white room where I always used to send it, back in the day, and flipped the internal switch that made my insides go dead. It was all way too familiar, too easy to go back to that place in my life. I barely noticed the elevator doors opening.

We stepped out into the hallway and made our way down to the room, passing the vending alcove where Mike Garrity was now positioned with his camera. Jeremy pawed at me all the way down the hallway. I stopped at the door to the room, my heart thudding in my chest at the thought of stepping inside. I couldn't do it. I needed a moment, I told myself. I needed to summon the courage to open the door. I turned around and leaned back against the door. I robotically put my hands on Jeremy's hips. I lifted my chin, exposing my neck. We needed to give Mrs. Knox a good show, after all. And Jeremy obliged. He could no longer claim entrapment. He was just a garden variety pig now. He dove in, rubbing his hands up my thighs and over my breasts, kissing my neck from ear to collarbone. He tried to kiss my lips, but I turned my head. No kissing on the mouth. Ever.

Despite my anxiety about entering the room, I also felt physically numb. It was almost too easy to make myself feel nothing, to turn my body to stone. Years of practice had made it almost automatic. Like riding a bike, right? I heard Jeremy's eager breathing in my ear as if it were coming from far away, happening to someone else. Perhaps it was happening to someone else—me, six years ago, eight years ago . . . But, no, it was happening now, to me, in this hallway. Jeremy unbuttoned the top of my blouse. That suddenly grounded me in the moment, and I forced myself to turn around. He pressed himself against me from behind and grabbed my breasts. I inserted the key card in the door and turned the handle. And then we were across the threshold, the door shutting behind us.

I felt like I was moving underwater, in slow motion. I stopped just inside the room. Jeremy moved past me and continued over to the bed. He sat and leaned back on his elbows. I remained frozen where I was. I knew I needed to turn around now and leave—Garrity had the footage he needed for Mrs. Knox. My work was done. But my feet were frozen to the floor. This hotel room, it was so similar to that one six years ago. It, too, had been a Hilton . . .

"It's okay, baby," Jeremy said. "Don't be shy. I won't bite. Unless you like that."

I had to leave. I had to get out of here. But I couldn't move. *Six years ago . . .*

Jeremy got up from the bed and came over to me. He took my hand and pulled. But I didn't budge. He pulled a little more insistently.

"Come on, Karen. It's okay."

I managed a hoarse whisper. "No . . ."

Jeremy cocked his head in a vaguely canine way. "No? What do you mean, *no*? I mean, we both know why we're here."

"No . . ." I reached my other hand for the door handle.

"You're not gonna get me all the way up here and say no now. Come on. I promise I'll make it worth your while." Jeremy pulled my hand even harder.

"No!" I screamed, my vision suddenly colored crimson. A jagged memory of blood everywhere. Blood spraying in a pumping squirt across my naked torso. White sheets a slick shiny red. Warm blood covering my hands, running in rivulets down my forearms.

Jeremy grabbed both of my wrists. "Hey, relax. Shhh. Calm down, you crazy bitch."

I tried to pull loose, but his grip was too tight. I twisted my arms, but he was too strong. He was now pulling me into the room, toward the bed. I could see the bed, covered in blood . . . *No . . . Not again.* Instinctively, I brought my knee up, driving it as hard as I could into his groin. I yanked my arms free and thrust the heel of my right palm up under his chin. I felt his teeth clack together and his head snap back. He stumbled backwards, dazed.

I turned and threw myself out the door and directly into the path of Mike Garrity, who was charging down the hall. He grabbed my arms to steady me.

"Sandra—are you okay?" His eyes were concerned, searching mine for trouble.

I managed a quick nod but was unable to say anything.

We skipped the elevator and headed down the stairs. Five minutes later, Garrity was driving me in his pickup to a nearby Starbucks so I could collect myself. He bought me a water and a decaf latte and we sat at a small round table in the corner for several long minutes before he finally broke the silence.

"I'm sorry," he said. I looked up at him, unsure of how to respond. "I shouldn't have made you go into the room with him. I could have gone to the client without that. Even without that, the footage was good. The audio was good. It would have been more than enough."

"It's okay," I said quietly. I didn't tell him about my issues with hotel rooms, but he probably knew. Garrity knew me then. He was there six years ago as the investigating detective, standing on the blood-soaked carpet, before either one of us had ever considered becoming private investigators. He knows who I am and what I was.

"As soon as I meet with the client and get paid, I'll send Billy a check for the job. All right?"

I nodded. "All right."

We sat in semi-amiable silence until our coffees were finished. Then Garrity drove me back to the hotel for my car. We made sure that Jeremy Knox was nowhere around before I slipped out of Garrity's pickup and into my Honda.

"You gonna be okay?" he asked.

"You know me," I said, which didn't answer his question. I kept the radio off and the windows open on the drive downtown to my little 1940s Craftsman bungalow. The warm nighttime spring air in my face helped. I imagined it blowing the events of the evening away so I didn't bring them into my home with me. They didn't belong there.

Tyler was already in bed when I came in, but Laura was up watching *Dancing with the Stars* on TV.

"How'd everything go?" she asked.

"Y'know. Fine. Do we have any wine?"

"Fine, huh? Yeah. There's a half bottle of Chardonnay in the fridge."

I poured myself a full glass. "How was your evening?"

"No problem. Tyler did his homework and we even read a chapter in that mouse book."

"*Stuart Little.*"

"Right. That's what I said."

Laura was ten years older than me but looked twice that. She appeared perpetually worn out, which, in truth, she probably was. She was in the life a lot longer than I had been, and that lifestyle will definitely chew you up. It certainly chewed her up. It almost literally killed me. Laura's unkempt brown hair was lighter at the roots, but she was unconcerned and made no attempt to hide it. My deal with Laura was free room and board as long as she stayed clean and sober and took care of Tyler whenever I wasn't around, the occasional evening glass of Chardonnay notwithstanding. My job often had me working weird hours, so I needed to know that Tyler was safe and fed. For the past three and a half years the arrangement had been working out. Knowing Laura as I did, I was keeping my fingers crossed.

I took my wine and tiptoed to Tyler's room. I quietly opened the door and slipped inside. He was visible in the dull, blue glow of the crescent moon night-light. He was lying in his bed, eyes closed, lips just barely parted. He seemed so motionless that I momentarily panicked and laid my hand on his chest to reassure myself that he was still breathing. His six-year-old chest gently rose and fell, and I felt the tender, rhythmic thumping of his heartbeat beneath his rib cage. I brushed a blond lock of hair away from his face and lightly kissed his cheek.

I crawled across the room and leaned my back against his dresser, pulling my knees tight up against my chest. Sipping my wine in the darkened room, I spent the next thirty minutes gazing silently at the very best thing I have ever done, a truly good thing to have come from a very bad life.

CHAPTER 2

THE NEXT MORNING, I walked Tyler the several blocks to the downtown Catholic school where he attended first grade. I loved that time with him. We held hands when we crossed the brick-lined streets, the dappled morning light peeking through the branches of the tall live oaks that hung over the sidewalks. Tyler wore his little white polo shirt with navy shorts and carried a Spider-Man backpack secured over his shoulders. He usually told me about what happened the day before or what he was looking forward to that day. Music, art, recess, and science were his favorites this week. He loved his teacher and, as far as I could tell, she loved him back. All his days were filled with wide-eyed possibility, and I so envied that. I tried to let just a little rub off on me. But my emotional calluses were so thick. Sometimes I felt like I would never regain any sense of that wide-eyed possibility. If anyone could ever bring it back to me, it was Tyler.

Spending that time with Tyler had put me behind schedule. When I finally got into the office, Billy was already there. He was smoking, as usual. I made a big show of coughing and waving my hands when I came in.

"You're late," he said.

"Good morning to you, too," I replied.

"Just 'cause you're my sister doesn't mean I won't fire you." His usual greeting.

"I know, Billy. But if you do that, who else would ever bring you Munchkins?" I plopped a carton of donut holes down on his desk. He offered a noncommittal grunt, which was how he expressed gratitude. He immediately popped two donut holes into his mouth.

"Did you finish that job for Garrity?" he said through his mouthful of Munchkins.

"Yep."

"You get the goods?" Another donut hole.

"Yep."

Another noncommittal grunt. Billy was my older brother by more than six years. His wiry black hair was noticeably thinning, and he was carrying forty pounds more than he should, but somehow, he made it work. Although he acted gruff, he had always been there for me and took care of me after everything happened six years ago. Truth be told, he had always taken care of me. He was the only one who had ever taken care of me. He was the one who made sure that Ryan and I were fed, that our clothes were washed, that we went to school most days when Mom was gone or unable to get out of bed.

He was also the one who, a few years ago, encouraged me to get my Florida private investigator CC intern license, which allowed me to work for him under his MA license. He needed the help, and I needed a job. I liked to think that it had worked out well for both of us.

Billy wasn't flashy and neither was his agency. We operated out of a nondescript office in a low-rent commercial building in a quasi-dodgy part of town. For his whole life, he always wanted to be a P.I. and, to his credit, the success of Class A Investigators was due entirely to him. The secret of his success was that he wasn't afraid of the grunt work—the workers' comp cases, the insurance and law firm stuff, process serving, even working the computer databases for hours at a time. And I was happy to take whatever assignments he gave me.

But he had never forced me to do the cheater stings. I did those voluntarily. It was one of the few areas where I could bring some added value to the agency. For as long as I was young enough and my looks held, I could occasionally dangle myself in front of unfaithful men to bring in revenue. It was usually easy money. When I first started doing the cheater stings, I wondered about the ethics of entrapment. But it quickly became clear that in the vast majority of the cases, there was a very good reason why the spouse or girlfriend was suspicious. Simply put, their husbands or boyfriends were philandering pigs. And, every once in a while, the guy turned out to be a decent human being and stayed faithful. I was always secretly glad when I got rejected. But, of course, I told myself that it was because he loved his wife and not because he found me unattractive.

Usually, the stings went off without any complication. Last night's flashback in the hotel room was an anomaly. The room looked so much like that same room six years ago. I hadn't had an episode like that in a long time. I would need to be more careful.

After Billy swallowed what might have been his twelfth donut hole, he tilted his head at me, remembering something. "Hey. You got a call. Before. She wouldn't leave a message with me. She only wanted your voicemail."

"Okay. Thanks." I slid behind my desk and punched in the code to access my system voicemail. In another moment, I heard a woman's recorded voice. Her accent was southern, almost twangy. She spoke haltingly, nervously, like she was looking over her shoulder.

"Hey, Diamond. It's me. Collette. Collette Green . . . Y'know, *Glitter*? Listen, I need to talk to you about somethin'. It's important. Real important. I'm gonna be at the Florida Mall at lunchtime, around noon. Maybe you can meet me in the food court. I just . . . I need your help. I don't know who else to call. Please. Okay? I'll, uh, I'll see you then. Okay. Bye."

I held the phone receiver frozen against my ear for an extended moment. *Hey, Diamond* . . . It had been a long, *long* time since anyone had called me that and, after my flashback last night, the timing was eerie. Just the mention of that name made my throat go dry. I listened to the message again before deleting it. I remembered Collette Green. We had shared an apartment for a few months with several other girls back in . . . Jeez, was it seven years ago or eight? She was younger than me by a few years, maybe more than a few. She was a new girl, fresh off the streets. A runaway who had made her way south from Georgia or South Carolina. I thought it might have been an Atlanta suburb. She had acted tough, but I knew she was scared. She had asked me a lot of questions. If she was still in the life, she certainly wouldn't be new anymore.

Billy had me doing filing and employment background check paperwork all morning, but I remained distracted by the message. I didn't know how she found me here, but I supposed it wasn't that hard. I wasn't hiding.

Hey, Diamond . . .

I told myself to ignore it. I had cut ties with all aspects of my former life. I couldn't meet Collette at the mall. There was nothing she could say that would be good for me. Whatever she wanted to tell me would only be bad, would only bring some ghost from the past back into my new life to haunt me. My life was different now. I had Tyler. *I* was different now.

But the more I thought about it, the more I wondered if I *needed* to confront her. To confront what she represented. Last night's episode had proven that, in some way, I was still not over what happened to me. The bloodstains were still there, even if I was the only one who could see them. Maybe facing Collette would help me remove those stains, exorcise my hidden demons.

Or maybe I was just rationalizing my own curiosity. Because, as much as I hated to admit it, I was curious.

Either way, I knew that I would be eating lunch at the Florida Mall food court today.

*   *   *

I spotted her easily. Her hair was darker than I remembered, dyed perhaps a little too black. Unnaturally black. She was picking at some lo mein and looking up occasionally. I remained out of sight for a few minutes, watching her, watching the people who passed by her, wondering if this was some sort of elaborate setup for me. But then I told myself I was being paranoid. A setup by whom? For what reason? I couldn't think of any. But, nevertheless, I got the sensation that something ominous was waiting for me at that small table with the paper napkins and Styrofoam cup of Diet Coke.

Even from this distance across the food court I could see that she was wearing too much makeup. Her eye shadow was too blue and her lips were too red. She was still pretty, though, under all that makeup. She sipped from her drink and went back to her noodles. I decided that she was probably alone and stepped out from around the corner where I was spying on her. I approached the table.

"Hello, Collette," I said.

She looked up from her food and offered a shaky smile. "Hey, Diamond."

"Don't call me that. That's not my name."

She considered me for a brief moment and her face registered concern at making a faux pas. "Sorry. *Sandy.*" Her accent was dripping with sugary southern syrup. In my hypersensitive mind, I translated her likely sincere apology into *It doesn't matter what I call you. I still know who you are.* "Why don't you have a seat?"

I sat across from her.

"Aren't you eating?" she asked.

I had no appetite. All desire for food left my body as soon as I heard her message earlier today. "Maybe later," I said. "So, how are you?"

"Oh, you know. Same old, same old. Still doin' that thing we do."

She had included me in the life I left long ago by using the word "we." I almost corrected her but decided to let it go. I didn't want to seem overly defensive.

She was probably only in her mid-twenties, but somehow she looked older. At first I couldn't put my finger on it. It wasn't her skin, which was almost flawless. No lines at the corners of her mouth. Her hair, while probably dyed, was cut well and looked good. Her clothes—a simple but nice t-shirt and a pair of jeans— looked almost stylish. But then I saw it. Her eyes. Her eyes were old. They were tired, and they had seen too much.

"You look good, honey," she said. "Really."

"Thanks." I took a deep breath. "I almost didn't come."

"I wondered if you would. But I'm glad you did."

"Why?"

"Because I need your help."

And there it was. This was the part that would end up being bad. I didn't yet know how, but somehow, some way, there would be trouble for me.

"Go on," I said.

"There's this new girl, a little Asian thing, I think from Thailand or the Philippines or Vietnam or somewhere. Her online name is Spice but her real name is Naomi. At least that's what everyone calls her. Naomi Nguyen, which ain't easy to pronounce, believe you me. But she taught me how to say it right." I could see that Collette was nervous. She was talking just a bit too quickly, looking down at her food. She tried sipping again from her drink, which was empty. "Anyway, she's been gone for over a week now and I'm worried. We're all worried."

"And . . . ?"

". . . and . . . we need somebody to find her."

"Me."

"That's right."

I snorted derisively. "You want me to find some poor girl so I can bring her back to a life of prostitution? Hell, if she got away, good for her. And even if I did find her, I'd give her some money and help her to keep going. You're asking for help from the wrong girl, Collette."

Collette shook her head. "No, you don't understand. We're afraid something happened to her. We're afraid maybe, you know . . ."

Ah. I got it now. She thought that this Naomi girl might be dead. I sat back in my seat, feeling like a heavy stone was settling in the pit of my stomach.

"Why do you think that?" I asked, my words careful and deliberate. "How do you know she didn't just run away? It's not exactly rare. Lots do." I looked at her meaningfully, reminding her of her own runaway past.

"Because, she never once talked about it. As far I know, she had nowhere to run *to*. She left all her stuff. *Everything*. All her clothes. Her makeup. Jewelry. Her shoes."

I shrugged. "Wouldn't be the first time a girl took off, leaving everything behind. Maybe a social worker found her. Maybe getting away was more important than shoes."

"Yeah. I know. But . . ." She took another sip from her empty cup. "See, she has this stuffed animal. A rabbit. I swear, she loves this thing like she's three years old or something. I think maybe her mother gave it to her when she was little. Anyway, she sleeps with it every night. Holds it when she's on the couch watching TV. There was this one time when she couldn't find it and she freaked out. And I mean *freaked*. We finally found it in the dirty laundry, but by then she was hysterical, in tears. I mean, she was literally shaking."

"Okay . . ." I said, knowing what was coming next. Collette reached down and pulled a dingy stuffed animal from her oversized purse. It was a mottled tan rabbit with floppy arms, legs, and feet. She placed it gingerly on the table, almost as if she might break it. I sighed and lifted it up, squeezing it slightly. "And I suppose you're going to tell me that she would never leave Mr. Cottontail here behind, right?"

"Yeah. Except his name is Thỏ. That's what she calls him. I think it means bunny or something."

I held Thỏ closer and peered into his shiny black button eyes. "I don't know, Collette..."

"I have money," she said quickly. "All the girls pitched in. Well, most did. We can pay you."

"I just... it's complicated." I looked across the mall. Of course, at that moment, I happened to see three young Asian tourist girls walking by, shopping bags filled with American goodies. "What about Omar?" I asked. "Is he still around?"

"Yeah... But you know Omar ain't gonna spend any time or money looking for her. To him, girls come and go. He's probably already got someone to replace her. And then, there's what he'll do to her if he does find her. You remember. He'll probably make an example out of her. Runnin' away costs him money and makes him look bad to his partner. We need to find her first, if she can be found."

I sighed, watching the tourists disappear into a candle store. "I don't know, Collette..."

"Sandy, please. We need *you*. You're the only one who can help. You know we can't go to the police. Plus..." She took yet another nervous sip from the empty cup, then looked down, avoiding my gaze. "You, of all people, *know*... The last time we saw her she was heading out to meet a client. But she never came back." Collette looked up and directly into my eyes. "That could've been *you*, honey. We both know it. And if it had been, you would've wanted someone to look for you. To care."

Collette's words hit me like a concussive blast. Although I remained still and calm on the outside, inside I had been thrown back against a wall. *That could've been you.* She was right, of course. I could have easily disappeared that night six years ago and never been heard from again. Would anyone have cared? I honestly didn't know. Maybe my brothers. Maybe. Perhaps one or two of the other girls. That was it. But no one would have searched for me. I didn't think that with any sense of self-pity. It was simply a fact. I would have vanished and faded from everyone's memory. My existence would have been forgotten like the fading ripples on the surface of a pond. Just another anonymous hooker who vanished. This girl—Naomi—she was alone, probably just a kid, an immigrant, likely brought here illegally for the sole purpose of working the sex trade. Who would know if she simply disappeared? Who would care?

Collette cared enough to offer to pay me to find her. Or least find out what happened to her. To help her, if possible. And if she was in fact already dead, to speak for her and acknowledge her existence by finding out what had happened to her.

Yes, I could've been Naomi. Perhaps, in some ways I still was. I gazed again into the black eyes of her rabbit, Thỏ. I saw my distorted, twin fish-eye reflections looking back. The toy seemed to be asking me a question, imploring me for an answer.

"Sandy?" Collette said.

"Yes," I replied. "I'll do it. Of course I'll do it."

CHAPTER 3

WHEN I WAS STILL IN THE LIFE, there were between four and six of us living in the apartment at any given time. I never knew for sure how many other apartments Omar had and how many girls, but the rumors were that he had one or two other apartments, each housing the same number of girls as my place. This was where we slept and ate, did laundry, watched reality TV, and pretended like we were sisters. But we all knew we were pretending. This was no sorority. We were just killing time between clients.

Omar managed the girls, and a business partner I never met fronted for the customers, marketed us on a password-protected website, and ran the finances. A couple of times a week, Omar would send each of us out to the hotels by the gigantic Orange County Convention Center, or by the attractions, sometimes other places around town, to have paid sex with men from out of town. While we would occasionally get a "date" with a local guy, our clientele was almost always the tourist and convention trade. I spent five and a half years in that apartment and in those hotel rooms, my soul withering a little bit for every day that passed.

I always lived in the A place. As long as you looked good and kept clean, stayed away from the hard drugs, and knew how to carry yourself, you were still marketable as an escort to the higher dollar clients served by Omar's secret partner. You were given an exotic moniker such as "Diamond," got to live in the nice apartment, and had your dates arranged. You had relative freedom to come and go, as long as you made sure you were always on call for dates. You got to keep a decent chunk of your earnings and could drive one of two shared cars. You could even have a bank account. Your value as a high-end call girl to Omar's partner protected you. However, as soon as your looks started to go, either through age or crystal meth or something else, you were no longer of value to Omar's partner and were moved down to the B place. Omar owned the girls at the B place outright without any partner and put them all on the streets, 365 days a year. They walked up and down Orange Blossom Trail in miniskirts and stilettos and had to meet $300-a-day quotas or they got their faces slapped bloody. The life span of the girls in the B place was only a few years. Some only a few months. You never wanted to get moved to the B place.

The girls who started there, never making the cut to live at the A place, were almost all runaways, often underage, and desperate to survive. They were all addicted to something. Omar would find them on the streets and prey on their weaknesses and desperation.

Using different tactics, he recruited girls for his partner, and for the A place, by cruising the college bars for coeds looking to make easy money and the strip clubs, where he could convince the occasional stripper to take her skills just a little bit further for the promise of a lot more money. Or, he sometimes found girls for the A place through referrals, like he found me. A friend from high school was already part of Omar's stable and convinced me to give it a try. At that point in my life, having just lost a low-end waitress job and way behind on rent, I felt I had nothing more to lose by trying. Little did I know I would lose my soul.

It was an eerie sense of déjà vu when I crossed the threshold into Collette's apartment. The apartment was different, but the girls looked the same, watching TV in sweatpants and tank tops. I could smell the pot as soon as I stepped in. The joint was gone, but the sweet, herbal aroma remained. The drugs were also around when I lived in an apartment like this, but I tried to stay away from them. I was no angel, but I avoided the really bad stuff. I knew that led to the B place.

There were three girls in the living room, two on the couch and one on a cheap lounge chair, watching E! on TV. I think I may have recognized one of them. But maybe not. I might as well have been right back there six years ago, it was so familiar. However, I was different now. Older. And the girls seemed so much younger. They looked up at me warily as Collette escorted me in.

"Girls," Collette said. "This is Sandy." The girls said nothing. "Sandy Corrigan," Collette clarified. "She's the one I told you about. She's going to find Naomi."

This got their attention. I stepped further into the apartment and said hello.

"I need to ask you some questions, okay?" I said and pulled a rickety wooden chair from the equally rickety dinette table into the living room. I pressed the TV remote and shut off the E! channel. "What are your names?"

Two of the girls deferred to the one in the middle, on the couch. She was a little older than the other two, African American, with short, close-cropped hair. A lot of the Black girls wore wigs on the job. Their short hair lent itself to wigs.

"My name's Midnight," she said. "This is Sunshine." She indicated the blonde to her right. "And that's Nasty," she said, nodding at the brunette on her left.

I chewed the inside of my lip and nodded. "Okay. But I'm interested in your real names. Your human being names."

They blinked at me for a second before the brunette said, "Melissa."

"Jordan," said the blonde.

The one called Midnight narrowed her eyes at me. "You used to hook for Omar back in the day, didn't you?" I didn't reply. But my silence answered her question. "That's right. I heard about you. Yeah, I heard *all* about *you*. Did you really cut that dude up like they say?" I remained silent. There was no way I was dredging all that up here for this audience. "Yeah . . . I definitely heard about that. Before I tell you my real name, my *human being* name, first you tell me your client name. Your *online* name."

Collette held up a hand. "Look, Sandy is here trying to help. You don't need to give her such—"

"It's okay," I said. "Diamond. My name was Diamond. But that's not who I am anymore."

"Not who you are anymore?" the one called Midnight said. "Girl, you are who you were and you can't change that. You think changing a name changes who you are? Just because you quit that name don't mean that the name quit you. So, what, you think you're better than us now?"

"No," I said carefully. She was one of those tough girls, hardened even more by the life she led. How could I explain my new sense of self—the purpose that Tyler's presence had given me? The self-esteem of a legit job? It was as if before I was some sort of caterpillar and now I was growing my wings. But I couldn't articulate that here in the A place. Instead, I simply said, "I'm just . . . different now. If you don't want to tell me your name, fine."

She considered me for a long beat. "Tonya," she finally said.

I nodded. "So, Tonya, where do you think Naomi is?"

"Me?" Tonya said. "Damn. The girl ran. She couldn't take the life. She was always . . ." She hesitated, reaching for the right word. ". . . miserable. No—worse. *Fragile.* Always crying about something."

I searched the eyes of the other two girls—Melissa and Jordan. "Do you think Naomi ran?" I asked them. There was a long pause, as if they didn't want to publicly contradict Tonya.

"No," Melissa finally said.

I held her gaze. "Why not?"

She shrugged. "Just a feeling. Y'know."

I turned to the blonde. "What about you, Jordan? Do you think she ran?"

Jordan looked sideways at Tonya and then shook her head slightly. Tonya rolled her eyes.

"How well did you know Naomi?" I asked.

"Well, she hardly ever talked to me," Tonya said. "I think she had a problem with Black people."

"No she didn't," Melissa said. "You just scare her."

Tonya twisted her lips. She wasn't buying it.

I turned to Melissa. "Why do you say that?"

"'Cause she's shy. We share a room, so I probably talk to her more than anyone else. She doesn't know a lot of English. But she tries. She's quiet and always homesick real bad. I don't know how old she is, but I doubt if she's even sixteen. All I know is that she hates being here and she hates tricking."

"Which is why she ran," Tonya said. "Hell, she could've made good money. Young, pretty Asian girl. Omar tried. He even gave her some presents after her first few dates. To encourage her. Some earrings. A bracelet. I saw Lindsey wearing them the next day."

"Lindsey?" I asked.

"Another girl," Collette explained. "Satin. She's . . . *out* right now." I nodded, understanding that "out" meant with a client.

"That's 'cause she didn't want them," Melissa said. "She didn't want anything to do with hooking or Omar."

"Then why was she here in the first place?" Tonya pressed.

"That's a good question," I added.

"I don't know the whole story. But I think she might have been taken. Kidnapped or sold or something back in Vietnam. One time I think she said something about her father selling her. But her English is bad, and I have a hard time with her accent. She said she was told that she had to do whatever Omar said—to have sex with whoever she was told to—or else someone would kill her whole family back in Vietnam. I think she said she had four younger brothers, parents, grandparents. She was really worried. She cries herself to sleep a lot."

"So that's why you don't think she ran," I said. "Because if she did, she was afraid that her family back home would be killed."

Melissa nodded. "She was terrified of that."

We were all silent for a few moments. Even Tonya looked down, contemplating the mental and physical torture Naomi must have been going through. This story shocked even me. When I was still in the life, in a nondescript apartment not too different from this one, the girls were a lot like me. Runaways or drifters. Down on their luck. Girls from broken homes or with

drunk or drug-addicted parents. Girls who had been abused—
verbally, physically, and sexually. We were all vulnerable and we
all found shelter and protection under the care of Omar and his
anonymous partner. He preyed on our weaknesses and exploited
us, providing the right amount of money at just the right times,
sometimes picking certain girls to sleep with himself. He always
provided and protected. Except when he was slapping one of us.
Like all pimps, he was also controlling and dangerous when he
felt disrespected or if he believed that a girl was holding back and
not giving the johns what they wanted. He expected us to per-
form, to "take care of business," as he put it, and make money for
him and his secret partner who managed the website and arranged
the dates.

However, not once in all my years did I ever hear of Omar
buying a girl. He found them on the streets himself and became a
grotesque sort of father figure/boyfriend/boss. International
human trafficking in that way was a new and dangerous low, even
for him. And Naomi's age was younger than I had ever heard for
the A place. The B place was said to have its share of runaway
minors but, to my recollection, my roommates and I at the time
were all over eighteen. Yet I had no doubts that what Melissa was
sharing was true. I just wondered how Omar got connected with
the kind of people who operated international underage trafficking rings. He was a local operation. And could this somehow be
related to why Naomi disappeared?

"Do you know where she was going the night you last saw
her?" I asked.

Shrugs and shakes of heads.

"A client," Melissa said. "Omar took her out. I think to I-Drive,
but I could be wrong. She couldn't drive so he took her himself."

I-Drive was shorthand for International Drive, the heart of Orlando's convention Mecca.

"Do you know which hotel?"

"Sorry."

"Now, Missy," Collette said. "Tell us what you know. If you care about Naomi, you gotta tell us."

"I really don't know."

"What about Brenda?" Jordan said, cutting her eyes nervously at Tonya.

"Brenda? Be serious, girl," Tonya said with a dismissive exhale.

"Who's Brenda?" I asked.

"Brenda Davis. She was Naomi's roommate before me," Melissa said. "She got moved down to the B place a few weeks ago. She got strung out on meth kinda bad."

"Bitch was starting to look like a skeleton," Tonya said. "That won't do for the A place."

"You think Brenda might know where she is?" I asked.

Melissa shrugged. "Maybe."

"Why do you think that?"

"They used to talk on the phone a lot. She was kinda like a big sister or aunt or something for Naomi when she first got here. Naomi was real broke up when Brenda got moved."

I leaned forward, elbows on my knees. "You know how I can get in touch with Brenda?"

"I don't know her number or anything," Melissa said. "And none of us know where the B place is."

"Ain't none of us *want* to know where the B place is," Tonya said.

"So you have no idea how to reach her?"

"You could ask Omar," Jordan offered.

Tonya looked at her like she'd just sprouted a third eye. "You're crazy, girl."

I had to agree with Tonya on this one. There was no way Omar was going to tell me how to contact Brenda or where the B place was. The risk of exposure was too great. Plus, I wasn't exactly his favorite person. After my own unfortunate situation six years ago, I heard there was a lot of heat brought down on him. While I never gave him up or told the cops anything—I valued my limbs and heartbeat too much—I knew that he had to scramble to move his girls before the cops closed in. It was an expensive pain in the ass for him and he blamed me, regardless of the actual facts of the situation.

"Well," Collette said hesitantly. "What about the Trail?"

Orange Blossom Trail. Also called the Trail or OBT. Or, more specifically, a relatively short stretch of it running north from Oak Ridge Road up toward Colonial Drive. Orlando's very own red-light district, with seedy strip clubs every other block and low-slung motels boasting hourly rates. That's where Omar sent his girls from the B place to walk the streets.

"You think I would find her there?"

"Where else?" Collette said.

Where else indeed. The four of them gave me a description of Brenda. Medium height, perhaps 5'6". Brown hair gone flat and stringy with the effects of the crystal meth. A once-shapely figure shrinking to a rail-thin husk. Dark, sunken eyes. That described half the hookers on OBT. Her online name used to be Misty.

I pressed them with a few more questions, but I had exhausted their knowledge. I asked for Naomi's effects—clothes, personal items—anything that might hold a clue. They produced a small canvas bag with all of Naomi's possessions. An entire life's collection in one small sack. At one time, my life could be measured similarly. Thô the rabbit went in on top.

I thanked the girls for their time and rose to leave. As I reached for the apartment's front door to exit, it suddenly opened.

Standing there on the threshold was Omar.

He looked surprisingly unchanged. His skin was still the same light mocha. His ethnicity was undetermined—Black, East Indian, Latino. Maybe all three in today's post-racial society. His tightly curled hair was cut close to his scalp. He was taller than I remembered. Close to six feet. His eyes were a brown so dark that they looked black.

With him was a skinny white guy with a blond crew cut whom I didn't know. Although he was thin, I could see the definition of sinewy muscles under the tank top he was wearing. He looked wiry strong, like a feral dog. He had yellow goatee stubble around his mouth and chin. His arms were colored with tattoos that worked their way up to his neck and behind one ear. Some of the tattoos were crooked and cheap-looking. Probably prison tats. He was chewing gum insolently.

Omar was as surprised as I was to find someone in the doorway. He narrowed his eyes at me, momentarily confused. His tapered, angular head tilted slightly to one side. I could almost see the thoughts racing through his mind, accessing his memory. Then he remembered. His eyes widened with recognition when he finally placed me.

"Well, well, well," he said. "Look who's here. My favorite murdering bitch."

"I'm just leaving," I replied.

"What's your rush? Sit down. Have a drink. You here to ask for your old job back?"

"I was just visiting Collette."

He curled his lip at me. Omar may have been a lowlife pimp, but he was no fool. He glanced at the canvas sack. "Uh-huh. What's in the bag?"

"Nothing. Just some of my clothes."

He paused and scanned me from head to foot. "You still look pretty fine for an old lady. I could make room for you here in the A place."

"No thanks."

"Too good for it now? Is that it, Diamond?"

"Don't call me Diamond."

"Yeah, you were popular back in the day. I remember. Made good bank. You weren't too good to spread your legs then."

"Step aside, Omar. I just want to leave."

"I asked you what's in the bag, bitch."

My hand instinctively slipped inside my purse, fingers groping for the mini tube of pepper spray I carried everywhere I went. "Step aside, Omar."

His hand then shot up with the speed of a bullwhip, his palm cracking me across the cheek with a severity that sent me sprawling stunned to the floor.

CHAPTER 4

I HIT THE LINOLEUM FLOOR. I tried to reach out my hands, to break my fall, but one hand was in my purse and the other was holding the bag of Naomi's possessions. I dropped the bag to prevent a broken nose. From the corner of my eye I saw the stuffed rabbit spill onto the ground.

In the moment it took me to recover my senses, I saw that Omar had leaned down and picked up the rabbit. I blinked myself back into coherence and pulled myself to my feet. My ears were ringing. My cheek throbbed like it had been scalded.

The whole apartment was suddenly still, as if charged with potential energy waiting to be ignited. The skinny white guy next to Omar was grinning through his rapid gum chewing, eyes wide, seemingly waiting for something.

Omar held the rabbit casually but squinted an eye at me. "What are you playing at?"

I swallowed a lump in my throat and felt the pain bloom sharper on the side of my face. I refused to react to his slap. To give him the satisfaction of an emotional response. This wasn't the first time he had slapped me. I wasn't big on obedience back in the day. But it was the first time in many years. I didn't remember it hurting this much. I quickly made a decision. As long as

Omar was standing here, I might as well see if he was good for any information.

"Do you know where she is?" I asked, looking him in the eye, something I knew he hated his stable of girls to do.

"You trying to find her?" Omar peered past me at the girls in the apartment. They sat like statues in the living room, waiting to see if this exchange would go even more badly and draw them into the maelstrom. He nodded at them. "Did *they* ask you to find her?"

"I would think that you, of all people, would want her found." A pause. "Unless you killed her."

"Killed her? Why the hell would I kill her? She was a damn money machine. Young little Asian like that. The johns can't get enough of that shit."

"So don't you care that she's gone?"

He shrugged. "Yeah. 'Course. But she was also a mopey bitch. Always crying. She probably wasn't gonna last anyway."

"So you don't know where she is?"

"Hell no. And I ain't asking."

That struck me as an odd response. "What do you mean by that?"

"Nothin'. She's gone. Girls sometimes run. I don't like it, but it happens. Just let it go."

"Why?"

He considered me for a beat. "Don't start looking for things unless you know what you gonna find. Let it go, Diamond."

I paused, letting the not-so-subtle warning hang there between us. Clearly something was going on and Omar either knew or had a hunch. He was far too willing to give up on Naomi, especially if she really was the money machine he claimed.

I reached for the stuffed rabbit, but he pulled it back, the way a schoolyard bully might take your book and taunt you with it.

"Hand it over, Omar."

He smiled. There was no warmth behind his thin lips. "Maybe we can make a deal. You do something for me and I'll give it back." I offered him a flat expression, not playing his game. "C'mon, Diamond. It wasn't that long ago. You remember what to do. Just like riding a bike . . ." He emphasized his meaning with a grotesque hip thrust. As a point of fact, I never slept with Omar, even when he was basically running my life.

"I'm only asking once more," I said. "Hand it over."

Omar's expression changed instantly, clouding to a menacing anger. "And what are you gonna do, bitch?" He grabbed the rabbit's head in one hand and the feet in the other. Then he started pulling.

I immediately pulled the pepper spray from my purse and unloaded it directly in his face. He yelped and clawed at his eyes, stumbling backwards. I snatched the rabbit and pointed the pepper spray at the skinny white guy, who was already reaching for something hidden under his tank top and tucked in the rear waistband of his saggy jeans.

"Don't," I barked at him, the pepper spray poised several inches from his nose.

Omar was growling, making guttural animal noises in his agony. "Shoot that bitch! Shoot her, R.J.!" He was rubbing his eyes, staggering toward the kitchen.

"Don't," I repeated to the skinny guy, whose name was apparently R.J. "I just want to leave."

R.J. held his hands out, palms facing me. He had an eyeball tattooed in the center of each palm. Classy. I got the distinct sense that if I depressed the trigger this wouldn't be the first time he had been pepper sprayed. He was still grinning and smacking his gum.

"This ain't over, babycakes," he said with a swamp cracker twang.

Babycakes? Seriously? Jeez ... Who was this guy? Omar was now splashing water in his eyes from the kitchen sink and making a growling noise in the back of his throat. He had it coming. Slapping me was bad enough, but there was no way in hell I was letting him tear apart that girl's rabbit.

I turned and sprinted down the stairs to the parking lot. R.J. did not, in fact, shoot me, for which I was more than a little relieved. I hoped that he had a cooler head than Omar, realizing that shooting someone in broad daylight the middle of a populated apartment complex might attract some attention and bring the police. Omar would be all right. Shooting me would unnecessarily complicate their lives.

However, if I knew Omar—and, unfortunately, I did—he wouldn't let this go. He couldn't afford to let anyone, and most especially a former girl, get over on him. It showed weakness. Vulnerability. He would want his payback and would be looking to get it in a time and place where the heat wouldn't be brought down on him. I would need to watch my back.

I sped home, taking an indirect, circuitous route to make sure that no one followed me. My address and phone number were unlisted, although I am registered through the state for my P.I. license. Plus, Omar was smart and connected. He could find me when he wanted. I simply needed to be ready when that time came.

* * *

I found my favorite priest in his usual spot, walking the seediest strip of sidewalk on Orange Blossom Trail. He was alone tonight, but I knew he was often accompanied by a case worker from Catholic Charities or a counselor from Anchor House, which was a home for runaway girls, especially the victims of human trafficking. His name was Fr. Francis Paulson, but to me he was simply Fr. Frank.

I hadn't seen him in a while, and the only difference I noticed was maybe a slight receding of his hairline and a few extra laugh lines around his mouth. Otherwise, he still seemed to be the same boyish guy I had known for years. He was maybe an inch taller than me, with a thin, runner's frame. He was quick to smile and had one just slightly crooked tooth that only seemed to give him character. His round, wire-rimmed glasses added a semi-studious touch.

As usual, he was wearing his Roman collar but no jacket. It was a typically warm, muggy Orlando evening. I parked in front of a taco stand and sat in my car to watch him for a moment. He was talking to a girl with an olive complexion. She looked like she might be Latina. She was wearing a tight miniskirt and precarious pink pumps. She was nodding her head. Fr. Frank leaned in close, shrugged his shoulders. She nodded again. Then he stepped back and blessed her with the sign of the cross. She followed by crossing herself and then disappeared down the sidewalk, teetering in her stiletto heels. I wondered if I had just witnessed a street corner confession. It wouldn't have been Fr. Frank's first.

I got out of the car and approached him. He didn't notice me right away. I was dressed in jeans and a plain blue t-shirt. I didn't advertise myself as a working girl, so his street radar missed me. But as I got closer, he turned to face me.

"Sandy Corrigan!" he exclaimed, the boyish smile bursting across his face.

"Hi, Father," I replied. "Can I buy you a coffee?"

"Of course." He linked his elbow through mine and escorted me, arm-in-arm, two blocks to a nearby Hardee's restaurant. I bought us each a cup of coffee and carried them to a corner booth where we sat across from each other.

He sipped his coffee and peered at me over the lid. "How's Tyler?"

"Amazing." I couldn't help but smile. "He's in first grade now. Loves science. He can name all the planets and tell you which dinosaurs are carnivores and which are herbivores."

He smiled to himself, holding his paper coffee cup in both hands. "Carnivores and herbivores. That's wonderful." He took a sip. "So, he's happy?"

I hesitated, a sudden, unbidden lump forming in my throat. The emotion came over me before I even realized it. It was a simple question, but it represented the most profound desire of my heart. *Is he happy?* That is all I ever wanted in this world, for Tyler to be happy.

"I hope so," I finally said, blinking away the moisture in my eyes. "I think so."

Fr. Frank took another sip. "And what about you?"

"Me?"

"Are you happy?"

I considered for a moment. "Tyler makes me happy."

Fr. Frank pondered my response. "That doesn't really answer my question."

I shrugged. "That's all I can say."

He nodded, almost to himself. "You look good, Sandy. Healthy. I'm glad to see it. Are you still working for your brother?"

I nodded, swallowing a mouthful of hot coffee. "He tries hard to be a grump, but deep down he's a softie. He's been good to me."

"I know. And what about Ryan?"

I chewed the inside of my lip and looked out the window. How could I answer that question? For all I knew, my younger brother, Ryan, could be out there in an alley off the Trail with rubber tubing tied around his bicep and a needle in his arm. Or maybe he was finally back at community college, studying computers and getting his life back on the rails. Or maybe he was dead.

"I don't know . . . I . . . I haven't seen him in a long time."

Fr. Frank nodded knowingly. "So what brings the prodigal Sandy Corrigan out on this particular night?"

"Do I need a reason to come see an old friend?"

"No. But this isn't a social call. Not here. Plus, you have that look in your eye."

"What look?" But I couldn't hide a self-conscious smile. "I'm looking for someone. Actually, I'm looking for two different people, but one is really just to help me find the other."

"Go on."

So I told him about Naomi Nguyen and how she had disappeared. I described her and produced a small photo I found at the bottom of the bag of belongings I took from the apartment. It featured Naomi, presumably shortly before she left Vietnam, holding a toddler boy, probably a baby brother.

Fr. Frank took the photo and studied it for ten or twenty seconds. Then he shook his head and handed it back to me.

"She's not working the Trail," he said. "I haven't seen her."

"What about Brenda Davis?" I asked.

"Who?"

"Brenda Davis. She's working for Omar. He sent her out here a few weeks ago. Brown hair. Meth addict. Used to be called Misty."

He considered for a few seconds and then nodded to himself. "Maybe. I might know her. I'll take you to Ramona when we're done." He explained that Ramona was a case worker from Anchor House, a former streetwalker who now helped trafficked girls get off the Trail.

Fr. Frank and I drank our coffee and didn't say anything for a full minute. We had known each other for close to ten years. He placed his palms flat on the table and peered at me for a long moment. I could almost see his mental wheels turning as he looked at me.

"What?" I said.

"Are you still going to Mass?"

I shrugged. "Yeah." I paused and then sighed. "Well, sort of. Sometimes. They have Mass once a month at Tyler's school, and I like to go to that. And we'll sometimes go on Sundays." It was a bit of an exaggeration. I had been to maybe a half dozen Sunday Masses in the last year.

I was raised culturally Catholic to a pair of parents who liked the idea of being Catholic a lot more than the actual practice of it. My brothers and I went to Catholic school for a few years until my father died of pancreatic cancer. His death triggered a dormant but debilitating schizophrenia in my mother—a condition from which she never recovered and still suffers from to this day.

That's when Billy stepped in and for several years acted as a surrogate father, even though he was just a teenager himself, making sure that Ryan and I were clothed and fed and made it daily to the local public schools. And he also dutifully took us to Mass each week where I prayed my mom would get better. She never did.

I eventually dropped out of high school and drifted through a series of minimum wage jobs. I had just been fired from my latest waitressing gig and was three months behind on rent with my electricity already turned off when a friend connected me with Omar. I was young, clean, and could easily satisfy the paying clients of Omar's secret partner. Because living in the A place afforded me a certain level of freedom that the B place girls didn't have, I sometimes slipped away and went to Mass, usually on my way home from a night-long "date."

Throughout my years as an escort, I regularly went to both Mass and confession. I recognized the irony of hitting the Saturday night confessional on my way to a date with a John, or attending Mass on Sunday afterwards, but I still went through the motions. It made me feel better, and I figured it couldn't hurt. That's where I first met Fr. Frank. He was my confessor.

Over the years, I shared more about my life with him, and while he was never successful in convincing me to leave the life, we did move out of the confessional and into coffee shops and fast-food restaurants. He was the first person I called on that horrible night six years ago. It was Fr. Frank who got me into a room at Anchor House, who connected me with Catholic Charities to get new clothes. I could never return to Omar's apartment, nor would Omar have wanted me there after the heat I brought down. As awful and terrifying as that evening was, it was probably the only way out of Omar's clutches besides death. Since I escaped the life, Fr. Frank and I had kept in touch. I even had him over to the house for a barbeque once.

He nodded at me from across the booth. "Good. I'm glad you're still going to Mass. It's important." He downed the last of his coffee and dropped a crumpled napkin into the cup. "Come on. Let's go see Ramona."

CHAPTER 5

WE WALKED A FEW BLOCKS SOUTH on OBT until we reached a single-story motel called the Paradise Inn. The walls were cinder blocks painted the color of dull straw, and the windows were covered with iron bars. A neon sign in the office window blinked "Hourly Rates." The parking lot smelled like urine and cigarettes.

Along the way we passed two hookers loitering on the sidewalk, one a dyed blonde and the other a tanned brunette. It's amazing what the sight of a priest's Roman collar will do. The brunette looked away and covered her face in a shame reflex. The blonde aggressively propositioned Fr. Frank, clearly getting a thrill at the possibility of making some cash off of a deviant priest. They were probably both lapsed Catholics.

Fr. Frank gave each of them a card containing information about Catholic Charities on one side and Anchor House on the other. The aggressive girl threw hers in the street, but I saw the one who hid her face slip the card into her plastic pink purse.

"That's Ramona's car," Fr. Frank said as we passed an older blue Ford Focus. We crossed the parking lot but didn't go into the office. "There." Fr. Frank nodded down the row of motel doors. Ramona was standing just outside the circle of light from an overhead lamp. She was African American, in her mid-forties, just starting to thicken in her hips. I took a step but before I could start walking toward her, Fr. Frank placed a hand on my arm. "Wait."

She was barely visible in the shadow, except for the blue glow from her cell phone, which she was poking at with a finger. We waited silently for a few minutes. Finally, the motel room door in front of her opened and a thin Black girl in skintight, spandex shorts stepped out. We could just barely hear their conversation.

"You still here?" the girl asked.

"I told you," Ramona said. "I'll be here as long as it takes."

"Well, you're wastin' your time."

"Maybe. But I got all night. I got all year, girlfriend. The only one wastin' her time is you, sweetheart. Stop layin' on your back for these pigs. For that pimp who bloodies your nose. Let me help you."

"You can't help me," the girl said more quietly, her voice becoming smaller, losing some of its bravado. "Ain't nobody can help me."

Ramona leaned in close. "I can help you."

"What do you know about it? You don't know what it's like . . ."

"Don't I? I *know* what it's like. I spent my time in rooms like this. I got my eye blackened by a pimp plenty of times." She pulled up the left sleeve of her shirt, turning her arm. "I got the cigarette burns when I didn't bring home enough cash. I know *all about* it, honey. I'm a damn expert."

The motel door opened and a disheveled white guy in his late-twenties, unshaven, emerged tucking in his stained golf shirt. He was surprised to see the girl and Ramona standing there. His eyes cut back and forth between them, sizing up the situation and trying to decide if there was a problem for him. He stepped around them like he was avoiding a pair of cobras and walked quickly into the shadows. Based on the expression in Ramona's eyes as she watched him, he was right to worry.

"Look," the girl said. "I gotta go . . ."

"Let me help you," Ramona said, touching her arm. "That's how I got out. Somebody helped me."

The girl hesitated. She looked down and shuffled her feet, contemplating her high-heeled purple pumps. She sighed, and I heard the telltale sniff of someone trying not to cry.

"I . . . I . . . gotta go." She turned and walked quickly away, passing right by us on her way to the street.

Ramona grimaced and balled her fists. "Damn." She saw us loitering in the parking lot nearby. She patted her hair, composed herself, and strolled over. "Evening, Frank."

"Ramona," Fr. Frank said. "I thought you might have had her."

Ramona sighed and rubbed her face wearily. "Yeah. Maybe. If the damn John hadn't come out when he did. It spooked her."

"How long have you been working on her?"

"Couple weeks. Tonight was close. She's not too hardened yet. She still hates it. She hasn't completely accepted it. Which means she doesn't always bring home her quota. So, unfortunately, she gets slapped around a lot." Ramona seemed to finally acknowledge me with her eyes. "But that next beating might be what drives her to me. If it doesn't kill her first."

Fr. Frank saw her eyeing me. "Ramona, this is a friend of mine. A private investigator. Sandy Corrigan."

One of Ramona's eyebrows went up. "Private investigator? Okay . . ."

"Can we go somewhere and talk?" I asked.

"Sure. I've had enough of the Trail for one night. Let's go for a drink."

*   *   *

To Ramona, there was only one drink suitable for washing away the filth of the Trail: a malted vanilla milkshake from Beebee's Diner on nearby Sand Lake Road. If this was how she unwound after trying to fish hookers out of the cesspool of OBT, I now understood the thickening of her hips. But I joined her by having a shake of my own. It was rich and creamy and made my eyes roll back in my head. I could see why she came here.

"Naomi Nguyen?" she said, wiping her lips with a paper napkin. "Not ringing a bell. I'll ask around. There's a little Asian girl who's been walking the strip for a few weeks, but I don't think that's her. I think her name's Ana and I'm pretty sure she's Filipino, not Vietnamese. But, like I said, I'll ask around."

"What about Brenda? Brenda Davis?" I asked. "She may know where Naomi is."

"Now Brenda I know," Ramona said. "I've been trying to help her, but she's a hard case. She's strung out on meth real bad. She's pimped by a thug named Omar, and if she doesn't bring home the cash, she gets a punch in the mouth. I'm afraid that it's a race to see which kills her first, the meth or Omar."

"Can I talk to her?"

Ramona shrugged one shoulder. "I dunno. Give me a number where I can reach you and I'll try to set it up." I pulled out a business card and scrawled my personal cell phone number on the back. I handed it to her. As she pocketed it, she eyed me carefully. "You already know the name Omar, don't you?"

I hesitated for a beat and exchanged a look with Fr. Frank. "I do."

Ramona nodded. "Just be careful, Sandy Corrigan. Unlike a fine wine, Omar gets worse with age." She noisily slurped up the remains of her milkshake. "You never walked the Trail, though, did you?"

"No," I said. "I was at the A place." Ramona nodded again. I continued, "Can I ask you a question?" Ramona raised her eyebrows in the affirmative. "When I went to the apartment, where the girls hired me to find Naomi, I ran into Omar and his buddy, a skinny guy named R.J. Omar basically said he wasn't actually looking for Naomi—even though she's run off and made him look bad. And he implied that if I was smart, I wouldn't be looking, either. That doesn't sound like Omar, does it?"

Ramona squinted an eye, considering. "Not only doesn't that sound like the Omar I've heard about all these years, but it doesn't sound like any pimp I've *ever* heard of. Pimps don't let girls go. Pimps punish girls who try to run. Pimps make examples of girls who run."

"Right. When I was in the life, we A place girls had a lot more freedoms than the B place girls. But there were still limits. I remember a girl who disappeared for, like, five days. She got drunk and high and was sleeping it off somewhere. Omar hunted her down and beat the crap out of her. That's the Omar I know."

"Yeah . . ."

"So, I've been thinking, why would Omar be so willing to let her go?"

"You tell me."

"I have no clue." I chewed the inside of my lip, thinking. There was a question that had been bouncing around inside my head for a long time—years actually—but had suddenly seemed more important since my encounter with Omar. "So, who is Omar's secret business partner for the A place girls? The one who runs the internet site, sets up the dates, and collects the money?"

"How should I know? My business is the Trail. The girls in the B place. The ones like Brenda who've been sucked dry by drugs and abuse."

"Well, help me think it through. Yeah, Omar would be inconvenienced by the loss of a girl from the A place. But who would really suffer? Who would it hurt more?"

Fr. Frank looked at me. "The business partner."

"Right," I said. "That's the deal, right? The partner manages the clients and Omar handles the girls. Then they have some kind of financial split. He's the wholesaler. Well, losing prime inventory would have to be bad for business. If I were the partner, who controls the cash, I'd be pissed if the merchandise disappeared. And I would assume that this partner would bring some sort of heat down on Omar about the lost girl. Especially a young Asian girl who might appeal to a certain clientele. Naomi represents money. Revenue."

"Maybe Omar *is* the heat," Ramona said. "You don't know how their relationship works."

"True, but it can't be good for either one's business for the merchandise to disappear. Why does no one seem concerned about Naomi vanishing—except the other girls?" That question hung ominously over the table for a moment. "Is there any way you can find out who the business partner is?"

"Me?" Ramona asked.

"Yeah. You're closer to the girls from the B place, including the ones like Brenda who've been shoved out of the A place. Maybe they know something. I'll see what I can find out from the girls who hired me. Maybe we can work it from both ends."

"Look, Sandy honey, I care about these girls. A lot. That's why I'm out here most nights a week trying to help them. But I'm just a social worker. You're the detective."

"Just promise me that if you hear of anything that you think might be helpful, you'll let me know. Okay? Please?"

Ramona sighed. "Okay. But don't expect much. My job is to get these girls off the street, not put their pimps in jail."

I reached across the table and grasped her wrist. "Thank you."

I bid good night to both Ramona and Fr. Frank and began my drive back to my bungalow downtown. I thought about how I had pepper sprayed Omar in the face and how angry he had been. So, I then started checking the rearview mirror every few minutes. Was it smart to start asking questions about the mysterious business partner? Did I really want to jab my stick further into Omar's hornet's nest? Did I have a choice?

At home I found Laura asleep, sitting up on the couch with the *Tonight Show* winding down. I placed a pillow under her head, shut off the TV, and covered her with a blanket. I checked in on Tyler, who was sleeping peacefully in his bed.

I double-checked the lock on the front door, brushed my teeth, and washed the grime of the Trail off my hands and face. Then I slipped into my cheap Walmart pajamas. I found Naomi's bunny, Thỏ, in the bag of her belongings and curled into bed. After a very long time I finally fell asleep, clutching the stuffed rabbit tightly in my arms.

CHAPTER 6

THE NEXT MORNING WHILE I was putting cereal bowls in the dishwasher it occurred to me that Naomi might not actually be missing at all. I mean, she could be somewhere, but whoever she was with didn't know who she was. Although I knew that she wasn't being helped by Anchor House, she could be hurt and lying in a hospital bed somewhere. So I spent the morning in the office calling every hospital in a five county area. None had admitted either a patient named Naomi Nguyen or a Jane Doe Asian girl of her approximate age. Of course, she could have been admitted under a fake name, but it seemed unlikely. Besides, I couldn't walk every floor of every hospital checking beds, so I would have to take the hospitals' words for it.

"What are you doin'?" It was Billy's voice, hovering over my shoulder.

"Working a case." I rotated around in my desk chair to look up at him.

"What case?"

"A case. Something I found myself."

"Oh yeah? You gettin' paid for this *case*?"

"Yes."

He hesitated, considering. "How much?"

"Five hundred. More if the case takes longer."

"Longer than what?"

"Longer than what I think it should take."

Billy snorted. "So you're an expert now. What's the job?"

"Skip trace. Missing girl."

Billy narrowed his eyes at me. I could see the wheels grinding inside his head. He knew that there was more to the story but decided not to press. "What have you done so far?"

"Talked to some people who might know where she could have run. I just called all the hospitals."

"Any credit cards or social security number?"

"No. She's kind of off the grid."

Billy nodded and scratched his unshaven face. "Have you checked the morgue?"

I opened my mouth to respond, but his question caught me off guard. I had not checked the morgue and, in point of fact, hadn't thought to. Perhaps I had blocked the idea, afraid that I might actually find her. Or, more likely, maybe I still had a lot to learn about being a P.I. "That was next on my list."

"Uh-huh."

Billy shuffled back to his desk. I looked up the phone number to the Orange-Osceola County Medical Examiner's office and placed the call. I pressed the requisite buttons to escape the recorded menu and talk to a human.

"District Nine Medical Examiner," said the female voice who answered.

"Hi," I said. "I'm a private investigator looking for a missing person and am wondering if she might be in your facility." I paused, unsure how to ask the next question. *How many girls are you currently storing? Housing? How many do you have in the cooler?* All seemed too callous. "How many unidentified females do you currently have?"

"We have nineteen unidentified decedents on premises. I would have to check how many are female. How long has the person been missing?"

"Not too long. A little over a week. She's young. A teenager. She's also Asian. Vietnamese."

The woman was silent for a moment. "Please hold."

After two minutes or so a voice came on the line. It was male, with a slight Hispanic accent. "Hello. This is Investigator Ruiz. Can I help you?"

I looked at the phone receiver for a moment before responding. "Are you a police officer?"

"I'm a medicolegal investigator for the M.E.'s office. I work with the police. I'm told that you're calling about a missing person?"

"That's right. A young girl. Teenager. Vietnamese."

"And how long did you say she was missing?"

"A little over a week." I was getting a sinking feeling in my stomach. "Should I come down and . . . see anyone?"

"I think that might be a good idea. And what is your name?"

"Sandy Corrigan. From Class A Investigators. I'm a private investigator."

"When can you come, Ms. Corrigan?"

I told him I would be by that afternoon. I couldn't commit to a specific time because I had to talk to Collette first. When I called her cell number, I got voicemail. I left a message for her to call me ASAP. Then I took a deep breath and called the A place apartment number she gave me. If Omar answered, my plan was to immediately hang up. But it wasn't Omar who answered.

"Hello?" It was a soft, female voice. Vaguely familiar. One of the girls I met? Maybe. What were their names—? I took a chance.

"Melissa," I said. "Is that you?"

"Who is this?"

"Sandy Corrigan. We met the other day. I'm the one looking for Naomi."

"Right. Okay . . ."

"Is Collette there?"

"She's . . . on a date."

Super. "Any idea when she'll be back?"

"No . . ."

I rubbed my face. "Okay. Listen. I need you to do me a favor. We have to go to the morgue."

*   *   *

Melissa didn't want to go. She was afraid Omar would find out that she not only left the apartment but left it with me. Apparently, Omar had made it clear to the girls that I was off limits, and that anyone caught talking to me would regret it. But when I told her that there was an unidentified Asian girl lying on a gurney in the morgue cooler and that I couldn't tell on my own if it was Naomi, she agreed to go.

She was quiet on the drive over to Michigan Street. Her face was pale under her brown hair, and she kept chewing her nails. She looked nervous and sick.

"Do you think it's her?" she finally asked, looking out the passenger window.

"I don't know," I said. But I was starting to feel nervous and sick myself.

We pulled into the parking lot of the new District Nine Medical Examiner's office, which was more of a small complex of buildings than a single facility. District Nine was responsible for Orange and Osceola Counties, covering metro Orlando and the tourist districts. I parked my Accord, and we walked across the scorching hot asphalt. It might only have been May, but summer had already arrived in Central Florida.

The lobby of the main administration building looked sort of like a doctor's office, with comfortable chairs in the waiting room and a long, raised receptionist counter. Melissa and I approached. An overweight receptionist in her late-thirties sat behind the counter.

"We're here to see Inspector Ruiz," I said.

"Please sign in."

I did as she asked, signing a paper log with the time of my arrival and the person I was seeing. I watched Melissa reluctantly do the same. We found a couple of seats in the waiting room. It wasn't long before a door to the side of the reception counter opened and a man stepped out. He was also in his late-thirties, with salt and pepper hair just starting to thin into a widow's peak. His complexion was dark but unlined by any wrinkles, with a mustache and goatee framing his chin. He was wearing blue jeans with a sport coat over a white Orange County polo shirt.

"Ms. Corrigan?" he asked. We stood and approached. "I'm Inspector Hector Ruiz."

"Sandy Corrigan," I said and shook his hand. He looked at Melissa.

"Lois," she said, looking at his feet. Fake name. I didn't blame her.

"She's just a friend," I said. "For moral support."

Ruiz nodded. "I understand. Follow me, please."

We followed him through the door and down a corridor, passing other doors to what looked like meeting rooms. Down one hall I thought I saw office cubicles. It felt like we could be in any business anywhere in America, a call center or a district sales office or a law firm. It was all too normal, too corporate, for the business of death.

Finally, we reached a door and Ruiz ushered us into a small room. A table with three chairs was set against a wall. On the wall above the table was a flat-screen video monitor.

"We do most of our identifications through photographs. But for some we now use closed circuit video," Ruiz said, gesturing at the chairs. "Please have a seat."

Melissa and I sat across from each other, and the uneasiness in the pit of my stomach grew. This was more than butterflies. This was dread. The monitor screen crackled to life, but no image appeared. It was filled with the empty blue of no input. Ruiz picked up a wall phone and pressed a button. He spoke into the receiver.

"Okay, George. Stand by." He turned to us. "If you were family, we would typically have a grief counselor present. But since you're a private investigator, that didn't seem necessary. Let me know when you're ready, ladies."

I exchanged a look with Melissa, who didn't seem to be breathing. "Okay," I said.

"Go ahead, George," Ruiz said into the phone.

The screen flickered momentarily, and an image appeared. Melissa's sharp inhale told me everything I needed to know. From the corner of my eye, I saw her right hand go shakily to her mouth.

The screen displayed a girl's face and bare shoulders on a light blue background. Everything below her collarbone was covered by a white sheet. Her features were clearly Asian, and she was undeniably beautiful. Flawless skin. Silken black hair. But the usual clichés didn't hold true—she did not look at all like she was sleeping. In the harsh oversaturation of whatever lights were shining on her, she looked dead. There was no warmth under that skin. No life behind those closed eyelids.

I looked over at Melissa. She was trying not to cry. Her eyes moved from the screen to me. She was distraught. Ruiz caught this look between us.

"Can you identify her?" he asked in a voice practiced with the question. He was gentle but professionally detached.

I sighed. "I'm afraid so."

Melissa suddenly stood up. "I need to find a bathroom." She was beyond anxious. She was shaking.

"Out the door to your left," Ruiz said, watching her carefully. After she was gone, he waited a moment, letting her abrupt departure hang in the air. "Who is she?" He nodded at the screen.

"Naomi Nguyen. From Vietnam. I'm not sure how old. Sixteen. Seventeen."

"And your relationship to her is . . . ?"

"As I said, I'm a private investigator. I was hired to find her."

"Hired by whom?"

"Uh . . . I'm not really at liberty to say."

Ruiz tilted his head at me. "Why's that?"

I looked over at the screen again. "What happened to her?"

"I said, why are you not at liberty to say?"

I continued looking at Naomi. I thought I saw some discoloration on her neck—what could be bruising. It was hard to tell. "What's the M.E.'s conclusion?" I asked.

"Ms. Corrigan," Ruiz said. "Who hired you to find her?"

I looked back at him. He moved away from the wall and was now standing over me, looking down. "A friend of hers. A friend who was afraid that I would find her exactly like this."

"What about parents? Relatives?"

I shook my head. "She's an illegal immigrant. She has no one here."

"Except this mystery friend. With money to hire a P.I."

"Right." I glanced back at the screen. Those definitely looked like they could be bruises on the neck.

"And tell me again who Lois is?"

I almost asked stupidly, *Lois? Lois who?* But I caught myself. "Like I said, she's just a friend of mine."

"She doesn't know the girl?"

"No."

"She looked pretty upset for not knowing her."

"Well, you know. I don't think she's ever seen a dead body before."

Ruiz nodded. But he wasn't buying a word of these obvious lies. He was no fool. "I'm going to have Detective Carlisle from the Orange County Sheriff's Office get in touch. He'll want to know the truth. The whole truth."

I suddenly realized that my life just got a lot more complicated. I again studied the sweet, silent face on the monitor. My eyes were drawn to the dark blotches on her neck. "What's the M.E.'s conclusion?" I repeated.

Ruiz looked at me for a long time. "It's an active investigation. Officially undetermined."

"And unofficially?" I asked.

After a long pause, he said, "Suspicious."

CHAPTER 7

COLLETTE DIDN'T EVEN HESITATE. "Find out what happened, Sandy," she said when we talked on the phone later. "You find out what happened to that poor girl. We have another five hundred to keep you going. You find out what happened." Her voice was calm through the receiver, but I could hear the bubbling rage beneath the surface.

"Okay," I said. I was home when we spoke, alone in my bedroom. Laura was making dinner. Tyler was watching cartoons on TV. I promised Collette that I would keep investigating and hung up. I lay back on my bed and stared up at the slowly swirling ceiling fan.

Ruiz didn't keep me much longer at the M.E.'s office after he shared the M.E.'s undetermined conclusion. I think he knew he had gotten everything he was going to get from me. I felt bad about withholding information, but I couldn't expose Collette and the girls to the cops. Who knows what Omar would do? Beatings were certain. Maybe worse. I couldn't take that risk yet. My plan was to keep investigating. See what I could uncover. I would then hand over whatever I found to the cops, without risking anyone's safety, most of all mine.

But what if Omar was the one who killed Naomi? That was always possible. I still didn't see the motive, unless she really did run, he found her, and then he made an example out of her. But if that were the case, he would have somehow subtly advertised her death—otherwise she wouldn't serve as much of an example. He hadn't yet said anything. I needed to get the M.E.'s report, which would have the estimated day and time of death. Until I knew more, Omar would stay on my list. But I also needed to find out who Naomi's last client was.

After Ruiz and I were finished at the M.E.'s office, I retrieved Melissa from her hiding place in a stall in the ladies' room and we drove in almost silence back to the A place apartment. The only noise was Melissa's quiet sniffling as she stared out the passenger window. When she got out of the car, she looked back at me, eyes red from crying.

"Just another dead whore, right?" she said. "Just another whore like any of us. Like me." Then she shut the car door and disappeared back up the apartment stairs before Omar could show up and realize that she was gone.

Now, as I stared up at the fan in my bedroom, her words ran hauntingly through my head. *Just another dead whore, right? Just another whore like any of us.* Was she including me in her collective "us"? It didn't matter. As much as I tried to I deny it, I had already been including myself since I accepted this case. I'm not Vietnamese. I wasn't sixteen when I was in the life. But I *was* Naomi Nguyen.

I had once felt the strong, trembling hands of a crazed John on my own neck, squeezing . . . squeezing. The stab of a knife into my upper arm, where a jagged scar remains as a daily reminder of my former life. I have secretly labeled it my Diamond Cut. The blinding terror of someone trying to kill me. If I had not been just slightly stronger than Naomi, just slightly luckier . . . If I hadn't been able to knock the knife from his hands and grab it myself . . . I would have been the dead girl on the morgue gurney. I would have been the anonymous dead whore. Forgotten. Erased.

Was Naomi killed by a client? I didn't know. But it was a reasonable theory. It was an occupational hazard, although it was an admittedly lower risk for the girls in the A place. Their dates were conventioneers, not the dangerous clientele of the Trail where the B place girls plied their wares. Even with their relative freedoms, the A place girls didn't get out enough in uncontrolled ways that a random crime or accident seemed as likely as something more nefarious.

Naomi was so young. She should have been in high school. Now she lay on a cold metal tray on the other side of the world from her home. Who would speak for the dead? Who would care? Who would have spoken for me six years ago? Who would have cared?

I lay there on my bed for a long time, feeling the room grow dusky with twilight. Perhaps I dozed off, but I didn't think so. I reached to the side and pulled Naomi's stuffed rabbit from the spot where it lay near my pillow. I held it close, hoping in vain that it would fill the hollow space inside my chest. I finally pulled myself up.

I went out to the kitchen and sat with Laura and Tyler at the dinette table. Laura made spaghetti with meat sauce. Tyler loved spaghetti. As a result of his eager slurping, his face had been slapped by sauce-covered noodles, leaving a reddish mess on his cheeks and chin. A milk mustache decorated his upper lip. I smiled at him. He was so innocent and oblivious. He caught my look and smiled back at me. His was a genuine, trusting smile. His happiness was pure and good. After my afternoon at the morgue, he was my reassurance that the world could still be decent and wholesome.

Laura joined our smiling. "Dear Lord, boy," she said. "Your face looks like a pizza that lost its cheese."

This made Tyler laugh, which caused me to laugh. Laura wiped his cheeks with a napkin and his face was restored to its simple perfection.

"You want a glass of wine?" Laura asked me, carrying the dishes to the sink.

However, before I could respond, my cell phone rang. When I answered it, I heard Ramona's voice.

"Sandy," she said. "This is Ramona Landry. You still want to talk to Brenda Miller?"

"Yes."

"Okay. She said you can have five minutes tonight. Right after ten. She'll be behind the 7-Eleven on OBT, two blocks north of Oak Ridge."

"I'll be there. Thanks, Ramona."

"Don't thank me yet. She don't want to talk to you. I had to lean on her pretty good. She might not show."

"I understand."

Ramona sighed heavily. "She's a mess, Sandy. The meth is killing her. Desperate people will do desperate things. Just be careful, girl."

* * *

Some evening clouds moved in after sundown and a misty sprinkle spritzed my windshield as I made the relatively short drive from my downtown neighborhood to the Trail. It was always a wonder to me how close these different worlds were, butted up against each other, usually segregated, but with chaos erupting on the occasions when one world happened to spill over into the other.

I found the 7-Eleven without any trouble so I was early for my rendezvous. I parked and went inside for a Diet Coke to pass the time. I sat in my car, drinking my soda, until nearly ten o'clock. Then I got out and positioned myself on one side of the building with a view toward the front so I could see anyone approaching. Nearly twenty minutes passed and I was about to give up when I saw a shuffling figure in the shadows walking from the sidewalk around the other side of the building. I presumed that was my cue.

I followed the figure around the building. At first, I couldn't find her. It was dark, with a dim pool of amber light illuminating only about a third of the space behind the building. Broken glass and cigarette butts littered the concrete. I could see a section of missing slats in a wooden fence that separated the back of the convenience store from the neighboring apartment complex. It was obviously a homemade shortcut for the apartment residents to access the store. A tin oil drum lay on its side near a scratched dumpster. Broken wooden pallets were piled in the corner. The misty rain and the amber light made the whole place seem otherworldly, like from some postapocalyptic movie.

Then I spotted her, a hunched, emaciated figure in the darkness, shifting her weight from foot to foot, and my film reference changed to a zombie movie. I approached slowly, like I might for an unfamiliar dog.

"Brenda?" I asked.

"Yeah." Her voice was hoarse, unnatural, without age or gender. It could have been a man's voice, a boy's voice, a woman's voice. It was a dry, used-up voice.

"I'm Sandy. The one Ramona mentioned."

"Yeah." I could see now that she was wearing a plain green t-shirt, with one arm across her abdomen holding the other elbow. What should have been skinny jeans hung almost loose on her bony frame. The drizzle made her dull brown hair lay flat and stringy on her head. Even in the shadows I could see the dark bags under her sunken eyes.

"I'd like to talk to you about Naomi Nguyen."

"I told Ramona. I don't know where she is. We got nothin' to talk about."

"Then why are you here?"

"To tell you that. So you go away. The word is out. Omar is gunnin' for you, and I can't have my name in your mouth. Leave me alone."

I nodded slightly. "Okay . . . Did you care about Naomi?"

Brenda was silent for a moment. She continued holding her elbow and shifting her weight. "Sure. I felt bad for her. She's just a kid. She don't want to be here."

"She's dead."

Brenda was quiet again, and I became very aware of the misty rain dusting my skin. Brenda looked off to the side, at nothing in particular. She was upset but pretending that she wasn't.

"Yeah, well . . ." she finally said, still looking off to the side. "That happens."

"Collette and the other girls hired me to find out what happened to her. I need your help."

"Sorry. I don't know nothin'."

"When did you last talk to Naomi?"

"I don't know."

"Brenda . . . please. I think she was murdered." I could see the anguish on Brenda's face. She wanted to help, but her streetwise sense of self-preservation was stopping her. I didn't want to push too hard and risk spooking her. "We're the only ones who can help her now. You and me. Help me find out what happened to her."

Brenda's breathing became just a bit more rapid. She wiped an eye with the heel of her hand. "She called me. I think the night she disappeared. She was scared."

"What was she scared of?"

"She saw someone. She kept saying 'I see Yvonne. I see Yvonne.'"

"Yvonne? Who's that?"

"Someone she talked about once or twice back at the A place. It was hard sometimes to understand her with her accent. But I could tell she was . . . terrified. I think this Yvonne is the one who took her from her home in Vietnam and brought her here. Or at least had something to do with it."

"So Naomi saw this Yvonne? Where?"

"At a hotel. She was walking through the lobby going up to a client and I guess that's where she saw Yvonne. I'm not completely sure. She kind of freaked. She called me from the elevator."

"She called you?"

"Yeah . . . You know, we all had cell phones, especially those who can't drive, like Naomi. They call to be picked up when the date is over. Or if there's a problem. She was almost hysterical."

"What was she afraid of?"

"I don't know. That she would be taken away again. That she would be forced to do even worse things. Seeing Yvonne was some sort of . . . I dunno . . . trigger or something."

"Did she say which hotel?"

Brenda coughed. It was a serious cough, the kind of cough that a character in a movie might have and then they were dead before you finished your popcorn. "I asked her. It was hard to understand her, especially when she got worked up. Her accent got thicker then. I think she might have said something like Olsen."

I nodded. There were three Olsen resorts clustered around the gargantuan Orange County Convention Center on International Drive. I had been to all three many times in my own former career. "What about her date? Did she say anything about the client?"

"I told her to tell me who she was meeting and what room, just in case. At first I thought she meant that she was meeting Yvonne, which didn't make any sense. But she said no, that his name was either Dan or Stan or something that rhymes with that. I don't remember the room number. I think it was on the fourth floor. Four something."

"What did you tell her?"

Brenda's face twisted up. Now she wiped both eyes with the heels of her hands. "I told her to calm down. That everything would be fine." She sighed deeply, her meth breath rasping out heavily.

"Yeah," I said and sighed myself.

"Look," she said, her voice thick. "That's all I know. Don't call me again. I won't know you."

"Okay." I took a half step backwards. "Omar never needs to know."

"Oh, it's too late for that," said a new voice from behind me. A male voice. A familiar voice.

Omar's voice.

CHAPTER 8

I DIDN'T TURN AROUND. I didn't hesitate. I ran.

But I didn't get far. Omar's tattooed buddy R.J. emerged from around the other side of the building.

"Hey, babycakes," he drawled.

My escape around the building blocked, I backed up, away from the building. I spotted the opening in the wooden fence next to me. I darted left and shot through the chunk of missing slats and into the parking lot of the adjacent apartment building. I could hear them crashing through the fence behind me. I ran between two of the apartment buildings, the sharp smell of curry wafting from a ground-floor window.

This route took me into a central courtyard of sorts. An aging set of a half dozen two-story apartment buildings were positioned around a neglected pool. I dashed off around the pool, leaping over a deck chair, silently grateful that I wore my sneakers. The rain-soaked patio was slippery and I almost lost my footing. But I caught my sliding foot and continued running. I could hear the pounding of chasing footsteps behind me, of patio furniture being kicked aside. They were faster than I was. They would catch me.

I continued between two more of the complex's buildings on the other side of the pool, past a bright, fluorescent-lit laundry room with spinning dryers. I emerged into another parking lot. It was too dark. There was nobody around. I needed to get to a public place. Somewhere with a crowd.

As I ran, I wondered if Omar would dare to shoot me. I honestly didn't know. He might. He told R.J. to shoot me in the apartment. I had disrespected him in front of his girls. He couldn't have anyone do that and not pay for it or risk losing his absolute control. More likely, though, was that he would catch me and do whatever he planned to do to me in front of the girls, as a message.

I ran past the apartment's darkened leasing office and out onto the sidewalk. Then I sprinted across the street. I wanted to cut left again, to work my way off the darkened streets and back toward the light and traffic of the Trail. But if I did anything but run forward, Omar and R.J. would have an angle on me and would be able to cut me off and catch me even more quickly. So I kept running forward.

I ran between two small, low-slung cinder block houses, the wet grass from the misty rain making squishing noises with each step. Up ahead a dog started barking. It could hear me coming and didn't seem at all happy about my approach. I ran between the two houses that backed up to these and saw the dog across the street. It was behind a tall chain-link fence. A Rottweiler, I thought. A good choice in this neighborhood.

I was getting winded and starting to slow down. Omar and R.J. would soon be on me. There was no way to make it back to OBT before they caught me. Without considering the consequences, I made a decision and charged directly at the Rottweiler. The black dog went nuts, barking ferociously and frothing at the mouth. It was unchained and practically throwing itself at the fence. Fortunately, the fence was too tall for it to jump over. But if it could, I had no doubt it would tear my throat out.

I picked my spot and positioned my back toward the fence, acting as if I were trapped. My breath was coming in deep, desperate heaves. I needed a break before I could run again. If I even got a chance to run again.

"You're gonna pay, bitch," Omar said, stopping at the edge of the yard. He was also breathing heavily.

"Look," I said, stalling for time. "Naomi is dead."

"You think I care?" He walked onto the lawn, R.J. a step behind and to his side. R.J.'s hand was under the bottom of his t-shirt, obviously on the butt of a pistol.

"Why did you kill her?" I asked between gasps. "Because she ran?" I silently urged him forward. Just another two or three steps. The dog was barking itself hoarse behind me.

Omar made a disgusted face. "Yo, I didn't kill that bitch."

"Tell it to the cops."

"That's real funny," Omar said, taking another step toward me. "And how are you gonna talk to the cops with your throat cut?" He brought his right arm up. There was now a knife in his hand.

I darted my eyes between Omar and R.J., who was stepping away from his partner, cutting off my escape route on either side. They weren't close enough yet, but I couldn't wait. They were being too smart, approaching me like pack predators.

I took a deep breath and turned around. I heard Omar and R.J. rush toward me. I had intentionally positioned myself in front of the fence gate. There was a latch but no lock. I immediately slid the latch and shoved up the U-shaped metal handle that held the door shut. Then I pulled the gate open as quickly as I could, staying behind it, sandwiching myself between the fence itself and the swinging gate.

The Rottweiler charged out from behind the fence as if from the depths of Hell and launched itself at R.J. He went down hard, screaming, with the dog tearing at him. Omar was paralyzed, at least for the moment, too shocked to move. I jumped out from behind the gate and swung it closed, sealing myself in the backyard. Then I turned and ran, praying that there wasn't another dog back there. The pungent smell of wet dog crap was strong.

I leapt onto the fence on the other side of the backyard and quickly started climbing. I could hear R.J.'s screams and the dog's snarling and growling coming from the front yard. Just as I swung myself over the top of the fence, I heard the loud pop of a single gunshot, followed by another.

I didn't know if the target of the gunshots was me or the dog. And I had no idea if the dog was hit or if R.J. had his throat torn out—or both—because I was again sprinting as quickly as I could. I cut left and was soon back on the Trail. I turned left again, running up the sidewalk, trying to get back to my car and get the hell out of here. I dodged a homeless guy with a grocery cart crossing the street and within a few minutes I was back at the 7-Eleven parking lot, gasping for breath and fumbling clumsily for the keys to my Accord.

I was soaked from sweat and rain and my hands were trembling with adrenaline. I dropped the keys on the ground, and when I reached down to retrieve them, I discovered that I had dog feces all over the side of one of my sneakers. I stood up and, in the distance, saw Omar and R.J. approaching up the sidewalk. R.J. was shirtless, his forearm wrapped in his now bloody t-shirt. His entire skinny body was tattooed. Based on the expressions on their faces, they were beyond pissed. Their eyes were murderous.

The dread settled on me when I realized that I couldn't get in the car, start it, and take off before they reached me. And I doubted that the public nature of the parking lot would protect me now. I swallowed and tried to remember if I had any pepper spray in my glove compartment.

Before I could check, a dark blue sedan with a flashing blue dashboard light abruptly pulled into the parking lot. The car angled in behind my Honda, blocking me in. The driver got out, leaving his door open, and addressed me.

"Ms. Corrigan?" he asked, although I'm pretty sure he already knew the answer. He was white, maybe 5' 9", with short, dark hair. He was wearing a sport coat but no tie.

"Um . . . Yeah?" I cleverly replied, still catching my breath from my sprint through the nearby neighborhood.

"I'm Detective Carlisle. Would you mind coming with us and answering a few questions?"

I looked past Detective Carlisle and locked eyes with Omar. He and R.J. halted their approach and slinked sideways into a shadow. I saw them turn casually around and disappear the opposite way down the sidewalk.

"I would be happy to, Detective," I said.

I got into the back of the car, hoping that Omar didn't smash my Honda while I was gone. Carlisle got back behind the wheel. In front of me in the passenger seat was a woman in her early fifties. She was trim, African American, with short, graying hair.

"This is Detective Benders," Carlisle said. I said hello. Carlisle eyed me through the rearview mirror. "You out jogging or something?"

"Yeah. Something like that. I kinda went for a run."

Benders crinkled her nose. "What's that smell?" she asked.

"Um . . ." I said. "I think I might have, y'know, maybe stepped in some dog poop."

"Terrific," Benders said and turned away.

"How appropriate," Carlisle mused and pulled the car out onto OBT.

* * *

We were relatively silent as we drove downtown to the Orlando Police Department headquarters. On the way I learned that Carlisle and Benders had stopped by my house, where Laura, thankfully, told them where I was going. Once inside the police department, Carlisle and Benders were kind enough to let me rinse off my sneaker in the ladies room before proceeding to a small interview room. I noticed the discreet video camera in the top corner as we entered.

"So, Ms. Corrigan . . ." Carlisle said once we were seated. "You want to tell me how you know the girl you identified at the morgue as Naomi Nguyen?"

I sighed. "Like I told Mr. Ruiz, I'm a private investigator. I don't know her. I was hired to find her."

"Hired by whom?" Carlisle was doing all the talking. Benders sat in the corner with her arms folded and a sour twist on her lips.

"Naomi was a prostitute. Probably trafficked here illegally from Vietnam. A group of her fellow working girls were worried about her when she went missing and they hired me to find her."

"We're going to need the names and contact information of these other girls."

I paused for a moment. There was no good way to say this. "I don't think I can give that to you."

"Oh? And why not?"

"Because that wasn't part of my deal with them. I'd need their permission first. It could be bad for them if the cops suddenly showed up."

Carlisle leaned forward. "That's why we need to talk to them. We don't want anyone else getting hurt. Who are you afraid will hurt them? A pimp?"

"It's possible," I said. "He's not exactly your biggest fan. Cops in general, I mean—not necessarily you personally."

"Who's the pimp?" Benders said from the corner. Her first words since we walked in the building.

I looked at her. "Omar."

"Last name?" Carlisle asked.

"Just Omar."

Carlisle looked over at Benders and raised his eyebrows. She nodded. "I've heard of him," she said. "Class A scumbag."

Carlisle turned back to me. "So, you think Omar killed Naomi?"

I shrugged. "I honestly don't know. He denies it, but, hey . . ." I let the sentence go unfinished. "The more I think about it, though, the more I doubt he killed her." I was thinking out loud now, trying to work it through. "He wouldn't kill her just for running, for disrespecting him. That would get a beating. She would be worth too much money to him. And if, for some reason, he *did* kill her, he would want the other girls to know it, so *they* learned not to run . . . No, I think it was something else. Maybe a date gone bad."

"Real bad," Carlisle said.

Benders considered me for an extra-long moment. "You seem to know a lot about what Omar would and wouldn't do." I said nothing. But I was pretty sure I knew where this was going. "Did the girls tell you all this?"

I stared down at my hands resting in my lap. Then I looked up pointedly at Benders. "Look, Detective, let's not play games. You know how I know. I assume you used to work vice or looked me up or something. Can we cut the crap?"

Now Benders leaned forward, her tone growing more aggressive. "Yes, let's do cut the crap. A girl—a child—is dead in the morgue. You have information that we need to solve the case and put the killer away. You also know the location of a house full of exploited, trafficked girls, as well as their pimp, who has worked these streets for a lot of years, doing a lot of damage to a lot of people and getting away with it." She bored her laser beam eyes into me. "Omar is a bad guy, Ms. Corrigan. You know that better than anyone. You wouldn't give him up six years ago. That's six years of damage *you've* let him get away with. If you had done the right thing back then, that little girl would not be in the morgue today."

Wham. It felt like she just hit me in the face with a 2 x 4. I opened my mouth to respond, to explain how she didn't understand. How, if I had rolled over on Omar, he would have killed me. Him being in prison wouldn't have stopped him. He would have had someone on the outside, someone like his tattooed pal R.J., kill me for him. I had just discovered that I was pregnant. I couldn't take that risk. It wasn't just my life I was worried about. It was Tyler's, too. The cops wouldn't have been able to protect me.

I wanted to respond, to articulate these extenuating circumstances to Benders, with her aggressive stance and tone. She wasn't in my position. She had no idea what it was like. How dare she judge me like that . . .?

But no words came out of my mouth. Because, deep down, I knew she was right. Had I helped put Omar away six years ago, Naomi might not be dead today. Brenda might not be a meth-hollowed shell shuffling like a zombie up and down the Trail. Who knows how many other girls might not have had their lives ruined . . . or ended.

If I had just made a different choice six years ago.

Benders leaned closer to me. She lowered her voice to almost a whisper. "Tell us where they are, Sandy. It's not too late to do the right thing."

CHAPTER 9

"I . . . I CAN'T," I said.

"Sandy . . ." Benders implored.

"Look, I have to talk to my clients first. You want to catch Naomi's killer. So do I. But you can talk all you want about ensuring the girls' safety and protecting them but the truth is that you can't. The minute that I tell you, they're in danger, no matter what you say."

"We can arrest you," Benders said. "For obstruction. You know that. You could sit in jail until you decide to cooperate."

I hadn't actually considered that. To put it mildly, getting arrested would truly suck. But it didn't change my answer. I needed to convince Benders and Carlisle that I was more good to them outside of jail than in.

"You could," I replied. "But I'm still not going to say anything. Plus, I'll lawyer up and then where will you be? I would honestly rather sit in jail than risk the safety of my clients."

"What about your son?" Benders asked. "Do you really want to go to jail?"

"Low blow, Detective. Of course I don't want to go to jail."

"What if another girl winds up dead?"

"Me sitting in jail isn't going to prevent that. Look, let me talk to the girls. Let me see what else I can find out. I want the same thing you do. I can help you. But I can't do anything if I'm in a jail cell."

Benders put the sour twist back on her lips. She exchanged a look with Carlisle, who offered a small shrug, deferring to her. My fate was up to Benders. She looked at me like she had indigestion. And she was angry about it.

"Talk to the girls," she said, pointing a long, thin finger at me. "Your job is to convince them to do the right thing. And the next time we talk, you better have something to say. You have a very short rope, Ms. Corrigan. Just enough to hang yourself."

I offered her my most disarming smile, which bounced off her hard, crusty demeanor with no effect. She and Carlisle walked me unceremoniously out of the building and instructed a uniformed officer to return me to my car in the 7-Eleven parking lot. Fortunately, I found it unmolested, right where I left it.

Once I returned home, I had a hard time falling asleep, even after two glasses of Chardonnay. My mind raced with the events of the day. Naomi's corpse. The meeting with Brenda. The chase with Omar and R.J. The interview with Carlisle and Benders. But most distracting of all was the notion that my failure to implicate Omar in my own incident six years ago had kept him on the loose and eventually resulted in Naomi's death. Was I too afraid? Should I have made a different decision? Had I agreed to be a witness, would a sixteen-year-old girl be alive today? The burden was almost too much to bear.

I clutched Naomi's rabbit, Thỏ, and pressed my face into my pillow, letting the pillowcase absorb my tears. At some unknown point in the early morning hours, I drifted off to sleep.

*   *   *

Collette and I agreed to meet downtown at Lake Eola Park. In case Omar made another appearance, I wanted to stick to public spaces with lots of people around.

It was a gorgeous spring morning. I walked Tyler to school and then crossed the street to the park. I found a seat under the shade of a live oak tree with a view of the school. Even on a weekday morning the joggers and dog walkers were out, working their way around the lake. The large fountain in the center of the lake added a serene white noise to the scene. Collette approached and sat next to me, offering a quick hug. She was wearing jeans and a nice blouse. She looked like she could have walked out of any of these office buildings, or even just dropped a child off at Tyler's Catholic school. She did not look like a call girl.

"Are you okay, hon?" she drawled.

"Sure. I'm fine."

"Word is that Omar came after you last night."

"I'm still here."

"Well, you just be careful. He's even crazier than he used to be."

"Listen, Collette," I said. "We need to talk." I shared my entire evening with her, starting with the meeting with Brenda and ending with the interview with Carlisle and Benders. I downplayed the chase with Omar and R.J., but I did mention that R.J. may or may not have been bitten by a Rottweiler.

"Good," Collette said about the Rottweiler. "Couldn't happen to a nicer guy. Although the dog may now need a rabies shot."

"So the cops want me to tell them who hired me and then have me roll over on Omar."

"Damn. What did you say?"

"I told them that I couldn't divulge my clients without their permission. *Your* permission."

"I bet they didn't like that."

"You could say. There were threats of jail cells and whatnot."

Collette clenched her fists and opened them. "I . . . I just don't know, Sandy."

"Think about it. They think it's possible that Omar killed Naomi. I'm doubtful. But if we turn him in, we may be preventing someone else from ending up in the morgue."

Collette nodded to herself and again opened and closed her fists. "It's not just me, you know," she said, looking down at her hands. "There are five other girls in the A place. And these girls are not like the B girls. The money is good, and you know we actually get to keep a good chunk of it. You know the drill. Most of us have chosen to be there."

"Not Naomi," I said.

"No . . ." Collette looked up at me. "But if I say yes and Omar finds out . . . If he doesn't kill me, Tonya will."

"I know. But we're talking about people's lives here. This is literally life and death."

"I just don't know . . . If we roll over on Omar, I'm done as an escort." She looked off at nothing in particular. "What else would I do? That's who I am . . ."

I reached over and grabbed her hands. I squeezed them and pulled her attention to me. "Hey," I said, perhaps more sternly than I intended, forcing her to look me in the eyes. "That is *not* who you are. It's what you've done for the past six years. You've made your choices and some money. But there are a lot of things you could do. Legitimate things that allow you to keep your dignity." I realized that I was talking to myself as much as I was to her. Collette realized it, too.

"You have a brother who hired you. I don't have anybody."

"Look," I said. "You're smart. You're pretty. You won't have any trouble getting a job. You could walk into any one of these buildings and be their receptionist or leasing agent or whatever you want right now. Today. And if you decide to go back to school, then the sky is the limit. As long as you stay with Omar, he is the limit."

"I'll think about it . . ."

"I almost got murdered and had to literally kill someone to get out. Don't go out like I did. It's too dangerous."

"Or Naomi," she said softly.

"Or Naomi . . ." I repeated.

I heard the class bell ring from across the street in Tyler's school. A swarm of children in yellow polo shirts walked from the old convent building to the gym. Those were the middle schoolers—seventh and eighth graders. The boys laughed and shoved each other. The girls huddled in small groups, whispering and giggling. I saw a long-haired Asian girl in one group and was immediately reminded of Naomi. This girl was thirteen or fourteen years old. A child. Yet Naomi was only two or three years older herself. The sheer magnitude of the evil that brought her here as a sex slave weighed on me.

"Sandy?" Collette asked, bringing me back from my reverie.

"What about this Yvonne that Brenda mentioned?" I asked. "Any idea who she is?"

"No clue. I can ask Missy back at the apartment. She roomed with Naomi after Brenda. But I've never heard the name before."

"At the moment, it's our only lead. The cops are only going to give me so much time. Then they're gonna show up and I'm either gonna tell them where to find Omar or I'm going to jail. And, Collette, I *really* don't want to go to jail. I have a kid. I *can't* go to jail."

Collette looked pained. She obviously sympathized with my predicament. Finally, she nodded.

"Okay," she said. "I know, hon. I know. When the time comes, you do what you have to do. But try to give me a heads-up, 'kay?"

I placed my hand on her forearm and gave it a little squeeze of assent. I could imagine texting her that I had just squealed on Omar and then the ensuing mad rush to evacuate the apartment forever. I would do it as long as I was not also warning Omar.

"You want a cup of coffee?" I asked. "I only live a few blocks from here."

"You have tea?"

"That could be arranged."

We walked down the sidewalk under the shade of the live oaks that lined the downtown residential sidewalks, passing more joggers and dogs on leashes. Although the temperature was starting to climb, it hadn't reached the early summer Orlando oppression. After a few minutes, we found ourselves standing in front of my little Craftsman bungalow.

"Oh, Sandy. This is yours?"

"Home sweet home."

She shook her head slowly to herself in disbelief. "My God. It's charming. You really did it." I could hear the emotion welling up in her voice. "You really got out."

I looped my arm through the crook of her elbow and walked her up the porch steps. Laura was out at the grocery store, so the house was quiet. I boiled some water for tea while Collette perused the photos on my fireplace mantel.

"Your boy is adorable," she said. "Taylor, right?"

"Tyler. And thanks. He's my life."

We took our tea under the shaded overhang of the back patio, sitting in plastic molded Adirondack chairs overlooking Tyler's turtle-shaped sandbox. After a few contented sips, Collette finally broke the silence.

"What do you think, Sandy?" she asked. "Do you think Omar killed her?"

I stared out at the backyard and the Tonka trucks half buried in the sandbox for a long moment, considering. "I don't know," I finally responded. "I think that he knows something, but I honestly don't see it. I don't know why he would kill her."

Collette nodded. "I've been with Omar for a long time. A little over six years. A lifetime in this business. There have been a few girls who disappeared, but they all told us they were going to run. None were a surprise like Naomi. I can think of two who OD'd, but the drugs didn't have much to do with Omar. They were both already a mess when they showed up. And Naomi didn't touch the drugs. In all my time at the A place, I'm not aware of a single time where I thought Omar killed one of his own girls. He's run a few down but he always brought them back. They were his moneymakers."

I nodded. "It's a question of inventory. Why ruin the merchandise, right?"

Collette smiled ruefully. "Right."

"But the inventory may be starting to change. Did Omar ever bring in foreign girls like Naomi before?"

"No. She was the first. At least at the A place. I don't know what goes on at the B place." Collette paused. "But she's not the last. Omar has a new girl at the A place. And I think you're going to want to meet her."

CHAPTER 10

THE GIRL'S NAME WAS MARTA and she was from Guatemala. She was petite, with caramel skin and full lips, her long brown hair pulled back into a ponytail. She was wearing a hunter green blouse and a denim skirt. Collette told me that Marta had been dubbed "Pepper" for the website, as in *Hot Pepper*. I couldn't help but be reminded of a pet's name, further dehumanizing her. She spoke very broken English, and I spoke very broken Spanish, so we were just barely able to communicate with each other. When I lived in the A place, one of my roommates was from a Puerto Rican family and she taught me a little "Spanglish."

Collette and I were operating under the assumption that Marta had been brought here in the same way that Naomi had and, by better understanding that process, perhaps we could glean some clue that would help us figure out how Naomi died. It was a bit of a stretch, but my leads were kind of slim at the moment.

Before picking up Marta in my car, Collette returned to the apartment and made sure that Omar and R.J. were nowhere in sight. Then the three of us rode in my Honda to a nearby Burger King restaurant. We found a booth in the corner and made ourselves comfortable. Marta wanted fries and a vanilla milkshake, just like any normal teenager. Except she wasn't. She was a trafficked child sex worker.

Like Naomi, Marta was young. She said that she was seventeen and I believed her. *Diecisiete*. After some fries and half a milkshake, we started asking Marta questions. It took a while to work out the language differences, but here's what I understood. A man came to her village and offered to take her and two other girls to the United States where they were promised jobs cleaning hotel rooms and doing laundry. They were to pay back the cost of their illegal passage for two years in these jobs. But it quickly became clear that the promise of legitimate jobs was a lie. A "mule" smuggled them through Mexico and into Texas, where another man drove them all night to a house in the country. There, they were chained to beds and each raped by various men who came and went. They stayed there for a week or two and were subjected to more forced sex. Marta was the first of the girls to realize that they were being prostituted and not simply tortured. However, when one of her companions objected and refused to cooperate, she was beaten severely in front of the other two, and Marta never had the courage to stand up and refuse. She did not want to be beaten like that.

One of the men who lived in the house came to her one day and told her that she had "potential" and was going to be moved. She was loaded into a car with two men and driven nonstop from Texas to Central Florida, each man taking turns driving while the other slept. They only stopped to use the restroom and pick up drive-through.

Once in Orlando, Marta was handed over to a different man with a strange accent—not American and not Mexican—she didn't know what it was. This man was very serious. He had blond hair and was very strong. *Músculos grandes.* He brought Marta to a house in a suburban neighborhood where she was kept for several weeks. She was given decent food and allowed to shower and pick out some clothes. She was not raped. A woman checked on her every day to see how she looked and to ensure that Marta's residual bruises and scratches from her time in the house in Texas were healing. There were several other girls in the house, but they were all foreign and no one else spoke Spanish, so Marta never really talked to anyone else. At least one of the other girls was Asian. One was blonde and spoke some sort of Eastern European language. The woman who checked in on her spoke some accented Spanish but she said little. Marta begged her to let her go but the woman told her that this was her home now.

Marta cried herself to sleep every night, desperately homesick for her village in Guatemala, for her parents, and her brothers and sisters. Since she was no longer being sexually assaulted, Marta thought that the worst part of her nightmare might be over.

One day the woman came into her room and instructed her to put on red lingerie. She applied makeup to Marta's face and styled her hair. The woman then set up some lights and took photographs of Marta kneeling on her bed. The man with the strange accent stood near the door with his arms folded, watching, his face a stern mask. He said nothing the entire time.

Once the woman decided that Marta's injuries had sufficiently healed, the blond man with the big biceps and the strange accent returned and had her pack up one suitcase worth of clothing. Then they got into a fancy black car and the man drove to the A place apartment, where he handed her off to Omar. She had been on two "dates" so far as an I-Drive resort escort.

I asked her if she wanted to leave with me today, now, and go somewhere safe. I could place her with Ramona or Fr. Frank and they would take care of her. But Marta refused. She said that her family would be killed back in Guatemala if she didn't do what she was told. This had been reinforced to her repeatedly since the house in Texas. I tried to convince her that this was just something that she had been told to get her to comply. They weren't going to bother her family. But she was unconvinced. She simply wouldn't leave with me. Collette patted her arm, promising to keep an eye on her.

The idea of a suburban house storing trafficked girls from other countries was somewhat horrifying to me. And if Marta was sent—or sold—to Omar, then where did the other girls go? Could they have ended up in other apartments under the control of other pimps?

The pictures taken of Marta in the red lingerie were clearly intended for the internet site. I'd had similar pictures taken myself once upon a time to go with my Diamond profile. Johns could go online to a password-protected website and order the girl they wanted from a menu of choices long before they ever got on an airplane to head to Orlando for their big industry convention. Except . . . I had my pictures taken at the A place. I didn't even remember who took them, I think one of the veteran girls, but I did remember where. If Marta had her pictures taken at the house, before going to Omar's, could that mean the woman and the accented man were somehow associated with the website? Just who were they?

I pressed Marta for some more details. "Tell me more about the fancy car. *¿El carro muy sofisticado? ¿Qué carro?*"

"*Un carro negro. Muy caro.*"

It took me a few seconds. Black car. Very expensive. "*¿Qué tipo?*" What type?

"*No sé.*" She didn't know. She reached into the french fry container and removed three fries. She placed them on the table and arranged them into an upside-down Y. Then she put her thumbs and forefingers together in a circle and held them over the french fries. I blinked at it for a second and then I got it.

"Mercedes." She was making the Mercedes logo with her fingers and french fries. She didn't know what it meant but she remembered it from the car. "Good girl," I said, squeezing her hand. "*Muy bien.* What about the house? *¿La casa? ¿Dónde está la casa?*" Where is the house?

Marta shrugged and shook her head. She had no idea. I couldn't realistically expect her to have any idea where the house could be.

"*Estaba cerca de un castillo,*" she said. "*Pude ver un castillo a través de la ventana.*"

I grimaced, trying to make sense of the words. I just didn't have the vocabulary. But a couple of the words in her statement sounded familiar. "*¿Castillo?*" I said, pronouncing the word like she did, *cas-tee-yo.* I remembered a class trip as a kid to the Castillo de San Marcos in St. Augustine. "A fort?" Marta scrunched her eyebrows together in confusion. "No? Not a fort . . . Castillo . . . Castillo . . . Wait—a castle?"

Marta tilted her head at me. She knew that word. She nodded. "*Sí.* Yes. Castle."

I imagined that all of these suburban, stuccoed homes, with their four bedrooms and two baths, manicured lawns and swimming pools, looked like castles to a poor girl from a remote Guatemalan village. I nodded back at her knowingly. "*Sí. Muchos castillos.*" Yes. Many castles.

Again her eyebrows squeezed together. "*No. Solamente uno castillo,*" she said holding up one finger. Only one castle. "*Pude ver el castillo a través de la ventana.*" I wasn't sure I completely understood this sentence. I thought *ver* was to look or to see or something like that. I drew a blank at *ventana*. "*¿Qué es 'ventana'?*"

Marta drew a rectangle around her face with her hands and then pretended to shield her eyes and look through it, like an amateur Latina mime. "*Ventana.*"

"*Ventana . . .*" I repeated. "A window?"

Marta nodded. "*Sí.* Window."

"You could see a castle out your window?"

"*Sí.* Yes. A castle."

I exchanged a confused look with Collette. A castle? In Orlando? It didn't make any sense. Where would you find a castle in Orl—

Then it hit me. Of course. Duh. But that *couldn't* be possible. Seriously.

Collette got it about a second after I did. "No way," she said.

I pulled out my iPhone and did a quick internet search. Within a few seconds I called up a full color photo of Walt Disney World's Cinderella's Castle. I showed it to Marta.

"*¿Este castillo?*"

Marta took the phone in her hands and studied it intently. Finally, she shook her head and handed it back to me, apologizing. "No. *Lo siento.*"

No need for her to apologize. It was a stupid idea. The Walt Disney World property sprawled for miles and miles across two separate counties. You had to drive through acres of Florida pine scrub just to get to the parking lot. There was no regular residential neighborhood anywhere in Central Florida with a view of the Magic Kingdom's Cinderella's Castle.

So, assuming Marta was telling the truth, where else could you see a castle from a residential neighborhood in Orlando? Maybe one of the more gimmicky tourist hotels. But none came immediately to mind. A themed restaurant, perhaps. There were a number of places from which you could see roller coasters. The neighborhoods adjacent to Sea World could spy the twisting colorful pipes of the Kraken and Manta roller coasters. Likewise, from the overpass on I-4 driving past Universal, you could see the snaking green tubes of the Incredible Hulk roller coaster at Islands of Adventure. But where else was there a castle like Cinderella's Castle? Then I remembered. And it seemed so obvious. I looked at Collette.

"Hogwarts," I said. She laughed and nodded. The towering Hogwarts Castle at the center of the Wizarding World of Harry Potter at Islands of Adventure was visible from some of the surrounding neighborhoods in West Orlando. In fact, you could see it from the football field of Dr. Phillips High School. So much for the Ministry of Magic's International Statute of Magical Secrecy. Yeah, I read the books.

I again poked at my iPhone and found a photo of the park's Hogwarts Castle, with the Gryffindor Tower rising up into the blue sky. I showed that to Marta whose eyes went wide. She nodded.

"*Sí. Sí. Ese castillo.*"

Collette and I again looked at each other. So, we knew that the house where Marta was held was somewhere in West Orlando, within sight of the Hogwarts Castle. This may be important in finding out what happened to Naomi. Or maybe not. If nothing else, it was a valuable piece of information to put in my pocket for the next time that Detectives Carlisle and Benders appeared.

Collette's phone buzzed in her purse. She pulled it out. "Damn."

"What is it?" I asked.

"Omar. He just texted. I have a date this afternoon. I have to be ready to go in thirty minutes."

I looked at my watch. "Damn."

Five seconds later we were all dashing out the door and running to my car.

CHAPTER 11

I SKIDDED INTO THE PARKING LOT of the A place apartment complex and stopped the car just long enough for Collette and Marta to throw themselves out. They sprinted up the stairs as I squealed my tires and hauled out of there. It took ten minutes, maybe less, to drive there, but Collette couldn't risk Omar's suspicions. I told myself that she would make it in time.

I sneaked peeks at the rearview mirror as I raced away but didn't see any signs of angry pursuit. I figured I was clear. Still, I made a few random turns and cut through a Publix parking lot, just in case.

It was early afternoon. I had some work that Billy had left for me on my desk, and I considered turning around and going into the office. However, I glanced up and saw the on-ramp for I-4, the main artery that cuts through Central Florida, and decided to head west. In less than fifteen minutes, I exited at Sand Lake Road and found myself at the intersection of International Drive.

International Drive, or I-Drive as the locals called it, was a touristy section of town on the west side, roughly connecting Universal Studios and the discount outlet malls at the north end to Sea World and the hinterlands of the Disney property at the south end, with the gargantuan Orange County Convention

Center positioned in the middle. Lesser-known attractions such as Wonderworks, Madame Tussaud's, and Ripley's Believe It or Not called I-Drive home, with hotels, shops, and chain restaurants pretty much a rock's throw away no matter where on the strip you might be standing.

Positioned near the Convention Center were three adjacent resorts owned by Jack Olsen, a local hotelier and resident millionaire. They were the Olsen Regency, the Olsen Premier, and the Olsen Suites Resort. They were beautiful hotels, tall and clean, with twisting fountains in the lobbies, leather furniture in the lounges, swim-up bars, and even a lazy river. The Olsen properties were popular with the convention crowd because of their proximity to the Convention Center. I had spent time in all three during my days as an escort.

Brenda had told me in the back of that 7-Eleven that Naomi had called her from one of the Olsen hotels the night she disappeared. She was freaked out because she had spotted someone named Yvonne in the lobby on her way in. It wasn't like I had an unlimited number of clues to follow, so this was at least something.

I drove around the Olsen Regency for a few minutes until I finally found a small sign for self-parking and located a spot at the far end of the sprawling lot. Clearly the intent was for guests to use the $35 per day valet service and avoid the forty-mile hike in the Florida heat from the self-parking frontier. Most arrived by taxi or Uber from the airport anyway. I made my way into the lobby and looked around.

It was even nicer than I remembered. There must have been a remodeling within the past six years. I wandered through the leather chairs of the lobby, past a black grand piano, and over to the lounge. I found a stool at the bar and settled in. The bartender was a woman, a few years older than me, perhaps pushing forty—maybe older, but she was pretty with brown hair and carried her age well. The place was quiet on a weekday afternoon, so she took my order without any delay. A Diet Coke.

As I sipped my drink, I considered how I should play this. When I was in the life, Omar—or someone—paid off employees in several of the regular hotels. It was just smart business to have that kind of inside insurance. This person would keep his eyes open—and it was always a guy—for any signs of trouble, especially cops. The Metropolitan Bureau of Investigation, or MBI, a multi-jurisdictional task force of local law enforcement agencies, often conducted stings in local hotels, catching both hookers and johns. This inside informant would let Omar know if he suspected a sting was going on. This insider could also be very helpful in getting a girl out of the building, through stairwells and service areas, should there be trouble with a client or if anything else went sideways on a date.

Before a date, if a hotel had such an informant, we would be given his name and cell phone number in case we needed it. Sometimes, in addition to cash, the insider wanted something more for his service. So they often got their own dates, free of charge. The couple of times I had to give a free date a hotel insider, I usually found them repugnant and entitled. They didn't treat me very well.

I still remembered the name of the Olsen Regency's insider. He liked me and often asked for me by name. *Diamond*. He was a clerk at the front desk named Scott Delaney. At the time, he was in his late twenties, thirty pounds overweight, with curly, receding hair, and stale coffee breath at all times of the day. But it was his arrogant attitude that was truly off-putting. He was a pig.

I drank my Diet Coke and was soon left with only ice cubes in the glass. The bartender wandered over.

"You want a refill?" she asked. She seemed very tired, with some extra makeup covering circles under her eyes. Her hair was pulled back into a utilitarian ponytail.

"Sure," I said. As she filled my glass with her soda gun, I tried to act nonchalant. "Does, uh, Scott Delaney still work here?"

She considered for a moment. "Scott Delaney?"

"Yeah. Do you know him?"

"I haven't heard *that* name in a long time." She returned the soda nozzle to its holder. She looked at me and said nothing for an awkward few seconds. "No," she finally said. "He doesn't work here anymore."

I nodded. "Is he at another Olsen hotel or is he, y'know, gone?"

"He's gone. Actually, I think he got fired or something a couple of years ago." She started wiping the bar with a towel. "Is there someone else who can help you?"

"Oh, I don't know. I stayed here a few years ago and Scott helped me with something. If he was still around, I thought I'd stop by and thank him."

The bartender nodded. "Sorry." She moved down the bar to attend to a couple who had just sat down. I nursed my Diet Coke and tried to think of what to do next. Without Scott Delaney, I had no idea how I was supposed to gather any information about a guest who may have stayed here. Hotels don't just hand over guest registry data to anyone who asks. They're funny that way.

Naomi had told Brenda that her date had been someone named Dan or Stan or something similar and that she was supposed to meet him in his room on the fourth floor of one of the Olsen hotels. It occurred to me that the cops could get the information from the hotel and perhaps I should have given the lead to Carlisle and Benders. I should have thought of this sooner. Maybe I should have called them at that moment.

But that would lead right to Brenda, which would ultimately get back to the A place, and I still didn't have Collette's permission to sic the cops on Omar and expose them all unless under direct threat of incarceration. No, I would have to keep working and trying my best to find out what I could until Carlisle and Benders reappeared dangling a pair of shiny handcuff bracelets.

I slurped up the last of the Diet Coke refill and rattled the ice in the glass. Satisfied that I had drunk it all, I pulled my wallet out of my purse and fished out a few singles. As I laid them on the bar and started to slide off my stool, I looked up and was surprised to see the bartender. She put a hand on mine and leaned over the bar.

"Listen," she said quietly, just above a whisper. "Since Scott isn't around anymore, you might want to talk to a guy named Jeff Walker instead. I don't know what kind of help Scott gave you, but Jeff is . . . kind of the new Scott. He's the one who helps people now. Like Scott did back then. You understand?"

I nodded slowly. "I understand. Thanks."

"You're welcome. But you didn't hear it from me. It's not like it used to be. There are some pretty scary characters running the shadow business around here now." She offered a half shrug. "Don't get your hopes up. Jeff may or may not help you. Just be careful."

"Thanks again."

She nodded and patted my hand. Then she walked off to check on the couple at the end of the bar. I put a twenty-dollar bill on top of the singles and slipped off the barstool.

I strolled back to the lobby and found the front desk. There were two people behind the counter, a man and a woman, both dark-haired and attractive. They must have been in their twenties, but they almost looked too young to have real grown-up jobs like this. I decided that the guy was my better option and sidled up to him.

"Hi," I offered with what I hoped was a disarming smile. His name badge read Justin.

"How may I help you?" Justin said.

"Well, I hope you can. May I speak to Jeff Walker, please?"

"Jeff Walker?"

"Yes."

"May I ask what this is in reference to?"

No, you may not, Justin sweetie, I thought to myself. But that's not what I said. "Oh, it's not a complaint or anything. We have a mutual friend, and I was told to look him up."

"A mutual friend. Certainly. Excuse me." I expected Justin to pick up the phone but instead he turned around and exited through a door behind the counter. He was gone for several minutes. The girl at the other end of the registration desk eventually looked up at me. I smiled at her. She smiled back with perfect, straight white teeth. Movie star teeth.

Justin finally returned. "Jeff will be right out. If you'd like to take a seat in the lobby, I'll send him over."

"Thank you so much."

I did as suggested and slid into a leather chair in the main lobby. The summer tourists had started to arrive and the place was actually fairly busy. Plus, it looked like at least one convention was in town. There were a lot of guys wearing sport coats with conference name badges dangling around their necks. I wouldn't have been surprised if Collette had been called down here today for her last-minute date.

"Hello?" A male voice. I tilted my head up. Standing next to me was a guy in his early thirties, decent build, brown hair, neat beard. He was wearing a black tie and a burgundy Olsen Resorts jacket. His name badge included the title Assistant Reservations Manager. "I'm Jeff Walker."

I stood and extended a hand. "Hi, Jeff. I'm Sandy." We shook hands.

He seemed harried. "How can I help you?"

"Well, Jeff, I'm doing some research and I think you might be able to help me."

"Okay. Like what?" He was impatient. Eager to be rid of me.

"I'm looking to find out the name of a guest who stayed here a few weeks ago. His name was Dan or Stan or perhaps something similar and his room was on the fourth floor."

Jeff's distracted impatience suddenly vanished. He was now focused on me entirely. He cocked his head slightly and narrowed his eyes. "What did you say your name was again?"

I smiled cheerfully. "Sandy."

"Well, *Sandy*," he said slowly and deliberately. "We aren't allowed to share guest records with anyone. Not unless you're a police officer. With a warrant or court order. I assume you're not?"

"Oh, no." I smiled and shook my head ruefully. "I'm a private detective. Look, I'll be happy to compensate you for the trouble. A hundred now and then another hundred in a few minutes when you deliver the name. Easy peasy."

He smiled at me. But this smile was definitely not sincere. "I don't know who you think you are but you're crazy if you think

I'm gonna do that." A beat. "Justin said you told him we had a mutual friend. Very funny."

"Jeff... I think it would be best if you just helped me. Make a quick two hundred bucks for five minutes' work."

"Forget it." He turned to leave.

"You really don't want me to tell Omar you refused to help."

That froze him. He turned back to me. "Omar?"

I smiled again. "Our mutual friend. I'd rather not involve him, don't you agree?"

"Omar sent you?"

"Just take the money. Five minutes. Ten, tops."

"You can tell Omar that this isn't part of the deal. I can get fired for this. That won't help either one of us."

"Oh, come on, Jeff. You can get fired for all of it. What's one more little favor?"

"No. I said forget it. They can log our records access. It's not worth it."

"Okay. A hundred now and *two* hundred when you bring the name back. I'll wait right here."

He hesitated for a second, considering. "No. It's not worth it."

I couldn't let this guy walk away. If I lost him, I lost any hope of getting that name. I had to do something—anything—so I blurted out, "And I *really* don't want to have to tell Yvonne that you wouldn't help me."

The color drained from Jeff's face. "Yvonne? You know Yvonne?"

"Just help me out. Five minutes. *Three* hundred bucks."

Jeff seemed to have lost his swagger. He nodded, more to himself than me. "Okay..."

"Our little secret," I said. I grabbed his elbow and led him to a darkish corner of the lobby where there wasn't so much traffic. I peeled off one of the hundreds that Collette had given me, provided the calendar date in question with a reminder of the particulars, and sent him back into his office behind the front desk. Then I made myself comfortable in another leather chair.

After fifteen minutes I started to wonder if I had just lost a hundred bucks. Perhaps the cops were about to charge in. Or maybe this mysterious Yvonne person was going to leap out from the shadows and stab me. At this point, nothing would have surprised me. But eventually, after precisely twenty-three minutes, Jeff returned. He looked even more harried than before. I stood to greet him.

As I reached my hand into my purse, he hissed, "Not here. Follow me." We walked around a corner to a small alcove where luggage carts were stored. He produced a piece of folded paper from his blazer and shoved it at me. "Here. I found two."

"Thanks," I said and slipped the paper into my purse. I gave him the two hundred bucks I promised. He suddenly seized my wrist. His grip was sweaty but strong, and it hurt.

"You never got this from me, you hear?" he whispered fiercely through gritted teeth. "And you tell Omar that this is a one time favor. This ain't part of the deal." I didn't like this guy and I didn't like the way he was twisting my arm, hissing hot breath in my face. I tried to pull away but he tightened his hold. "You like to drop names, but I don't know you. I think you might just be a lying bitch. So I'm gonna call Yvonne myself and find out the truth."

"Fine," I said, mustering all my courage. "Now you let go of my arm this second or I'm going to kick you in the balls so hard you'll taste them."

He offered one last sneer and then shoved me away, releasing my arm. We each stormed off in opposite directions, him toward the reservation desk and me toward the front door. I rubbed my wrist where he'd held me. It was red and sore, maybe bruised, but I would be okay. I made my way out to the self-park lot and found my Honda. I slipped behind the wheel and took a deep breath.

I thought about the wisdom—or lack thereof—of using my real first name. I also thought about Jeff Walker's threat to call Yvonne. At the moment, I could only think of one way to respond to such a threat. I closed my eyes, put my forehead on the steering wheel, and muttered, "Craptastic . . ."

CHAPTER 12

THE NEXT MORNING BILLY WAS his usual charming self.

"You're late again," he barked. "I should just fire you once and for all."

"Good morning to you, too, bro."

"You take advantage of being my sister. You think I won't do it. If you worked for someone else—a law firm or a bank or something—you wouldn't be able to get away with the garbage you pull here."

I sat at my desk and sighed. "Don't worry. I've been putting in a lot of hours on a case."

He looked up and scratched his unshaven neck. "Case? What case? Your missing person?"

"Yeah."

"You still getting paid for this *case*?"

"Of course."

"How much?"

"A thousand bucks."

"Where's the money?"

"In my purse."

"Dammit, Sandy. We have accounting standards, you know. Bank accounts and statements and crap. You can't just walk around with a grand in your purse. Plus, we have to keep track of hours spent so we can get paid for the actual work we do. You may not care about losing money, but I do." He sighed dramatically. "Give me the damn name. *I'll* find 'em. You can go serve these papers." He lifted a file from the corner of his desk.

"I . . . I already found her." I looked away. "She was in the morgue." The thought of Naomi on that fluorescent-saturated gurney filled me with sudden grief. Billy sensed my tone and softened his bluster.

"Who was she?" he asked, putting the file back down.

"Just a kid. An immigrant. She was alone here."

Billy seemed to realize something. He was no fool. "And . . . who's your client?"

"The girl was an escort. She was trafficked here from Vietnam. Someone from my former life got worried when she disappeared and hired me to find her."

"Your former life? Sandy . . ."

"Billy, it's fine."

"I don't like it," he said. "It's dangerous." He scratched the thick stubble on his chin. "I don't care how much money it is or how much we may need the cash. You never have to get involved in that world again. I'd rather close the doors first."

I stood and crossed to his desk. Then I leaned down and kissed him on top of the head. "You're a good brother, Billy." He waved me away and I sat back down.

But then something occurred to him. "Wait. You said you were putting in a lot of hours. If you already found her . . . ? You're done putting in hours, right?"

"My client asked me to find out what happened to her. The death was suspicious."

Billy closed his eyes, which appeared to get swallowed by his bushy brows, and shook his head. "Sandy. Sandy. This ain't good. I got a bad feeling. You need to drop it."

"It's okay. I've got it under control."

"Finding out what happened is the cops' job. We serve papers, track down deadbeat dads, and expose workman's comp cheats. We don't solve murders. Close the file. You're done." He paused and I was silent for a moment. "Sandy, you hear me?"

"I hear you." How could I explain to him that I felt compelled to solve this case? That solving this case now felt somehow linked to my own bloody exit from the life six years ago? I knew that sounded crazy, but that's how I felt. I needed to atone for my own cowardly silence. I could have easily been Naomi. Dead on that gurney. Who would have solved my case?

"Sandy?"

"It's fine, Billy." I grabbed the file from the corner of his desk. "I'll take care of this." Before he could protest, I was out the door.

The papers to be served were intended for a guy named Joe Spinelli from his soon-to-be ex-wife. Or, to be more precise, the papers were from his soon-to-be ex-wife's new lawyer. The simple act of me handing him an envelope today would forever change his life. He will divide his life according to this new historical demarcation line: pre-divorce and post-divorce. BS—Before Sandy—and AS—After Sandy.

Joe worked at Universal Studios in an overnight maintenance role. He got off work within the hour. So I hopped onto I-4 and headed west. Since I couldn't get into the parks without forking over twenty bucks to park and more than $100 just to walk through the gate, not to mention the interminable death march from the parking garage to City Walk and the actual theme parks,

I decided to catch him getting into his car in the employee lot off Turkey Lake Road.

The file told me that he drove a red 2003 Hyundai sedan. I also had his license tag number. I pulled into the employee lot and started driving up and down rows of cars, looking for the red Hyundai. I jokingly thought that I should also start scanning for a black Mercedes, too. After all, if Marta was right, then the house where she had been held wasn't too far from here. But then I asked myself, *why not*? I mean, really, how much different would it be to drive up and down the streets of the nearby MetroWest neighborhoods looking for a car than driving up and down these parking lot rows? Was it really that far-fetched? Granted, even if I were in the right neighborhood on the right street, the odds of seeing the car were still remote. The Mercedes might not even be there, or might be hidden inside a garage. Plus, there were more than a few Mercedes sedans in the nearby neighborhoods. But, still, it might be worth a shot. There were only a couple of neighborhoods where you could even see the Hogwarts castle.

After nineteen minutes of driving up and down rows, amazingly, I located the Hyundai. I also found an open parking spot not far away with a convenient vantage point from which to see Joe when he approached his vehicle. I parked, rolled down the windows, and settled in for a mini stakeout. I had a can of Diet Coke and a vending machine bag of Doritos to tide me over. I opened them both. We were entering the hot season in Orlando, but bearable for the moment.

While I sat, I pulled out the paper that Jeff Walker gave me yesterday. He printed out two hotel records on a single sheet listing the names, addresses, and phone numbers of two guests who had stayed on the fourth floor of the Olsen on the night that

Naomi disappeared. Each of their names matched the kind of name that Brenda remembered. She said that when Naomi called her, she was going on a date with a john named Dan or Stan or something similar. If anything unusual happened during that date, or if Naomi said anything or left something behind, perhaps one of these guys could fill me in.

The first name was Sam Coleman. He lived in Stamford, Connecticut. Apparently, he was a member of the Olsen Medallion Club, and I even had his rewards account number. He checked in the day before Naomi disappeared and departed three days after.

The second name was Dan Bishop. He hailed from Naperville, Illinois. He arrived two days before Naomi vanished and checked out the next morning. I saw no Medallion Club number on his record.

I tilted the bag of Doritos to pour the last few crumbs into my mouth and debated how I should use this information. I should probably hand it over to Carlisle and Benders but that would lead to Jeff Walker, which would lead to Omar, which would lead to Brenda and the girls. I'd go there if I had to, but for now I thought I could dig a little more dirt before hitting bedrock.

Aw, hell. I pulled out my cell phone and punched in the first phone number for Sam Coleman. I had no plan. I knew that I should definitely have a plan, but sometimes you just have to jump into the pool and assume you can swim.

"Hello?" A woman's voice. A little deeper than mine, maybe a few years older?

"Hello," I said in my most professional tone. "May I speak with Sam Coleman, please?"

"Speaking."

I blinked my eyes twice while her statement registered in my brain. At first it made no sense. Sam is a man, right? It took me a second to realize the fallacy of that assumption.

"Hello?" she said again into my surprised silence.

"Uh, *Sam*? . . . Sa-*mantha* Coleman . . . ?"

"That's right. Can I help you?"

"Yes," I replied. "I am, uh . . ." I am, uh, totally floundering. Then I got an idea. A crappy idea, but any port in a storm, right? "I am calling . . . uh, from the Olsen Regency Hotel in Orlando. You recently stayed at our property, and this is simply a follow-up guest satisfaction survey."

"Oh, well, actually, I'm right in the middle of someth—"

"This won't take a minute. How was everything during your stay?"

"Fine."

"Did you use all the amenities, such as the pool and restaurants?"

"Some. The pool. The breakfast buffet."

"Were you here for business or pleasure?"

"I guess a little of both. I had a meeting in Orlando and brought my family with me. We stayed a few extra days and went to the parks."

This smelled a lot like a big fat dead end. If she was telling the truth and was, in fact, the same Sam Coleman who stayed at the Olsen Regency the night Naomi disappeared, I sincerely doubted that she was Naomi's date. Not with the whole family camping out in the room. A quick scan of the hotel record confirmed the number of room occupants during the stay: five. I hadn't noticed that.

"Oh," I said. "And how old are your children?"

"Thirteen, ten, and seven."

"Did, uh, did they enjoy the property?"

"I suppose." Sam Coleman sighed loudly. "Look, are we almost done? I really am busy."

"That's it. You've been very helpful. Thank you for being an Olsen Regency guest."

I hung up. Dang. I wasn't exactly sure what I expected but that certainly wasn't it. As soon as I started to ponder the implications of my call with Sam Coleman, I saw a tired-looking guy with an insulated lunch bag walking down the row of cars. Before I could consciously wonder if he was the Joe Spinelli whose life I was about to change, he stopped at the red Hyundai. I sprang out the door and darted over to him with the envelope.

"Mr. Spinelli?" I called as I approached.

He stopped and turned to me. "Yes?"

I handed him the envelope, which he innocently accepted. "You've been served."

He almost seemed to visibly deflate. "My wife?"

"Sorry," was all I could offer.

He sighed. "She's sleeping with my cousin."

I nodded as if I already knew this. "Sorry," I repeated.

He tucked the envelope under his arm and, without another word, slipped into his car. In another moment the taillights of the red Hyundai were pulling out of the parking lot. He had just entered the AS portion of his life. Good luck, Joe.

I got back into my Accord and stared at the paper Jeff Walker printed. The more I considered the conversation with Sam Coleman, the surer I became that she was on the level and that she had nothing to do with either Naomi or her disappearance. Maybe I should have asked her if she happened to see a young

Asian girl wandering the fourth floor during her stay, but I had no idea how I could have asked that without arousing suspicion.

The next name on the list was Dan Bishop. With my luck this one would turn out to actually be Danielle Bishop. The number of room occupants on this record was only one. I punched in the phone number and let it ring a couple of times. I was about to give up and press END when the ringing stopped.

"Hello?" A man's voice.

"Dan Bishop, please," I said.

"Can I help you?"

"Are you Mr. Bishop?"

"Yeah. Who is this?"

I put a smile in my voice. "Mr. Bishop. I'm calling from the Olsen Regency Resort in Orlando. I just have a few questions I'd like to ask, if that's okay."

There was a long pause. A very long pause. A weirdly long pause. I could hear his faint breathing so I knew he was still there.

"Mr. Bishop?" I finally said.

"Yes." Another pause.

"Is everything okay?"

"Fine. What sort of questions?"

My girlish intuition was going off like a smoke alarm inside my head. But I didn't want to spook him. "Oh, you know, just a routine survey about your stay."

"Oh. Just routine. Okay."

Yeah. Something was definitely up with Mr. Dan Bishop. "That's right. First, how was everything during your stay?"

"It was good. Fine. Great. You know."

"Super. And did you use any of the resort amenities?"

"Amenities?"

"The pool, the fitness center, the restaurants . . ."

"Oh. Yeah. The food was real good. I liked the omelet station."

"And was your visit for business or pleasure?"

"Business." He answered quickly. Too quickly? Perhaps I was being hypersensitive. Perhaps I was reading too much significance into his awkward responses because I wanted him to be a link to Naomi. Maybe I simply caught him on the toilet. I had to avoid jumping to conclusions.

"Do you mind if I ask the nature of your business?"

"Uh . . ."

"Knowing what brought you to our property helps us to tailor future programs to better meet our guests' needs." Damn. Not bad, I thought,

"Yeah, okay. I'm an actuary for an insurance company. I was there for a conference at the convention center."

"Great. Thank you. Was there anything special or . . . out of the ordinary that you did during your stay?"

Another pause. "Nope. Everything was pretty normal."

"So, no special extracurriculars?" I was pressing.

"What do you mean?"

I decided to press some more. "Oh, you know. Did you do anything *out of the ordinary*? Anything *special* in your room?"

Another longish pause. "I still don't know what you mean. Everything was normal."

"Did you experience any problems and, if so, were they fixed to your satisfaction?"

"Yeah. I mean, no problems." A cough. Was that suspicious? I didn't know. I wanted to think so. "Everything was fine."

And did you pay to have sex with an underage immigrant from Vietnam?

Of course, I didn't ask this. But I was dying to.

"Is there anything else you would like to share about your visit?" I asked.

"No. Nothing else."

"Okay. Well, thank you for your time and for being a loyal Olsen guest."

Click. He hung up before I even finished my sentence. Yeah, Mr. Dan Bishop, there was definitely more going on than you were telling me. I turned the key in my ignition and cranked up the Honda. Before I had even pulled out of the parking spot, I had already decided that Mr. Dan Bishop needed an in-person visit.

CHAPTER 13

I COULD THINK OF TWO CHOICES. I could hire a local P.I. in the greater Chicago area to go visit Mr. Dan Bishop and ask a series of questions that I would provide. Or, I could go myself.

Sending someone else would probably be easier and likely cheaper, depending upon airfare and hotel costs. Billy had hired distant P.I.s several times since I'd been working for him, mostly for lawyers who needed interviews conducted with witnesses who were no longer in the area. It worked well but the limitation was that they could really only work from a set script. They didn't have the case background to improvise.

If I went myself, it would probably cost more. I would also be away from Tyler for two or three days. I hated being away from him. But I would have the advantage of being able to both work from a script and wing it. Maybe it was really an aversion to the hard work of preparation, but I seemed to operate best without a net. I liked being able to throw an unexpected question out there. Sure, it sometimes backfired, but it could also be very effective.

I went back and forth between these choices and the relative benefits of each as I drove to the A place apartment. I planned to slip into the parking lot, text Collette to come down and get in the car, and then go somewhere we could discuss my two phone conversations. No matter which option we chose—hire a local P.I. or send me, or maybe neither—Collette would be paying for it, so she had to approve the plan.

I turned my car into the A place apartment complex and my antennae were up for any signs of Omar or his tattooed buddy R.J. I was so focused on not being spotted by them that I almost missed the big black sedan pulling out of the parking lot.

Almost.

I turned my head just in time to see the Mercedes logo on the car's hood. It took a second for the logo and its significance to register in my brain. However, as soon as that second passed, my brain kicked in and I whipped the wheel around. By the time my car was pointed out of the apartment complex parking lot, the Mercedes was already zooming down the street.

I floored it across the road, turning left and scraping the under-carriage of my car on the curb gutter. This might be a wild goose chase. I might be completely wrong that this was *the* black Mercedes that Marta mentioned. But I couldn't take a chance.

The A place apartment was in a decent complex in a middle-class neighborhood. The regular residents would proba-bly have been shocked to discover that the second-floor apart-ment in the #3 building by the pool housed a collection of professional escorts. It wasn't some tenement. The idea of an apartment resident somewhere in the complex owning a Mercedes wasn't completely unrealistic. But it would certainly be the exception.

So chasing a black sedan on the off chance that it was in fact Marta's Mercedes was a risk worth taking. And, from what I could see, this was an especially nice, new-looking Mercedes, not a base level or older model. I caught up with the car at a red light. The windows were tinted illegally dark so I couldn't see any driver or passenger. After a minute the light turned green and we were off.

Whoever was driving had a serious NASCAR complex and I struggled to keep up. We went a few blocks with me trailing at a respectable distance. The car made a right into a Publix shopping center—with no signal. I missed the entrance that the Mercedes turned into and instead used the plaza's second entrance farther down. The Mercedes pulled up to a Starbucks and the driver's door opened.

A big, good-looking blond dude got out. He was built and flaunted his physique in a tight black t-shirt and blue jeans. Dark sunglasses hid his eyes. There didn't appear to be any passengers in the car.

I parked across the lot and stayed in my car. The thought of him going in for a coffee suddenly made me have to pee. Seriously? Now? Damn that Diet Coke. I sat for a minute, debating whether or not I might have time to run into Publix and use the restroom. Finally, I decided I better go now or not at all.

I opened the door, but then saw the blond dude come back out of Starbucks with a venti cup of something. Crap. I closed my door and started up my car. In another moment I was again chasing him down the street.

He was hard to keep up with. I didn't want to get spotted, so I avoided the weaving in and out of traffic that he was doing. But I also didn't want to lose him. Thankfully, there were occasional red lights to slow him down, plus the standard Orlando gridlock. I had to push two yellow lights to avoid getting separated. I prayed that they didn't have red light cameras.

I had a feeling I knew where he was generally going, and when I saw him getting onto the I-4 on-ramp I knew I was right. I

stayed in a different lane a few car lengths back. I couldn't afford
to get made. Fortunately, we weren't on the highway long enough
for me to lose him. Soon we were zooming off the interstate and
I noticed that I was not far from where I had handed poor Joe
Spinelli his divorce papers earlier in the morning.

My heart started to race as we got closer to the MetroWest
community. This might still all be a coincidence, but the odds
were going down. The number of people who would drive a black
Mercedes from the A place complex directly to the neighborhood
described by Marta had to be pretty small, right? Plus, the driver
with the biceps fit Marta's description of the blond man with
músculos grandes whom she saw in the house where she was held
when she was first brought to Orlando.

Staying unnoticed would get more difficult now that we were
off major roads. We turned down Hiawassee Blvd. and then into
a neighborhood called Osprey Cove, complete with a large, landscaped entrance sign. There was no way to avoid being seen now.
I could only hope that the blond dude hadn't noticed me earlier.

When he turned onto a small side street, I made the quick
decision not to follow. It would have been way too suspicious. I
slowed down and craned my neck to see if I could spot where he
was going. But he rounded a bend and then I was past the turn.
What should I do now? Double back? Go forward and hope that
the road connected again farther down?

I quickly pulled over to the side of the road and took out my
antiquated iPhone. I opened a map app and located myself on the
GPS. The road that the Mercedes drove down was called
Waterview St. It didn't connect back to the road I was on, which
was the main thoroughfare through Osprey Cove. But I did see
another entrance. It would take a few twists and turns through

the manicured lanes of upper-middle-class suburbia, but I could come back up Waterview St. from the opposite end. If I was lucky, I would spot the Mercedes in a driveway. If I was unlucky, it would be inside a garage or would have turned down the connecting road and be gone. Or the blond dude would be sitting on the hood waiting for me.

In another few minutes, I had navigated my way to the other end of Waterview St. and was slowly driving back toward where I had entered the neighborhood. I saw a white Mercedes and a black Lexus, but so far no black Mercedes. I was tracking my progress on the map app on my phone and was quickly running out of road.

And then, finally, I looked up from the smartphone screen and saw it. Just peeking over the tops of the shingled roofs was the distant, looming Gryffindor Tower of Hogwarts. It was an odd, incongruous sight, this fantasy castle turret set against a foreground of upper-middle-class tract homes. There were no wizards on brooms darting through the air, but I almost expected to see them. And directly in front of me was the black Mercedes. It was parked in the driveway of a nice, middle-class ranch house located just this side of the bend in the road. Two-car garage. Beige stucco with white trim. Decent window treatments. The Mercedes was the only car in the driveway. I didn't see the driver, and I didn't want to get spotted. So I rolled past the house, committing the address to memory. 1622 Waterview St.

My brain was racing. Between the discovery of this Mercedes and my phone calls, especially my suspicion that not all was kosher with Mr. Dan Bishop, I needed a moment to collect my thoughts and reflect. I also still needed to talk to Collette. But most of all, I *really* needed to pee.

I drove out of the subdivision and parked at a Taco Bell. I hopped out of my car and fast-walked into the ladies' room. My bladder situation was starting to get critical. After I washed up, I got a burrito and another diet soda. Might as well start refilling my reservoir, right? My diet cola addiction would not be denied. The food helped me calm down. Once I finished my burrito and was working on a cola refill, I texted Collette. She was available now. Neither Omar nor R.J. were at the apartment. They were both there earlier, so it was unlikely that they would be back. I told her I would pick her up.

A half hour later she slipped into the passenger seat of my Honda and we drove and talked, with no particular destination in mind. I recapped my day, telling her about the Mercedes first, then the two phone calls.

"I saw him," she said in her Georgia drawl.

"Who?" I asked.

"The blond guy. In the Mercedes. He was in the apartment earlier with Omar. I don't know who he is. But I think he might be the same guy that Marta talked about. He had a funny accent. German or Russian or something."

I twisted my lips. What the hell was Omar doing with a guy like that? Was he maybe the secret partner who ran the website? Or some new character swirling around Omar's cesspool of a business?

"Have you ever seen him before?" I asked.

"No, but two of the other girls say that they've seen him a couple of times in the last few weeks."

"Did you hear what they talked about?" I navigated around a UPS truck blocking traffic.

"No. He was only in the apartment a minute and then they stepped outside."

We drove in silence for a moment.

"What about the guy in Chicago?" I finally said. "What do you want to do?"

"Hell, Sandy. How should I know? You're the professional here. What do you think?"

"It all depends on how much money you want to keep investing. Airline tickets ain't cheap."

"I got money, honey. You know that. And the other girls are still willing to pitch in. Well, except Tonya."

"Plus, my time," I said, thinking about my conversation with Billy.

"Just tell me what you think, Sandy."

"I think he knows something." I chewed the inside of my cheek. "I want to go see the guy myself."

"Okay, then. You go and see what you can find out. I know you'll keep the expenses to a minimum."

We circled back around to the apartment and Collette ran upstairs. She reemerged a few minutes later with a wad of cash. She pushed it at me through the open driver's window.

"Here. Five hundred more for your time and another five hundred for travel. Two of the other girls pitched in."

I reached out and held her hand. "Collette. The truth is—I really don't know if this guy has anything to do with it. What if it's a dead end? Or, what if—" I grimaced. "Look, I'm not the most experienced private investigator. I may not even be any good at it. I just—I just want to be honest. I don't want you to waste your money."

Collette regarded me for a moment and then kissed my forehead. "Honey, you're the only one I would trust with this. You go find out what happened to that poor girl. If this fella in Chicago knows anything, I'm sure you'll get it outta him." She gave my hand a reassuring squeeze. Then she was gone, back up the stairs to the apartment.

I lingered for a moment and then pulled the car out of the complex for the third time today. Then it hit me—I had never been on an airplane in my life. I needed to get to a computer and make an airline reservation for my first ever flight.

CHAPTER 14

IT WAS VERY HARD TO LEAVE in the morning. *Very* hard. I had been away from Tyler overnight before, working on jobs, tailing workman's comp cheats, whatever. But I had never been *away* from him before—as in a different state in a different time zone. What if he got sick? Or something happened at school? What if he had a nightmare and I wasn't there to comfort him? What kind of mother was I?

"For God's sake, Sandy, everything will be fine," Laura tried to reassure me. But I was far from reassured.

I saw Tyler standing there in the kitchen in his little uniform and his Spider-Man backpack, holding a brown paper sack containing a peanut butter and jelly sandwich. His eyes were huge and guileless. He didn't know about, nor would he understand, my horrible past. He only knew me as his mother. My chest ached just looking at him. I could still cancel my plane ticket. I could do it in five minutes on the phone in my purse.

I swallowed the lump in my throat and hugged him close, embracing him much too tightly, fighting desperately not to bawl.

"Mommy, you're squeezing..."

I loosened my grip and quickly wiped my cheeks. Kneeling, I held him away from me by his shoulders and forced a smile.

"You're my big boy, Tyler. Can you be good for Miss Laura while I'm gone?"

He nodded. His absolute willingness to do whatever I asked pierced my heart. I kissed him on the cheek and stood, composing myself. I went over my itinerary for the eleventh time with Laura.

"My plane gets into Chicago around noon. That's Central Time. I won't check into the hotel until—"

"Sandy," Laura said in her raspy voice. "I got it. It's all written down in the kitchen. Don't worry. Everything will be fine."

"I plan to be home sometime tomorrow. But I might have to stay longer. I won't know until I get there."

"We'll be fine. Just call and let me know."

"Okay." I hesitated, rubbing my fingers through my hair. "Right. Okay."

Laura fixed me with one of her trademark Laura looks. "Go."

I swallowed again. Nodded. Gave Laura a quick hug and then I was out the door before my resolve crumbled, trailing a wheeled overnight bag behind me and breathing heavily.

As conflicted as I felt about leaving Tyler, I felt almost as guilty about Billy. I hadn't told him that I was leaving town. He had made it pretty clear that he wanted me to drop the case. He certainly wouldn't be on board with me making this trip. He would tell me to call the cops and let them handle it.

While he was probably right, these were leads that, to my knowledge, the cops were neither finding nor following. If my unique position could help move this case along more quickly by working for Collette, I wasn't quite ready to bow out yet. The cops would get everything I had anyway. In fact, I would probably call Carlisle and Benders as soon as I got back from Naperville and hand over my whole case file.

No, Billy didn't need to know. I'd called late last night and left him a vague message on the office voicemail informing him of my absence. I would tell him about my adventure to the Land of Lincoln when I got back and after I talked to the cops. Long after.

I made the drive out to the airport on a sort of autopilot. Was I crazy to be chasing someone halfway across the country on a hunch? Absolutely. I followed the signs for airport parking and eventually found a spot in the busy garage.

Although I had never actually set foot on an airplane before, I had spent plenty of time at Orlando International Airport. There was a swanky Hyatt built right into the airport overlooking the B Terminal. I'd spent my share of nights on dates in that hotel.

Sometimes, when leaving one of those Hyatt clients, I would rest my head on the big glass windows overlooking the security gate and terminal trams below and try to forget what I had just spent the night doing. I would gaze at the weary business travelers, the families sporting mouse ears, the young couples holding hands, and long to jump into the security line right behind them, slipping onto their planes and going wherever they were headed. I would have gone anywhere. I didn't care where, as long as it wasn't here. I'd fantasize about a whole new life in Phoenix or Seattle or Philadelphia or, yes, even Chicago. A fresh start.

The thought that I was now about to board one of those planes and actually go to Chicago was surreal. I did get my fresh start, after all. I had indeed come a long way in six years. I tried not to think about the fact that it took me literally killing someone to get here.

I managed to pass through security and onto the plane without incident. It mostly seemed to be a matter of attaching myself to the right crowds of people—this terminal instead of that terminal, this tram instead of that tram, this gate instead of those gates. I checked in twice more with Laura, who assured me everything was fine. Tyler made it to school before the bell. She told me to relax. I wouldn't be able to relax until I was back on the ground in Orlando with my child in my arms.

We boarded like hogs being corralled into a chute and I settled uneasily into my seat. As the plane accelerated down the runway and I felt myself pressing back into my seat, I glanced around at the other passengers to make sure that this was normal. No one seemed concerned. Across the aisle, an older guy in a wrinkled suit was even sleeping. A few moments later the plane left the ground and we became airborne. As the plane quickly rose, a corresponding queasiness descended into my gut. I again looked around for reassurance when I heard a disturbing whining noise from under the plane, followed by a terrifying thumping sound. Nobody else was even slightly bothered. I looked out the window and saw nothing out of the ordinary, unless you counted the receding landscape of Central Florida. I had no idea how much water there was. Lakes, canals, ponds, and other assorted bodies of water were literally everywhere. It's not something you notice as you're driving around.

The terrifying noises seemed to abate, and I decided that maybe what I heard was the landing gear going up. Maybe? It just seemed awfully soon after takeoff. What if there was a problem and we needed to land again? Was putting them up so quickly really prudent? At various points the plane tilted one way or the other or bounced unexpectedly, and each time my heart skipped a beat and adrenaline tunneled my vision. However, looking around at the rest of the unconcerned passengers encouraged me that the plane was, in fact, not plummeting uncontrollably to the ground.

The flight was just over three hours long and, when I was not busy fretting about a fiery crash, I spent every minute of it agonizing over my strategy for dealing with Mr. Dan Bishop. I had done some research in the databases last night and drew up a quick bio. He was a divorced father of three. Forty-four years old. Worked as an actuary for National United Insurance Company in Naperville, Illinois. He'd been there twelve years. Lived in a three-bedroom townhome he purchased for $325,000. I even had his driver's license picture. Kind of a saggy-looking white dude with thinning hair and dark circles under his eyes.

As we approached O'Hare International Airport, I saw the Chicago skyline out the window. It looked unreal, like something from a movie. Huge, mountainous buildings jutted up out of the earth on the shores of a lake so big it looked like the Atlantic Ocean back home. The midday sun glinted off the glass facades of the skyscrapers, making them appear to shift their positions in a gigantic, synchronized dance as we flew over. I couldn't take my eyes off the sight and watched for as long as I could while the plane turned, until my neck craned painfully and my eyes squinted through the oval window. I was actually here. *I was in Chicago.* I whispered it aloud so that I could make myself believe it.

The plane landed and the rugged thump of touchdown gave me another tunnel-vision adrenaline rush. I almost embarrassed myself by shrieking uncontrollably, but managed to refrain as I soon realized that all was fine. We disembarked in single file and I joined the shuffling herd on a rental car shuttle. Another crowd of people to attach myself to. The air was wonderfully temperate—warm, but a noticeable change from the sweltering humidity of Orlando. Pretty much everyone else on the shuttle seemed to be in some sort of business suit, mostly white men but a couple of women, too. The business road warriors were shuttling along to claim their chariots. And here I was riding along with them, just another cosmopolitan traveler on a business trip. Sandy Corrigan: globe-trotter.

Even after I got the car—a squat, lime green subcompact hatchback—and started driving west out of Chicago, I still had no idea how to play my approach to Dan Bishop. The thought of pretending to be a cop occurred to me, but I quickly discarded it. Impersonating a police officer was big trouble if I got caught, especially if Bishop turned out to be a dead end.

It took about an hour to get near the National United headquarters, which sat in a nondescript office park in the outer suburbs. By the time I arrived, my stomach was audibly growling. It was midafternoon for me. I had no idea that even one hour's difference in time zones could have such an effect. Although I was anxious and actually sort of queasy from nerves, my body was telling me it needed food. I grabbed a turkey sandwich at a nearby sub shop and thought some more about how to play the interview. I was stumped.

Finally, I decided, what the hell—I would wing it. It wouldn't be the first time. I drove over to the National United building and parked in a visitor's spot. I fixed my makeup, threw on a navy suit jacket to dress up my jeans, and entered the building. It was a five-story office building, with no receptionist or guard in sight on the first floor. However, there was a wall directory near the elevators. I saw that the Actuarial Department was on the third floor. I pressed the elevator call button. Okay, here we go . . .

I arrived on the third floor and looked around. To the left of the elevators was what looked like a combination receptionist / administrative assistant desk. A middle-aged woman with a brown perm was busily typing on a computer keyboard. I took a deep breath and approached her. I offered my most disarming smile and waited. After a moment, it was clear that she had no intention of acknowledging me.

I cleared my throat. "Hi."

She tilted her eyes at me without actually adjusting any other part of her body. An impressive feat. "Can I help you?"

"I hope so. I'm looking for Dan Bishop."

She pursed her lips thoughtfully. "Okay." Pause. "Do you know where he sits?"

I blinked at her. No third-degree questioning? No sign-in? I guess this National United place wasn't exactly the tightest ship in the insurance biz. "Actually, I don't. Can you direct me?"

"Down this hall." She gestured behind her. "First right. Then down on the left." She immediately returned to her typing.

I nodded my gratitude and stepped cautiously down the hall. I had no idea why I was stepping cautiously, but it seemed like the appropriate thing to do. I passed the restrooms and, after a few strides, found my confidence. I made the first right turn onto an entire floor of modular office cubicles. It was clearly what I had heard others describe as a cube farm.

I walked down the first row of cubicles on the left but didn't see Dan Bishop's name on any of the placards affixed outside each one. I walked up another cubicle corridor and then down another. I was about to ask one of the many keyboarding cubicle inhabitants where to find Dan Bishop when I finally spotted his name. I froze. It was a decent-sized space in a corner, with plexiglass walls and a built-in desk. It looked like a small glass office with no roof.

I peered through the doorless entrance but discovered that no one was present. However, the computer was on, with some sort of spreadsheet visible on the monitor. I stepped into the space like I would a darkened room, careful not to bump anything. I did a quick visual sweep, trying to spot anything that might help my investigation. It wasn't like I expected to find a photo of Naomi taped to his whiteboard, but I didn't see anything. Not even a program guide from the convention he attended in Orlando.

I hovered in the center of the space, my arms held slightly away from my body, wondering what to do. My heart was pounding. What next? How would I respond when he returned from the break room with his coffee, or the restroom, or a meeting, or wherever he was at the moment? What would I say? Had I over-played my hand by coming here, to his office? What if he had nothing to do with Naomi when he was in Orlando?

The weight of these questions pressed down on me and I felt my legs getting weak. I slowly sank into his desk chair and con-centrated on not hyperventilating. I swallowed the golf ball form-ing in my throat. I clenched my eyes shut to reset my nerve and when I opened them, I saw the doughy, balding figure of Dan Bishop standing curiously in the entrance to his plastic-walled office, a can of Dr Pepper in his hand. He was wearing a pair of brown Dockers pants and a white golf shirt. He had a bewildered but slightly offended look on his face, with a trace of a curl on his upper lip. It was apparent that he was bothered by the boldness of some stranger plopping down in his private personal chair.

"Uh," he said. "Can I help you?" He said it in a way that implied he really had no interest in helping me.

I blinked at him for a beat. For whatever reason, I simply didn't like his attitude. I had no reason to be offended myself. I was, after all, sitting in *his* chair. But, nonetheless, I didn't appreciate his "tude." And I certainly didn't like people sneering at me. It was in that instant that I decided how I was going to play this. All my nervousness and anxiety seeped away. Right or wrong, I decided to go with the douchebag approach.

"Hello?" he said with more agitation. "Can I help you with something?"

I smiled and rotated the chair seat around in a playful half circle. "We'll see," I said.

Now it was his turn to blink. He grimaced in confusion. Looked left and right in the cubicle corridor, as if some explanation was waiting out there for him. It wasn't.

"Look," he said. "Seriously. I'm very busy. Do you want something?"

I stopped spinning and gave him a stone cold stare. "Yeah, Dan. I want something. I want you to tell me about the little Asian girl in Orlando. That's what I want."

Any doubt I had about whether or not Dan Bishop had been Naomi's client vanished completely when the Dr Pepper can slipped from his hand and the blood visibly drained from his face.

CHAPTER 15

HE APPEARED TO HAVE STOPPED BREATHING. Soda was gurgling out of its red can into the fibers of the gray commercial carpet. But he remained paralyzed.

"You're ruining the carpet," I said pointing at the can at his feet.

This snapped him back to life and he bent down and picked up the can, which continued to drip onto the carpet. He stood back up and looked at the wet floor for a moment.

Finally, he said, "Who are you?"

"Tell me about the girl, Dan," I said.

Long pause. "I . . . I want a lawyer. I don't have to answer any of your questions."

I gave him my best bemused face. "Oh, you think I'm a cop? That's cute. Really. No, I'm not a cop. I'm a lot worse than a cop. And you *do* have to answer *my* questions."

"Why is that?" He was trying to put forward a tough bravado, but it was fake. I had totally freaked him out. "Who are you?"

I let him dangle uncomfortably for a few seconds before responding. "I represent the owners of the Intimate Encounters website. Let's just say that this is a follow-up."

"Jesus. You came here—to my work? Are you nuts?"

"Would you prefer to talk somewhere else? That's fine. Let's go."

"Go to hell. I'm not going anywhere with you."

I smiled coldly. "Yes, you are."

"Yeah? And—and why's that?"

"Because I'm not leaving until you talk to me. I am going to sit right here and get louder and louder as the day goes on, asking what I imagine will be very uncomfortable questions about how you spent your time during the"—I mimed air quotes—"big conference in Orlando."

"Like hell you will. I'm calling security."

"No, you're not. If I even see a security guard, your boss and your boss's boss will start getting emails and phone calls detailing how you"—I raised my voice to an awkwardly loud volume— "*pay for sex*"—back to normal volume—"with underage girls while on business trips. I'm sure that will go over real well during annual performance review time."

"Shh! Shut up. Goddamn. Keep your voice down. I *work* here. Are you nuts?" His front crumbled. "What the hell more do you people want from me? I've already paid you seven thousand goddamn dollars. I don't *have* any more money. I'm tapped."

I blinked at him. Seven thousand dollars? Did I hear that right? That was an astronomical amount of money. It made no sense. I had no response. Fortunately, Dan Bishop was still talking.

"You can't—you can't come here to my work. I could lose everything. Please. *Please.* You have to go. Just go."

"Okay . . ." I said quietly, still stunned by the amount of money he had paid. "But you're coming with me."

His face blanched again. "No," he said, shaking his head. "No. Like hell. I don't know you."

"Look, Dan, I'm not here for money. I promise. I just need to ask a few follow-up questions."

"Follow-up questions? Since when? I've never gotten follow-up questions before."

"Have you ever paid seven grand before?"

A long pause. I assumed he had never paid that much before. "You could have just called me on the phone. Why show up here *at my work*?"

"Really? Would you really have talked to me on the phone?"

His silence indicated that he would not, in fact, have spoken to me on the phone. When I saw him hesitating, I decided to press him further.

"Plus," I said, swiveling the chair slightly with my foot. "I don't think you want me calling Yvonne . . ."

"Yvonne . . . ?" I saw his Adam's apple bob with a big swallow. "Why would you do that?"

"Only if I have to." I fixed him with my gaze. "Do I have to?"

Very long pause. He blinked his eyes three times. "No."

"Great," I said. "Then where would you like to chat? We can talk here or go somewhere a little more private. It's entirely up to you."

The choice wasn't hard. I followed Dan Bishop out of the building and then tailgated his white Nissan Altima with my snot-green rental out of the industrial office park. We drove a few miles down the road to a municipal baseball park. With school still in session, the park was empty except for a couple of random joggers in the distance. We parked the cars and he led me to a seat in the bleachers by one of the Little League diamonds.

"So," he said, after we were seated. "How long will this take?"

"It depends on how honest your answers are."

"This is a goddamn nightmare. What else can I tell you? What else is there to say?"

"Let's start with the basics. How many times have you hired a girl?"

A big sigh. "Ever? Or from your service?"

"Both."

"What is this? Some kind of hooker market research?"

I shrugged. "Yeah. Something like that. Just answer the question."

"I dunno. A few."

"C'mon. You're going to have to do better than that."

"Whatever. Maybe twice a year. Maybe three or four times with you guys total."

I looked out at a male jogger in the distance and wondered about the seven thousand dollars. He definitely didn't pay that three or four times. "So you'd consider yourself a regular?"

"Yeah, I guess." He glanced away, disgusted. "Look, if you're really from the website, you already know all this. That's why I was offered the special."

"Yeah, okay. Relax. I'm getting to that." In fact, I had no idea what I was getting to. I had no clue what "the special" was. There was no special service that I recalled from my days in Omar's employ. "So why did you want the special?"

"I dunno. I guess I got tired of the same old same old. After I booked the date online, the woman from the website called and told me that I could spice things up if I wanted. Only available to regular, trusted clients. I got the link to the restricted section of the website. There were only two girls in the gallery. One called Lucky and, of course, Spice. She was so beautiful and . . . exotic.

She was the one. I could spice things up with Spice. That sounded pretty good, y'know?"

I wondered to myself if Dan Bishop was aware that Spice, aka Naomi Nguyen, was an underage child forced here against her will. I wondered if he cared. But I bit my tongue to keep him talking. To my knowledge, he was the last one to see her alive. I needed to know what he knew.

"What were you looking for?"

"I dunno. Just different."

"Different how?"

"I don't know! It's your goddamn service." He took a deep breath and looked down at his hands, which were opening and closing into clenched fists. I didn't like this dude and a seriously hostile vibe was starting to waft off him like an odor. I started peering around my surroundings for escape routes or something to defend myself. Bishop continued speaking quietly, but with a malevolent intensity that gave me the heebie-jeebies. "It was the five-year anniversary of my divorce. My ex was being a total bitch about my kids. A total, raving bitch. I was just really, y'know. On edge. I had some money from Vegas that she didn't know anything about. So when I got offered the special, I thought, why the hell not?" He kept clenching and unclenching his hands. "I was told that for two grand I could have her all night and do whatever I wanted. No rules. Whatever. I. Wanted. If I got rough, that was okay. I could go as far as I wanted."

"And how far was that?" He gave me a malevolent glare. "Just tell me what happened."

"I have to go through this again?"

"You think I like coming all the way to Chicago? Hell yes, you have to go through it again. You either go through it with me or I start making calls. And then you'll wish you were telling me instead. We know the story. But now I need the details."

More clenching and unclenching. "Fine. I got a little carried away. I thought it was part of the fantasy, right? I thought I was paying for no rules. A little choking, maybe a slap to the face. Some spanking. I mean, I was paying *two grand* after all." He looked up at the outfield and his eyes went distant. I didn't think he was looking at the baseball field anymore. He seemed to be back in the hotel room now. "So just as I was, y'know, finishing, I kind of choked her. I thought she was into it. But she scratched my arms with her nails and then her eyes rolled back. I jerked back and smacked her. My arms were cut and bleeding. It hurt like hell. I kinda lost my temper. I guess I smacked her a few more times. Then I saw the bed. She had crapped and pissed all over the sheets. It was completely disgusting. Then she rolled over on her side and started coughing real bad. I guess from the choking. Like I said, I thought she was into it. I told her to go in the bathroom and clean herself up. She was a goddamn mess. She didn't move at first. She just laid there, coughing and crying. She was saying something in another language but I had no idea what. Snot started running out of her nose. I got dressed and then told her again to go to the bathroom. It smelled awful. She just laid there crying and sputtering in her own filth. Finally, I grabbed her arm and pulled her out of the bed. I dragged her to the bathroom and told her to clean herself up."

I looked down and realized that I had involuntarily clenched my own fists. This story was turning my stomach. That poor girl. What must have she been feeling? What dehumanizing fear?

Bishop had gone silent. I verbally prodded him. "So, what then?"

He was breathing more rapidly. His hands stopped clenching and unclenching, instead freezing themselves into a crooked position between the two that looked almost like rigor. He continued talking to the outfield. "So, she closed the door to clean up while I stripped the sheets off the bed. After a while, I finally heard the tub faucet running." His voice grew flatter, slightly more monotone, distant. "I piled the dirty sheets into the corner. And then I waited for her to come out. Ten minutes. Fifteen minutes. I don't remember when the faucet stopped running. I wasn't really paying attention. After about twenty minutes I knocked on the door. But she didn't say anything. I tried opening the door, but it was locked. I pounded on it and told her to open up. But she ignored me. By this time I was pretty pissed.

Finally, I called the number from the website and talked to some woman. I told her that her girl had locked herself in the bathroom and wouldn't come out. I gave her my room number and she said someone would be there in a few minutes. He must have been in the lobby because it was literally like only ten minutes before I heard the knock on my door."

I immediately wondered who it was who had come to the door—Omar or R.J., or maybe Jeff Walker, my buddy from the front desk. But I dared not ask. If I were really representing the website, I would probably know that particular detail.

"Well, you probably know the rest," Bishop continued. "Yvonne pounded on the bathroom door and barked something at her in Russian. But the door stayed locked."

Now I blinked. *Yvonne?* I thought he said that "*he* must have been in the lobby." It didn't make any sense. Russian? I only knew one possible Russian in this story—the guy with the biceps in the Mercedes. But his name couldn't be Yvonne, could it?

And then it hit me. I could be so stupid sometimes. *Ivan.* Ivan, pronounced the way a Russian might pronounce it. Not "Eye-van," but "Eee-vahn."

In my surprise, as I was working this out in my head, Bishop was still talking.

" . . . by this time he had found a small screwdriver in a little leather kit he had in his pocket. He worked at the lock for a minute or two and then I heard it click. He turned the knob and swung the door open. The girl was in the bathtub, eyes closed. Still naked. Her head was sort of flopped over to one side. The water was about half full and was completely red. Ivan kneeled down and reached into the water. He pulled her arm up and I saw that she had sliced her wrist open in three jagged lines. They almost looked like tiny gills. We figured out that she had found a little grooming knife I had in my toiletry bag, climbed into the tub, and cut both her wrists. Then she sat in the warm water and bled out."

I said nothing. I was too stunned to respond. I swallowed the lump in my throat and let him go on.

"Ivan checked for a pulse. He lifted her eyelids. Finally he said that she was dead." He paused for a moment. "I was numb, you know. I didn't know what to do. Should I call the cops? An ambulance? When I asked, Ivan grabbed me by the shirt and told me to do exactly as he said. I was panicking and he's a scary dude. I said okay. There was no blood on the floor or towels or anything. It was all in the tub. He told me to wait in the room. He would be right back. So I sat there with a dead girl for almost an hour. I was kind of freaking out. When Ivan got back, he had rubber gloves, a sheet of plastic, towels, some duct tape, and a big roller suitcase. First we put on the gloves. Then we drained the tub, rinsed her off a couple of times, and used the towels he brought to dry her. Then he wrapped duct tape around her wrists to keep them from bleeding any more. He opened the suitcase, lined it with the plastic, and then folded her into it. He threw in the towels and her clothes, and sealed up the plastic with some duct tape. Then he zipped the suitcase. He told me that after he left I was supposed to rinse out the sheets and take a shower myself. He also wanted me to scrub the tub and the faucets and the handles with soap. And wipe down everything she could have touched with a towel. After that I could call housekeeping and tell them I had an accident and needed new sheets. He wanted me to put the sheets on myself. No one else was to come into the room that night." Bishop took a long, deep breath. He said the next few sentences with his eyes closed. "Before he left, he told me that if I wanted to off the girl I should have paid for it up front. I argued and said that I didn't. She killed herself. I just wanted to play rough, not kill anyone. He said that she was still dead on my date. So there would be a surcharge for the cleanup." He opened his eyes. "It turned out to be another five grand. What could I say? I did everything he told me to do and then let them take another five thousand dollars from my credit card. I'm maxed." He looked down at his still crooked fingers. "It was the single worst moment in my entire life. I am never calling another escort, ever."

I rubbed my face. It was his story, his experience, but I was drained.

"So," he said, finally looking at me. "Are you happy now? Is that what you wanted?"

I couldn't meet his gaze. I was disgusted. It may have been the information I needed, but hearing that story was probably the very last thing that I wanted.

CHAPTER 16

I DROVE THE RENTAL CAR back to Chicago. I had no appetite. My hands trembled the whole way.

The turn-by-turn navigation on my phone guided me to the airport Hampton Inn hotel and, like a mindless robot, I did as instructed. Left turn here. Exit in five hundred feet. It didn't tell me to stop and park, but I did. I sat with the engine running for several minutes, my mind blank and empty.

They stuffed her into a suitcase and wheeled her out through the lobby under everyone's noses.

I considered flying back that night, paying the exorbitant change fee just to get out of there, to not have to share the same metropolitan area as Mr. Dan Bishop. But the flights were all booked. I was stuck in Chicago until 6:45 the next morning Central time, when, God willing, my plane was scheduled to pull back from the jetway gate.

I took several deep breaths, exhaling slowly, screwing up my nerve to walk into the lobby. When I booked this trip and reserved the hotel, I knew I would be spending the night. Overnight was part of the deal. But, as I may have already mentioned, I hadn't spent the night in a hotel in six years. Not since the night I earned the scar on my arm. My Diamond Cut.

I shut off the engine and pulled my suitcase from the trunk, involuntarily envisioning a slightly larger version that could hold the folded body of an innocent Vietnamese teenager stuffed into a plastic bag. I shook the thought from my mind. Or I at least tried to. I checked in at the front desk, saying little other than a few monosyllabic confirmations.

A few minutes later, I found myself standing in the hallway outside room 318 with my plastic key card in hand. I stared at the card as if it held the answer. It might if I only knew the question.

This was ridiculous. Just put the card in the slot. Finally, I did.

Once in the room I immediately hung the Do Not Disturb sign on the outside handle and then locked and bolted the door. I turned on every light. I turned on the TV and found the Food Network. I stared for a few moments as several chefs tried not to get chopped. Then I stripped off my clothes and took the hottest shower I could stand, just this side of scalding. I lathered up a washcloth and scrubbed my body from face to toes. No matter how hot the water or how hard I scrubbed, I couldn't remove the image of Naomi Nguyen's lifeless face from my memory.

I hadn't seen the cuts on her wrists on the coroner's video screen, but I had seen the bruises on her neck from Dan Bishop's hands. The bruises, the absence of blood at the location where her body was found, the residue of tape on her wrists—or even the tape itself—maybe other clues as well. All of these had led the medical examiner to declare the death suspicious. Naomi's death was probably listed as a likely homicide, although Inspector Ruiz would have never disclosed that to me.

Was it homicide? If Dan Bishop was telling the truth, Naomi may have been the one to cut her own wrists, but who really was responsible? Bishop? Omar? Ivan? The trafficker who took her from her village? Her father for selling her? All of them? None of them?

Or was it me, for not rolling over on Omar six years ago? If I had cooperated, would Naomi still be alive today?

I finished my shower but I didn't feel any cleaner. As I dressed, I looked at my phone and saw that I had a voicemail from Billy. I couldn't face listening to him yell at me about not being there, or whatever other deficiency he had found in my work. I couldn't do it now. Later.

Instead, I dialed Laura.

"Sandy!" Her raspy smoker's voice felt like a comforting, warm blanket. "How's it going?"

"It's . . . going."

There was a short pause. "What's wrong, honey?" Laura knew me too well.

"I'm okay. It's been a day. I'm just spent."

"You get what you came for?"

"Yeah. I think so."

"You sure you're okay?"

"No," I said. "Is Tyler there?"

"Sure. Hang on."

I heard the phone thump down on a hard surface. Then the sweet voice of my precious boy.

"Hi, Mommy."

And my eyes instantly filled with tears. "Hi, baby. How was school today?" He proceeded to tell me of his wonderful, perfect day. His class drew the state of Florida for art. He even added an alligator to Lake Okeechobee. They played kickball at recess and he scored a run. It rained but he didn't get too wet. Father Tim, the young priest assigned to the nearby cathedral, visited their class and played the guitar. I squeezed the tears from my eyes and kept them shut.

"That's wonderful, Tyler." A deep breath. "I miss you."

"Me, too. Miss Laura says that I can have ice cream if I do all my homework, but I'm not supposed to tell you." I couldn't help but laugh. I heard Laura's faux chastising voice in the background.

"That's okay, baby. You can have ice cream. I'll see you tomorrow, okay?"

"Okay."

"I love you."

"I love you, too."

I took the opportunity to sniffle while the phone was handed back to Laura. I reminded her of my flight arrangements and let her know when I would be home. She told me to take care and we hung up. I sat on the edge of the bed, cradling the cell phone in my hand. Without really thinking about it, I lay gingerly back onto the bedspread, as if it were a hot bath and I didn't want to burn myself. I was careful to keep both feet planted flat on the floor.

When I had booked the hotel, I had made sure to reserve a room with a couch. I hadn't slept on a hotel bed in six years. I vowed I never would again. The couch would be my sleeping surface tonight. Yet, here I was now, reclining on the top of the bed, trying it out.

It made my skin feel weird. Prickly and flushed, like hives.

The popcorn ceiling. The fire suppression sprinkler head sticking out. How many times had I lain on other hotel beds, looking up at similar ceilings, at similar sprinkler heads? Lying there with my feet up on the bed while some nameless stranger lay on top of me, crushing my dignity, suffocating my soul. What was the ceiling like six years ago when I had last lain on a bed like this? I honestly didn't recall. But everything else about that night came flooding back, unbidden.

*   *   *

The date had started like any other. I went to the room. He let me in. He was in his mid-forties, hair just starting to thin on top. About my height, meaning a little short for a guy, kind of overweight. His extra weight was soft—fat, not muscle. He said his name was Gary, although I later learned that it was really Gerald.

We took care of the payment and then I disrobed. He liked dirty talk and kept saying what he was going to do to me, "his whore." I had heard that sort of thing before, the dehumanizing fantasy that some guys have. They bought me and would do what they wanted. Since I had heard it before, I likely missed any possible warning signs. Plus, by that point in my career I had grown pretty jaded and calloused in the life. I was also slightly nauseous from what I later learned was my pregnancy. All of this together caused me to not have my guard up as I usually would.

He climbed on top of me and got started. After a few minutes, after I had already sent my mind to the empty white room, he slapped me hard across the mouth. That brought me immediately back to the moment. I tasted the metallic tang of blood where my lip had been split. I tried to get up, to squirm out from under him, but he pressed his palm on the side of my face and pushed me back, leaning all his weight on me while he continued pushing himself into me.

I started to panic and began to flail. He leaned harder on me and pinched my nipple with his other hand so hard I my vision tunneled. I opened my mouth to scream, but he shifted the hand on my face to cover my mouth and nose. I tasted his sweaty palm, felt his fingernails digging into the skin of my face. I couldn't get any air. I was going to suffocate.

Then I felt his hand slide under the pillow behind my head. I saw the glint of the knife in the bedside light as he slid it out. He showed it to me, touching the blade to my nose, a horrific grin on his face. It was a kitchen steak knife with a black handle. He enjoyed seeing the fear register in my eyes. It turned him on.

"You like that, whore?" he said. "Are you scared, whore?"

He raised the knife up, pausing for just a moment, and then jabbed it down. I don't know what he was aiming for—it seemed like the side of my face or my ear—or maybe it was just a sick feint to frighten me, but I twisted violently to avoid it. At the same time, I bit down as hard as I could on the meaty palm pressing on my open mouth. He made a shrieking noise and jerked back, the knife cutting deep into my upper left arm. I bucked with all my strength and suddenly he was off me. I kicked wildly, trying to drive him back.

My arm screamed in pain. My mouth was covered in blood, both his and my own. My nipple was throbbing from his pinch, my cheek scratched from his fingernails. I rolled aside to get off the bed, to escape, and I saw the knife on the sheet. Maybe I knocked it loose. Maybe he dropped it. Regardless, I snatched it up and rolled onto the floor, holding it up to keep him away.

He was clutching his bloody hand, with a look of shock and rage on his face. He was now off the bed, standing naked in front of the TV. I pointed the knife with a trembling hand.

"Stay away!" I screamed.

But his eyes were crazed. "You bitch!" he barked. "Put that down!" He charged me, arms outstretched, yellowed teeth bared. I took a step back, trying to get away, but I knocked into the other bed in the room, falling involuntarily backward as he threw himself on me. My awkward fall caught him off guard, and he stumbled forward into me and directly onto the knife. The blade disappeared into his throat, leaving only the handle visible. Leaning over me, I saw his eyes register what was happening.

The sight of the knife jammed into his throat, my fingers on the handle, freaked me out and I yanked it free in a panicked spasm. Blood spurted out in a red spray across my chest. He pushed himself back up and stood there wavering for a few seconds, blood pumping out from the slit in his neck and running down his bare chest. His eyes stared blankly at me. His mouth opened but made no sound, blood bubbling up between his lips. Then his legs gave out and he collapsed in a bloody pile on the floor.

That's how the homicide detective had found him. That detective happened to later become my P.I. friend Mike Garrity, when he was still a cop with the Orlando Police Department. He took my statement, tried unsuccessfully to get me to roll over on Omar, and let me call Fr. Frank. I was taken to the women's shelter where I was cleaned up and given some decent hand-me-down clothes.

"Sometimes," Fr. Frank said to me that night, "it is only by passing through fire that we can escape hell. But the burns will heal." He pressed a rosary into my hands. I clutched the rosary in my tight fist during that first night in the shelter, whispering the two prayers that I remembered over and over. I couldn't remember the Apostle's Creed but I knew the Our Father and Hail Mary. I said them over and over until the words became meaningless noise. But the ritual provided some comfort, distracting me from the thirty stitches in my arm and bandaged fingernail cuts on my cheek. I clenched my eyes and imagined my mother in younger, more lucid days standing at my bedside, watching me, offering reassurance that I was okay—would be okay—reassurance that her schizophrenia would have made her incapable of actually providing. I still had that plastic rosary in my jewelry box at home. Sometimes, I would take it out and hold it. I never seemed to muster the energy to actually recite the prayers, but just holding it comforted me.

The days that followed remain hazy in my memory. Interviews with cops, assistant state attorneys, my court-appointed lawyer, Fr. Frank, and my brother Billy. After a few days Billy took me in and cared for me, as he always did, as he always has. At some point in this process, I started feeling nauseous, and the hospital that was checking on my injuries ran a pregnancy test. Congratulations, Ms. Corrigan, you're going to be a mother.

I had no idea who the father was and had less than zero interest in finding out. I suspected that the only one who wanted to know who the father was less than I did was the actual father himself, living blissfully unaware somewhere far, far away. If there were any doubt that my escort days were done, my pregnancy confirmed it forever. I swore I would never again lay on a hotel bed.

*   *   *

Yet here I was, lying back on this bedspread, staring up at the popcorn ceiling and fire-suppression sprinkler head. Yes, my feet remained firmly on the floor. And I certainly wouldn't be sleeping in the bed. But just lying there like that represented remarkable progress for me. Really.

I had not been with a man since that night. Sure, I'd gone on a handful of dinner dates with a couple of guys. Friends of Billy's or someone I met through one of the law firms we work with. I suppose they were nice enough. One or two seemed genuinely interested in me. Of course, they had no idea what my former career had been. I have no doubt that their interest would have evaporated the moment they found out.

Plus, if I was truly trying to live out this rediscovered faith of mine, sex outside of marriage shouldn't even be on the table, right? But, if I was really honest with myself, my chastity was for other reasons altogether.

The hard truth was that I have had more than a lifetime of interaction with men. And my experiences weren't exactly with the kind of men whom you might bring home to meet Grandma. I didn't have any model of a normal romantic relationship growing up and I didn't quite develop myself to understand them any better by choosing the career I did at such a young age.

For five and a half years I sold myself to them for their pleasure. I was not a person to them. They were not people to me. Any relationships I had were transactions. There was never any true human connection. No affection. Despite the nature of our transaction, there was not a single moment of any true intimacy. Intimacy requires an opening of yourself, a vulnerability, a deep knowledge of your partner. I never wanted to know the johns on my dates and there was no way that I would ever let them truly know me. They never even knew my name. To them I was simply Diamond.

How could I even think about a real, genuine relationship now? The life damages you. Yes, I had physical wounds, but my emotional scars are much deeper and possibly permanent. And, before you ask, yes, I have considered therapy. But, really, why would I seek therapy when the only reason to go would be to help me have a normal relationship with a man, and I genuinely had no desire for that? I would spend a lot of co-pay dollars to help me prepare for something I didn't even want.

But then I considered Tyler. At some point a strong male role model would be important for him. Would Billy be sufficient? Perhaps, but I doubted it. So, sometimes I thought that maybe I needed to fix my issues for Tyler's sake, not mine.

These were the thoughts I tried to distract myself with to avoid thinking about the story that Dan Bishop told me. But I couldn't shake the image of Naomi lying dead in a bathtub full of blood. The image of her lifeless face on the morgue monitor, bruises clearly visible on her neck. And suddenly the idea of lying on this bed started to freak me out. I could feel the mattress pressing against my back, as if a weight were forcing me down. My breathing was becoming labored. I swallowed hard, clutching the bedspread in my fists. The pressure on my chest grew heavier, pushing down on me. I saw a flash of crimson splash across my vision—

And I lurched upwards, spinning sideways off the bed and stumbling, catching myself on the nearby credenza, causing the flat-screen TV to wobble. I gulped a few deep breaths to try to steady myself, to slow my racing heartbeat. For a few moments, the blood felt like it was rushing down out of my head, and I was afraid I might faint. But I kept my hand on the credenza and, finally, I was okay again.

I found a spare blanket in the room's closet and pulled a pillow from the bed. Then I rummaged through my suitcase and retrieved Naomi's stuffed rabbit, Thỏ, whom I had carried with me from Orlando. I held him close and sat on the couch. As I brought my knees up to my chest, I saw my cell phone on the desk. The red number "1" on the phone icon indicated a voicemail waiting. Billy's voicemail. With an audible sigh that only Thỏ understood, I grabbed the cell phone and played Billy's message back on speakerphone.

"Sandy!" Billy's gruff voice intoned. "Dammit. Answer the phone. Where the hell are you? You wanna tell me why two cops—two *homicide* cops—showed up at the office today looking for you? You told me you were dropping that case. You did drop that case, right? I swear to Christ, if you're still working that case, you can find a new job. I'm not kidding this time. Where the hell are you?! Call me as soon as you get this."

"Click!" Even his electronic hang-up sounded pissed.

I sighed again. Looked at Thỏ. Together we decided that we had no choice. There was really only one thing we could do at this point that would do any good at all.

So we went down to the lobby and bought a pint of chocolate Häagen-Dazs from the gift shop freezer. Thỏ wasn't hungry so he generously let me eat the whole carton.

CHAPTER 17

I DECIDED NOT TO CALL BILLY BACK. I knew I should, but if I didn't call him, then I didn't have to tell him that I was actually in Chicago. I had a 6:45 flight in the morning and would be back in Orlando before lunchtime. I would call him then, when I was back on Florida soil, and explain that my cell phone battery had died. A lie, I know. But it was a relatively small sin to save us both from much greater sins: wrath for Billy and unemployment for me.

The flight back was uneventful. I clutched the airline seat armrests with white knuckles every time the plane bumped or dipped but, again, no one else seemed concerned. So I tried not to show any outward signs of my anxiety. Well, except for the white knuckles. And the occasional sharp intake of breath.

Once we landed, I quickly found my car in the garage and was soon whisking down Semoran Blvd., heading for the office. I figured that it would be best to face Billy in person, pull off the Band-Aid quickly, and try to get back to a normal—well, normal for us—routine. And I further decided it wouldn't hurt to swing through Dunkin' Donuts for a box of Munchkins.

I also needed to talk to Collette and bring her up to speed on the investigation. It turned out that her faith in me wasn't as misplaced as I had originally thought. My hunch about Bishop was right. And I got him to confess the whole sordid story. All within twenty-four hours. Not a bad day's detecting.

Lurking at the back of my thoughts was the fact that I had to figure out my strategy for meeting with Detectives Carlisle and Benders. If they had really come by the office yesterday looking for me, it probably meant my time was up. I was going to have to either give them Omar and the girls or get fitted for a stylish orange jumpsuit to wear in my stylish new jail cell. And I've never looked good in orange. I'm more of a "winter."

I took a deep, fortifying breath before pushing through the office door, Munchkins in hand. But the door was locked. I let myself in and looked around. Billy wasn't there. While it was kind of a relief, it was really just postponing the inevitable scolding. I checked the office voicemail. Nothing from Billy. Just a few messages from regular clients at two different law firms. I placed the Munchkins on the desk and called his cell.

His gruff recorded voice greeted me and requested that I leave a message.

"Hey, Billy. It's me. Got your voicemail last night. I can explain everything. I'm in the office now but I guess you're out." *Yeah . . . duh.* "Anyway, give me a shout when you get this. Bye."

I then texted Collette and asked if she was able to meet me.

R U free? Major news from Chicago.

She didn't reply.

Next, I called Laura to check in on her and Tyler. She didn't answer the home phone, and I elected not to leave a message. She sometimes went to Lake Eola after dropping Tyler off at school and walked a few laps. So I called her cell but got voicemail. I left a message letting her know that I was back and would pick up Tyler from school later.

Just as I was beginning to think that everyone in my circle was intentionally avoiding me, the office phone rang. I picked it up.

"Class A Investigators. Can I help you?"

"Sandra? Is that you?" A man's voice.

"Speaking."

"It's Mike Garrity. I was hoping to catch you."

"Hey, Garrity. What's up?"

"A job. Maybe. If you're interested. I'll buy you lunch and try to talk you into it."

I smiled. A new paying job might soften Billy's anger. Plus— why hadn't I thought of it before—Garrity might have some advice for dealing with Carlisle and Benders. He used to be a police detective. He knew the species in their natural habitat. Lord knows I couldn't talk to Billy about it. But Garrity would understand. And he would be discreet. It's like when doctors call in a specialist for help. What do they call it? A professional consult. Garrity would be my specialist.

"Sure," I said. "Lunch sounds great."

*　　*　　*

We met at a Chinese buffet and Garrity pitched his job. It wasn't a cheater sting this time. He wanted me to tail a woman who was suspected of faking an injury for a workers' comp claim. He needed a woman detective to follow her into her female-only Curves gym and see if the suspicions were true. What did she do in the gym, and was it consistent with her injury claims? It might not be a glamorous Hollywood-type investigation, but it was a

real case for a real detective. I wasn't just bait for an unfaithful
husband or process serving some poor schlub's divorce papers. Of
course I accepted.

Then I asked him about my case. I filled him in on the basics.
He listened quietly for a long time. I wasn't used to having a
man listen to me like that. Without planning to, I noticed his
mature face in a way I never had before. Kind eyes, despite the
things he had seen on the job. An unlined face, weary but quick
to offer a wry smile. Hair flecked with white and receding a bit.
I could kind of imagine what he looked like ten or fifteen years
ago. I pushed the thoughts out of my head. Jeez, stay focused,
Sandy.

"So what about Omar?" Garrity asked when I finished. "Does
he know you've been looking for the girl?"

"You could say. And . . . I may or may not have sort of pepper
sprayed him in the face and sicced a Rottweiler on him and his
friend."

Garrity pursed his lips and nodded. "I see. Well, Billy is right.
You have to give the cops what you've found. You've done well,
Sandra. Really well. But you've probably gone about as far as you
can. Let the police take it from here. They have the resources, the
professional skills, and, frankly, the jurisdiction. We're talking
about both domestic and international human trafficking, suspicion of murder, and if what you suspect is true, a prostitution ring
that is potentially selling girls to be killed if a client is willing to
pay. This will probably end up in a federal jurisdiction with the
FBI and a U.S. Attorney. Trust me, if you come clean, the cops
will leave you alone. I don't know either one of these detectives,
but that's what I would do in their place. You'll have to give up
Omar. But I think you know that. You also know it's the right

thing to do. The cops won't give you the thanks you deserve, but they won't throw you into a cell, either."

Now it was my turn to nod. "I guess so . . ."

"And, most importantly . . ." Garrity said, fixing me with a serious look. "You'll know in your heart that you were responsible for Naomi's justice."

I nodded again, touched by Garrity's recognition of Naomi's worth. He might be a hardened ex-cop, but he had always been a decent person. He was to me six years ago.

I offered to pay for my lunch, but Garrity insisted on picking up the tab. We agreed to talk in the next day or so to arrange the details of my recon for his suspected workers' comp cheat. He had to talk to his client first at the insurance company and clear the extra expense. He doubted it would be an issue.

I hadn't been home yet, going straight to the office from the airport this morning and then to lunch with Garrity. I decided to swing by my house and drop off my suitcase. I might even be able to sneak in a quick shower before picking up Tyler from school. I wished I could have driven straight to his school this morning and walked right into his classroom. I would have scooped him up in my arms and hugged him tighter than I ever had before. Being so far away from him like that, in another time zone, felt like having a smoking hole in my chest where my heart should have been. Only by returning home could the hole be filled. My squealing, scampering, irreplaceable six-year-old heart. In truth, Tyler had filled the hole in my chest that had been growing bigger and darker for many years. He had saved me in so many different ways. He still saved me every day.

I pulled into the driveway and saw Laura's dented, rusty Hyundai parked. I retrieved my suitcase from the trunk of my car and wheeled it up the front walk, thumping up the three low steps onto the porch. I reached the front door and before I fumbled for my keys in my purse, I took a chance and turned the handle. It was unlocked.

I pushed it open, silently chiding Laura for not keeping the front door locked. Yeah, this was a nice, quiet neighborhood, but we were still downtown. You still had to be smart.

"Laura!" I called, wheeling my suitcase in. No lights were on in the house, making the place look much darker than it should for the middle of the day. And it was strangely silent. The only sound was the faint whir of the refrigerator in the kitchen. I dropped my purse on the small table by the door.

"Laura!" I called again. I was starting to fear that Laura's sobriety may have suffered a setback. She hadn't had a relapse since we agreed to our arrangement, but you never knew. I should have come home sooner, straight from the airport.

I flipped on a few lights and made my way down the hall. That's when I saw her feet protruding from the bathroom door. I felt my spirit deflate. I couldn't keep Laura in her caretaker role if I couldn't depend on her sobriety. And I honestly didn't know what I would do without her. Who else could I trust with Tyler, the most precious thing in my life?

I stopped in the doorway and looked down at her. She was fully dressed, passed out on the tile. Although it had been several years, this was not the first time I had seen her like this. I sighed and kneeled down next to her. I gave her shoulder a small shake.

"Laura. Laura, wake up. It's Sandy." I shook her a bit more vigorously and her head lolled to one side, revealing a blackened eye and a bloody gash across her forehead. Blood had puddled into a small pool under her head, matting her straw-like hair into a red nest.

"Laura!" I shouted, suddenly frightened, shaking her again. "Laura!" I reached over and turned on the faucet in the bathtub and ran some cold water on my hand. I splashed it across her face, wiping the blood from her cheek. I grabbed a washcloth and pressed it against her forehead. The blood was no longer gushing, meaning that whatever happened had happened a while ago. Still, I used the washcloth to put pressure on the wound.

I splashed more water on her face, soaking the washcloth and squeezing it out over her head. The cloth turned pink from blood and water. Come on, Laura. Wake up. I smelled no trace of alcohol. Only the faint whiff of cigarette smoke infused in her clothing.

Just as I was about to call 911 and get an ambulance, her eyelids opened and closed groggily.

"Laura! That's it, girl. C'mon. Wake up." I shook her again, tapping her cheek gently. Her eyes opened and closed again. More water from the washcloth. "Laura! Open your eyes!" Her eyelids fluttered for a moment and then opened. She stared up at the ceiling, not seeing, not registering. Not yet really awake.

I held her chin and turned her to look at me. "Laura. It's me. Sandy. Laura! We need to get you to the hospital." She blinked numbly at me. Her lips parted, almost as if she might respond, but no sound emerged. I focused on her eyes. "Laura—can you stand? Or should I call an ambulance?"

"Suh . . ." she croaked. "San . . . dee . . ."

"That's right, honey. It's me. Sandy. I'm going to help you. Let's see if you can stand up."

"What happen . . . ?"

"I don't know. We'll figure that out later. Right now, let's get you taken care of. Here, put your arm around my shoulder and hold on. I'm going to try to help you stand. Okay?"

"Oh . . . kay . . ."

I wrapped one of her arms around my shoulder and held her hand. With the other I tried to brace her back and pull her into a standing position. We didn't get far. Her knees trembled as we attempted to rise, but we made it to the side of the bathtub, where she sat.

"Okay. That's good. Rest for a sec and then we'll try to get you on your feet. We're going to go to my car and then I'll drive you to the emergency room. If you don't think you can make it, let me know." By the blank stare I was getting I wasn't sure she was comprehending anything I was saying. Maybe I should have just called 911. But instead I said, "All right. Let's try again."

I sat beside her on the edge of the tub and put her arm back around my shoulder. I put my arm around her waist. Then I leaned slightly forward and rocked us up into a standing position. She swayed for a moment but found her balance, leaning most of her weight on me.

It was at that moment that I saw the life return to her eyes. She blinked twice and I sensed that she was back. She suddenly squeezed my shoulder very hard. So hard it hurt.

"Ah," I exclaimed. "Are you okay? Are you in pain?"

"Oh my God, Sandy. Oh my God."

"What is it?" I looked at her but she wasn't looking back. She was staring over the bathroom sink at the vanity mirror. "What the hell . . . ?"

Written large across the mirror in red lipstick were the words *NO MORE QUESTIONS*.

"No more questions?" I said aloud, confused. "What the hell is this?"

Laura turned to me. "I remember. I remember what happened. Oh God—where's Tyler?"

"Tyler—? Why?" I demanded, the panic raising my voice.

"They were here. They mentioned Tyler."

I started to comprehend and my breath caught. "What? Who was here? What did they say about Tyler?"

"They just—they said his name. The big one, he had an accent. I couldn't really understand him."

"When did you see him?" I was holding her upper arms, shaking her, screaming in her face. "When did you last see Tyler?"

"I—I don't . . ."

"When?!"

"This morning. I think I took him to school . . ."

"You think? You *think*?! Did you or didn't you?"

"You're hurting me . . ."

I let go of her arms and she collapsed back onto the floor. I bolted from the bathroom, skidding on the hardwood floor of the hallway, desperate to get to my phone.

CHAPTER 18

I FUMBLED THROUGH MY PURSE for my cell phone. Tyler's school was entered as a favorite and I jabbed at the contact name with a trembling finger. I let the purse fall to the floor and pressed the phone against my ear. The electronic ringing went on too long. How many times did it ring? Three? Thirteen? I had no idea.

Finally, a female voice answered. "St. James Cathedral School. How may I direct your call?"

It took all of my strength to not scream or sob. "This is Tyler Corrigan's mother." The words gushed out in a torrent. "I need to know if he is there. In class. I need someone to go right now to his classroom and make sure that he is there in his seat. First floor. Mrs. Campbell's class. I need someone to do that right now—"

"Is everything all ri—"

"No! No, everything is not all right. Please. You have to help me. Just confirm that Tyler Corrigan is in the building. Please. Do that now. Please. Now. Please."

"Okay," she said slowly, affecting an exaggerated calm as I amped up. "Okay. Just one moment. I'll check myself."

I heard a click and was put on hold. I was starting to hyperventilate. *Please, God, let him be there. Let him be there. Please,*

God. Please. Please. She was gone a long time, or what seemed like a long time. My skin was tingling, like it didn't fit, like it was too tight, pulling taut, about to tear off my body. *Oh God, please.* I saw Laura emerge shakily from the bathroom, holding the wet washcloth on her head. She leaned a hand on the wall and looked at me, her face contorted into a silent, desperate question. I had no answer to her question. I had no answer. *Please.* How long had I been on hold? Minutes. Hours. Tyler. My baby. If anything happened to him, I would literally not survive. I would be incapable of going on. He is my life. More minutes clicked off the clock. I should call the police. Send them directly to the school. *Where is he? Where is my baby?* Laura managed to shuffle halfway down the hall. I shook my head in answer to her pleading look. My grip on the phone tightened. I was gasping for air. I was sweating. My skin was stretched, reaching the point of ripping off my bones in great strips of flesh as my insides boiled and exploded.

Then finally there was a click. And the female voice. "Ms. Corrigan?"

"Yes," I gasped. "I'm here."

"One moment." The phone rustled. I heard it bump. Then—

"Mommy?"

And I burst into tears. "Oh, Tyler . . . Oh, baby. Are you okay?"

"I'm okay. Are you okay?"

I laughed through my sobs. "Yes, honey. I'm okay. I just—I just missed you from my trip and wanted to make sure you were okay."

"Okay."

"I love you, Tyler. I love you so much."

"Okay. I love you, too." A pause. "Mommy?"

"Yes, baby?"

"Can we have chicken nuggets for dinner?"

I laughed again. "Of course, baby. You can have as many chicken nuggets as you want."

"Okay. With barbeque sauce?"

"Whatever you want."

"Okay. I like chicken nuggets."

"Me, too, honey."

"Okay. Bye."

Before I could say another word, I heard the phone being handed off and Tyler was gone.

"Ms. Corrigan?" The female voice. "Is everything all right?"

I tried to recover my composure, but I was still blubbering and sniffling. "I think so. Thank you."

"Is there anything we should know?"

"I've been out of town. There was a home invasion while I was away. I was just afraid that—" I couldn't finish the thought. I couldn't even comprehend the thought.

"I think I understand. Is there anything we can do?"

"Yes. Have Tyler go to aftercare today. But please make sure that no one picks him up except me. No one except me, understand?"

"I understand. I'll make a note and I'll talk to the aftercare team."

"Thank you. Thank you so much."

"You're welcome. We love Tyler. He's family here. We'll watch over him. Don't you worry."

"Thank you . . ." But the words were lost in my renewed sobbing.

* * *

The emergency room took Laura straight back with no wait, and within an hour she was admitted for observation. She had a concussion, and her facial bruises now reached their full purple bloom. One eye was swollen shut and her head laceration took six stitches to close. She looked the worst I had ever seen her, and I had seen her at some pretty low points in her life.

I sat with her for an hour or so as she drifted off into a painkiller-induced slumber. I looked out the window of the hospital, across the gravel rooftop of the wing below me. Air conditioner boxes sat in a line like giant versions of the Legos that Tyler loved so much. A dark gray thunderstorm was approaching on the horizon. As I watched the distant flash of lightning, I considered the fact that I had brought this storm into our lives. A swirling vortex that had sucked me, Tyler, and Laura up into its winds and tossed us around.

Once Laura had been admitted, I knew that I had to talk to Billy. But I couldn't deal with a phone call with him at that moment. I couldn't force myself to wade through the inevitable recriminations and lecturing before I could explain everything. Once he understood the seriousness of the situation, I knew that he would be there for me, as he had always been. But I was simply too tired to do the work to get him there.

So, instead, I had texted him a cryptic message about being in the hospital. That Laura was being admitted and that I would explain everything in person. And now here he was, leaning on the doorframe to Laura's room.

"Is she okay?" His voice was gruff but not angry.

"She will be," I said. "She looks pretty bad. They want to keep her for a couple of days. But she's tough and she'll recover."

Billy nodded and folded his thick arms. He was unshaven. He looked even more tired than usual.

"What happened?" he said, looking at Laura's battered face.

"The short version is a home invasion."

"Damn . . . Were you there? Or Tyler?"

"No. Neither one of us was home." I decided that now was not the best time to confess my little jaunt to Chicago. "But there's more to it. I don't think it was a random break-in. I think it was related to my missing persons case."

"That's why the cops came to the office." It wasn't a question, but I nodded anyway. "Why do you think that?"

"Nothing was stolen. And there was a . . . warning written on the bathroom mirror."

"Damn, Sandy . . . What did it say?"

"No more questions."

"*No more questions*? What does that mean?"

"I assume it means that I need to drop my investigation or they will do something worse to Laura or me or . . ." I couldn't finish the sentence.

"Or Tyler." Billy completed the thought. I nodded. "What have you gotten yourself into? This is serious trouble, Sis."

"Yeah. I know."

"Who is it?"

"Some bad characters from my former life. It involves international trafficking and . . . possibly worse." I took another deep breath. "I need a favor, Billy. And I don't want a lecture or an 'I told you so.' I just need your help."

"What do you need?" I could tell he was wary, but the protective older brother was kicking in. The same one who took me in six years ago and helped put me back on my feet.

"Laura said that the guys who broke in knew Tyler's name. They said his *name*, Billy. I need Tyler to stay with you for a while. To keep him safe. They know me. They know where I live. Laura is out of commission. Until this gets resolved, it's dangerous for him to be around me."

"Wait—you don't plan to come with him?"

"No."

Billy shook his head. "I don't like it. You both come stay with me. Lay low until this blows over."

"No. Tyler needs to be away from me for a while, for his own safety. I'll be fine. Once I turn everything over to the cops, I'm done. Then we can all go back to normal."

"Sandy—"

"No, Billy. It has to be this way. Just for a little while."

Billy pursed his lips. Sighed. "You promise you're going straight to the cops?"

"I promise."

"Okay. What does Tyler know?"

"Nothing. It looks like it all happened after Laura took him to school. I'll pick him up from aftercare in a few minutes and bring him to your place. I'll set it up with the school so that only you or I can pick him up. If anyone else tries to take him, they'll call me and the police." I looked over at the sleeping Laura, snaking tubes taped to her arm. "We'll tell him that Miss Laura had an accident, but she's going to be fine. And that I need to take care of her for a few days." The thought of more time away from my precious boy almost forced an involuntary sob from my throat, but I maintained my composure. The mere idea that he could somehow be in danger—because of me—was almost too much to bear.

"Yeah, well . . ." Billy muttered. "He'll be fine. We'll eat pizza and watch baseball. We'll do some male bonding."

I forced a smile and wiped a tear that managed to escape from the corner of my eye. "Thank you, Billy. He's everything to me."

"I know, Sis. I know."

When I arrived at the school and entered the cafeteria where many of the kids were playing, I spotted Tyler at a table with two other boys. I watched him silently for a minute as he built something unrecognizable from Lego blocks. He looked so small in his little white polo shirt and blue shorts. His face showed the concentration required to engineer his little plastic structure. When he finally looked up and spotted me, the smile that flowered was filled with genuine joy. I knew that as he grew older, especially in the teenage years, things would change. But right now, at this moment, he was my little boy and he was always glad to see me.

"Mommy," he said through his smile. We embraced and again I fought back tears. "We're gonna have chicken nuggets!"

"Yes, baby," I said. "Chicken nuggets." I squeezed his shoulders. "Go pack up your stuff, okay?"

As Tyler scurried off to shove papers into his Spider-Man backpack, I turned to Mrs. Hanover, the aftercare supervisor. She was a wide, stocky woman with dyed brown hair and a broad, open face. I explained to her that only Billy or I would be permitted to pick up Tyler until further notice. I would call the office in the morning and make it official. The only other person on my approved list for picking up Tyler was Laura, and she would probably be unable to do so for the balance of the school year, which was quickly coming to an end.

"Of course, Ms. Corrigan," Mrs. Hanover assured me. "Oh, and I almost forgot." She reached into a desk drawer and retrieved a plain letter envelope. She handed it to me.

"What's this?" I asked.

"I don't know. I was asked to give it to you."

"By whom?"

"Why, the office, dear. Is everything okay?"

I tried to reassure her with a smile. I glanced briefly at the envelope before sliding it into my purse. Written on the outside in unremarkable handwriting was "*Ms. Corrigan.*" Tyler wrapped his arms around my leg, and we made our way out into Central Florida's bright late afternoon sun.

It was only later while eating chicken nuggets in a plastic McDonald's booth that I pulled the envelope back out. Tyler was playing with a windup toy from a Happy Meal. I slid my finger under the flap of the envelope and opened it.

Inside was a piece of penmanship paper from Tyler's handwriting workbook. His name was scrawled at the top. His teacher had placed a smiley face sticker in the corner. A series of solid and dotted lines cut horizontally across the page. In the first row Tyler had written CAT CAT CAT CAT. In the second row was DOG DOG DOG DOG. And in the third row was written PIG PIG PIG PIG. His letters were strong, sometimes veering over the line, and indicative of pressing too hard on the pencil—what his teacher called "the death grip."

But it wasn't Tyler's penmanship that caught my attention. My gaze was fixed on the large letters written in red marker diagonally across the page: *NO MORE QUESTIONS.*

CHAPTER 19

I'D PACKED A BAG FOR TYLER before picking him up from
school. Once we were done with our dinner of fine chicken nug-
get cuisine, I took him over to Billy's. I watched the rearview mirror for anyone who could be following me. I made a few random
turns. I didn't see anyone back there, but the truth was that I
really didn't know what I was doing.

Tyler was excited to stay at his uncle's house. I told him that
Miss Laura would be fine and that I would be back to get him in
a few days. His main concern was ensuring that his plush panda
bear Bobo wasn't forgotten. He wasn't. I pressed the doll into his
eager arms and he was content.

I again thanked Billy and promised to keep him informed. He
followed me out the front door of his suburban ranch house and
closed it, leaving Tyler inside watching the Disney Channel.

"Here," he said, pushing a folded string bag into my hands.
Whatever was inside was hard and heavy. "Take this. Keep it in
your purse." I looked inside the string bag and saw a small holstered semiautomatic pistol and two boxes of 9mm ammunition.
"No argument? I know you don't like guns."

"No argument," I said. When I joined his agency, Billy had
insisted that I take some basic firearms classes, as well as secure a

concealed carry license. Every month or so, he took me to the range and insisted that I practice. But I didn't actually own a firearm myself. I didn't feel comfortable having one in the house with Tyler around.

"It's small. But if you think you're in danger, use it. It's one of my regular carry guns. I sometimes wear it on my ankle. Ruger EC9." He held it up and showed me as he talked. "Nine millimeter. Single stack, seven in the mag, plus one in the chamber. Trigger safety. You've shot this pistol before. Not a lot, but a couple times. Remember your training."

"Thanks," I said. "I will."

"It's just regular range ammo. Not hollow point. So if you do have to pull the trigger, you keep pulling till it's empty. Got it?"

"Got it."

"Sandy." Billy looked at me for a long beat.

"What?"

"Seriously. If you need to use this, do not hesitate." His dark eyes bored into mine, underscoring his words.

I nodded. "I know. Thanks again. For everything."

"Yeah. Just, y'know. Be careful. Don't be a hero."

I kissed his scratchy cheek and slid into my Honda. My mind was blank on the ride home. I considered visiting Laura again, but I needed to extricate myself from this case first. Things had gotten too far out of hand. Like Garrity had said, the cops had the resources and jurisdiction to deal with this. All I had was . . . Tyler. And that was everything.

I got home and, while still sitting in my driveway, I texted Collette:

THINGS HAVE ESCALATED

TIME HAS COME. HAVE 2 TELL COPS ABT O

GET OUT NOW AND I WILL COME 4 U

I waited for a reply or the little dots that indicated she was writing a response. Nothing. I prayed she got this message before the cops burst in looking for Omar. I also prayed that the cops found Omar before he found me.

Once inside, I was careful not to touch anything. I used my cell phone to call the number on a card Detective Benders gave me. After a few rings she answered.

"This is Detective Benders."

"Hi. This is Sandy Corrigan."

"We've been looking for you, Ms. Corrigan."

"Yeah. I know. Listen, there was a break-in at my home while I was out. My friend Laura was attacked. I believe it was related to the missing girl."

"Why do you think that?"

I explained about the warning on the mirror and on the piece of Tyler's handwriting work. "They are threatening my son, Detective. My—son." My voice caught as the fury surged up my spine. The mere thought of those monsters circling my son, making veiled threats about him, was enough to make my vision tunnel with rage.

Bender's voice was understanding but serious, which was exactly how I would want her to sound given what I had just told her. "How do you think they got your son's classwork?"

"I assume they took it from here in the house. I think I had it on the refrigerator. But they specifically wrote their warning on *his* work. Then they put it in an envelope with my name on it and delivered it to his school. I called the office and they said it was a large blond guy with an accent. I know who he is. Sort of. These are not coincidences, Detective."

"No, they're not. Have the police processed the crime scene yet?"

"Crime scene?"

"Your house."

I nodded in understanding, even though I knew she couldn't see it. "No. With everything happening, I haven't really had time to think. Once I made sure Tyler was safe, I drove Laura to the hospital and got her settled. Then I . . . took care of Tyler, and came home." I didn't plan to tell anyone where Tyler was. Even the cops. "And now I'm calling you. I haven't touched anything since I got Laura up and took her to the hospital."

"You should have called us a lot sooner. But okay. I'll take care of it. We'll get a unit out there to fingerprint and see what else we can find. I'll try to reach Carlisle and we'll come out to see you. Are you ready to make a statement and give us what we're asking for?"

"I'm ready. Yeah, I am definitely ready."

*　*　*

The CSI unit arrived within twenty minutes along with two uniformed officers, and they got to work. They photographed the entire interior of my house, spending a lot of time in the bathroom. I didn't know everything they were doing, but they were like ants on a mound. Dusting, measuring, inspecting. It was like on TV, but it lasted a lot longer and was a lot more tedious.

Finally, after almost an hour, Carlisle and Benders showed up. Carlisle looked annoyed, like I'd spoiled whatever plans he had for the evening. I'm sure I did. We exchanged short, perfunctory hellos and moved into my living room. I sat on a chair. They took spots on the couch. Benders pulled out a notebook and pen while Carlisle chewed the inside of his lip.

"Okay, Sandy," Benders said, fixing me with a look. "Where do you want to start?"

I decided to start with the hotel. Without going into too much detail, I told them about the tip that Brenda gave me behind the 7-Eleven, before my footrace with Omar and R.J. Based on that tip, I was able to get the names of two guests who might have been the last john to be with Naomi.

"And how did you get these names?" Bender asked.

"Three hundred bucks and some threatening lies."

She nodded and wrote something on her pad. I thought I detected just the slight hint of a wry smile on her lips. "We'll come back to that. Keep going."

So I kept going. I told them about the phone calls. One was the woman whose family was with her in Orlando and the other was Dan Bishop. I thought Bishop was hiding something, which took me to Chicago. And I was right.

"Wait a minute." This time it was Carlisle. "How did you know it was this guy Dan Bishop? Why exactly did you think he was dirty?"

"He seemed, I don't know, shifty. On the phone. I had a hunch."

"A hunch? You flew to Chicago the next day on a hunch?"

"Yeah."

"Bullshit. There's more going on here. How did you know he would even be there? What if he was out of town or something?"

I opened my mouth, but it hung agape for a second. "I guess I didn't really think it through. Like I said, it was a hunch."

"I don't buy it."

"We'll fill in the details in a minute," said Benders.

"She's hiding something," he said.

"I am not," I said.

"We'll fill in the details in a minute," Benders repeated, this time to Carlisle with a distinct edge in her voice. She turned back to me. "How did you find out you were right about this guy Bishop?"

So I told them Bishop's whole, twisted tale. How he strangled Naomi, terrified her, treated her like she wasn't human. How it must have been the final straw for her. Seeing no way out, she cut her own wrists in the bathtub. How Ivan was summoned and cleaned everything up, disposing of her body. How it was clear that the escort service run by Omar's partner—who was possibly, maybe, Ivan—was pimping out girls to be beaten or maybe even killed for a premium price. And that they were trafficking girls from all over the world—minors—for the service.

Carlisle and Benders were silent for a moment. Maybe it was more than they were expecting, and they seemed surprised that I had been able to secure the story from Bishop.

"Well," said Benders. "Damn."

"Yeah. Damn," I concurred. "There's more." Benders raised her eyebrows and cocked her head, a gesture encouraging me to continue. "I know where the house is."

"The house?" Benders asked.

"Ivan's house. Where he keeps the girls. The foreign ones for sure. Maybe others."

"And how did you find *this* out?" This time it was Carlisle asking the question. His tone was skeptical. Almost sarcastic.

"I followed him from Omar's place. He drives a black Mercedes."

"So where is it?"

"The house? West side. MetroWest. Dr. Phillips area."

"Could you find this house again?" Benders asked.

"Sure. I can give you the address."

"Great. But first, I want to go back to something you said before. You said—"

"We should go," Carlisle interrupted. "We should go see the house. Omar's place, too."

"What—now?" I asked.

"Yeah. Why not? Your son isn't here, so you don't need to stay to watch him."

Benders looked at him and furrowed her brow. "We should probably finish the interview. Then we take everything and bring it to the task force."

"We'll take her with us. She can show us the house and we can do the interview in the car."

There was an extended pause before Benders replied using a measured tone. "If you need to leave, that's fine. I can finish the interview and catch a ride back with the CSI or one of the uniforms. Then we take it to the task force."

Carlisle stood up and straightened a crease in his pants. "We *will* take it to the task force. I just think it makes sense to put eyes on the place. We'll just roll by, get a lay of the land, and then we'll have more intel for the team."

Benders' lips tightened. "Can I talk to you in the kitchen?"

Carlisle nodded and the two of them stepped into the kitchen, which was presently free of technicians. I heard muffled voices, like Mom and Dad trying not to fight in front of the kids. It was probably three or four minutes before they came back. Benders was silent, arms crossed, standing behind Carlisle.

"Okay, Sandy," Carlisle said, clapping his hands once. "Let's go."

They assured me that if the crime scene techs finished before I got back, they would lock the house when they left. A few minutes later, I found myself sitting in the back seat of a dark blue sedan. This must have been a detective car because there was nothing to indicate its law enforcement purpose except a police radio along with the bubble light on the dash and a row of lights in the back window. There was no prisoner cage or shotgun mount. I dutifully buckled my seat belt and started directing Carlisle to the house where I saw Ivan pull in.

The detectives' moods seemed to have completely switched. Carlisle was now chatty and cheerful as he drove while Benders was silent and sullen, looking out the passenger window. Mom brooding after the fight in the kitchen.

"So, tell me again, how long were you in Chicago?" Carlisle asked.

"Just overnight," I replied.

"Right. Right. And what do you think this guy Bishop did after your chat?"

"I have no idea. He seemed pretty shaken up. But mostly about the money."

"Uh-huh. How much again?"

"Seven thousand. So he said."

He let out a low whistle. "Seven Gs. That *is* a lot of money. And your theory—if I have this right—is that this escort service— Ivan and Omar's—is selling a special premium service where the johns can abuse the girls for extra money?"

"That's right. Maybe worse."

"Maybe worse," he repeated.

This type of conversational inquiry continued for the entire journey, interrupted only by me offering navigational directions. Exit here. Turn left there. Benders said nothing during the whole ride. Finally, we turned into the Osprey Cove neighborhood and onto Waterview Street.

"That's it up ahead," I said. "On the right."

Carlisle rolled up slowly and craned his neck. Benders eyed the house coldly, her face a stone mask.

"No lights on," Carlisle said. "And I don't see your Mercedes."

I didn't know how to respond so I said nothing. Carlisle slowed the car and we passed the house. We pulled over at the home next door to 1622 Waterview.

Benders turned deliberately to Carlisle and in a measured voice asked, "What the hell are you doing?"

"I don't think anyone's home. Let's take a quick look," he said. "See the landscape. Fences, doors, dog, whatever. More intel for the task force." He looked back at me. "You stay right here. Don't move. We'll be back in thirty seconds. You understand? Do. Not. Move."

I nodded.

"Like hell you are—" Benders protested but Carlisle popped open the driver's door and got out. I thought fire might literally shoot from her eyeballs. She clenched her teeth and followed him out of the car.

I twisted in the back seat and through the back window I watched them walk down the sidewalk toward the house. I didn't know the first thing about police work, but I had to admit that I had no idea what was going on. There definitely seemed to be a difference of opinion on strategy. As they got close to the house,

Carlisle stepped off the sidewalk and onto the grass. Benders was a step behind him.

It was late. I wasn't sure exactly what time it was, but it had to be after midnight. I was exhausted. I had woken up early this morning in Chicago and, with everything that had happened with Laura and Tyler, I'd had an eventful, emotional day. The neighborhood was dark. The streetlights were staggered every few houses, alternating on each side of the road. There was no lamp directly in front of Ivan's house.

Benders quickened her step and caught up with Carlisle. She grabbed the sleeve of his sport coat and pulled him to a stop. I saw them talking quietly for a second before Carlisle nodded. Obviously, I couldn't hear anything they were saying. He pointed down the narrow strip of grass between the house and its neighbor, as if he were talking about the large, gray air-conditioning unit set along the side of the home.

Benders looked between the homes. Then back at Carlisle. He nodded. She looked again, taking a half step in that direction. Carlisle took a step back and reached under his jacket, along the back of his belt. I saw his hand emerge holding a pistol. I took a deep breath and held it. My heart rate jumped into overdrive. What did they see that needed a drawn gun?

The gun was silhouetted against the reflected light of the house's white stucco and it appeared to have an especially long barrel. I then saw the movement of another figure step out from the shadow of one of the shrubs that flanked the garage.

In one swift motion, Carlisle raised the gun. But his aim was not at the shadow. There was a single loud pop and Benders' neck jerked forward. Against the reflected white of the house I saw the front of her forehead burst open in a spray of dark pulp. Her knees buckled and she collapsed face down in the grass, one arm twisted awkwardly to the side.

The entire world paused for a half second. I could not process what I had just seen. I finally exhaled. What should I do?

What should I do? There was only one thing I could do.

Run.

I grabbed for the door handle. I pulled it frantically but nothing happened. I scratched at the lock mechanism but it didn't respond. They must have had the child safety locks set on the doors. They wouldn't open from the inside.

I peered back through the rear window and saw Carlisle and a hulking figure I assumed was Ivan standing over Benders' body. Carlisle suddenly looked up, eyes wide, hair hanging over his forehead. Our eyes locked and he began walking quickly toward me, raising the gun as he approached.

CHAPTER 20

I IMMEDIATELY THREW MYSELF over the seat back and into the front seat, landing awkwardly on the police radio. I felt a stabbing pain shoot into my right thigh from the corner of the monitor display. I grabbed the handle of the driver's door and shoved it open. I crawled across the seat and past the steering wheel, flopping out onto the street on my hands and knees.

Then I was up and running. I didn't look back. I darted straight across the road and into a suburban yard, tearing between two well-landscaped, multi-bedroom ranch homes. I didn't know if Carlisle was shooting at me, but I assumed he would soon if he was not already. I just witnessed him murder his partner. He had to eliminate me.

Was he chasing me? I didn't know and I didn't dare slow down enough to glance back. All I could hear was my heartbeat pounding in my ears. My only thought was to put as much distance between me and him as quickly as possible.

I cut a hard right and ran through two backyards. Both homes had swimming pools enclosed by large screens. A row of tall, beautiful queen palms separated the two yards. I ran right through them. I made a left and dashed out between two more houses. I risked a glance behind me to see if Carlisle was there. I didn't see him, but I didn't slow down. I was now across another street and sprinting between two more upper-middle-class houses. Their colors were all pale—beige and white, blue and coral—especially muted in the moonlight and street lamps. I continued running between homes and through backyards. Every fourth house or so had a fence, forcing me to turn.

My breath was coming in heavy gasps and I considered pounding on the front door of one of these houses. But it was after midnight. By the time someone answered and I tried to explain what was happening through a closed door, Carlisle could easily show up, flash his badge, and haul me away. And if he didn't and I asked them to call the cops, how would I know who was working with Carlisle and who wasn't? He might have already instructed an accomplice to come to the area so they could be the first responder if a call came in.

I didn't know how many yards I ran through. I turned randomly left, right, crossing streets, driveways. My adrenaline burst was wearing off quickly and I was crashing. Just as I was deciding which house to wake up, I saw the lighted entrance to the Osprey Cove development. However, this was not the same entrance we had entered through. This entrance was on a main road—which one was it?—and across the street I saw a small strip mall shopping plaza. The stores were all closed, except for a Taco Bell, which by its lights appeared to be open. It was the same Taco Bell where I had used the restroom the last time I was here.

I pushed forward, exposing myself to the open road and the streetlights, and sprinted across the asphalt toward the restaurant. I didn't even check for oncoming traffic. Fortunately, the streets were relatively quiet at this hour.

I stumbled into the Taco Bell, sweat-drenched and gasping. The kid behind the counter looked wide-eyed at me. The ladies' room was off to the right, and I managed to lurch inside and twist the dead bolt to lock the door behind me. It was a single-use bathroom with one commode and a sink.

I suddenly panicked, praying that I did not leave my cell phone in my purse back at the house. Or in the back of Carlisle's car. But, by some miracle, there it was, still tucked into the back pocket of my jeans.

Would Carlisle think to come into the Taco Bell? Would he come into the ladies' room? Of course he would. He would show his badge to the kid at the register, who would immediately give me up.

I racked my brain for whom to call. My first thought was Billy. But I couldn't call him. He would have to either bring Tyler with him or leave him at home and it would be unacceptable to risk exposing him. Carlisle could not know where Tyler was. Ever. But if not Billy, who?

Laura was unconscious in a Florida hospital bed. I couldn't call the cops—at least not yet. Not until I knew who I could trust. And then it occurred to me. I found the number in my contacts. It was 1:12 a.m. I pressed CALL.

Please pick up. Please pick up.

"Hello? . . . Sandy?" It was Fr. Frank. "It's pretty late. Is everything all right?"

"No, it's not. I'm in trouble, Father. I need you to pick me up."

"Pick you up? . . . Okay. Uh, tell me what's going on."

"I don't—I don't have time. I'm hiding in a Taco Bell in MetroWest. I just need you to come get me as soon as you can."

"Sandy—"

"Someone is after me. I think he wants to kill me."

"Kill you? Sandy—have you called the police?"

"Father—It's a cop who's trying to kill me."

"Dear Lord. What have you gotten yourself into?"

"Please. I don't know who else to call. Please."

"Okay. I'll be right there. I'm on the Trail. It might take twenty minutes."

I opened the map app on my phone and found my location. I relayed that to Fr. Frank.

"I'm trapped in the ladies' room," I said. "I don't know where he is or if he will track me in here. But I don't know where else to go."

"Are you hurt?"

"No. No. I'm okay."

"All right—Can you lock the door to the bathroom or something?"

"Yeah. It's locked. A dead bolt on the door."

"Okay. I will text you when I arrive."

"Hurry. And pray."

I didn't hang up, but the connection cut off after a few seconds when Fr. Frank ended the call. After running for my life through the suburbs of West Orlando in the muggy Florida night, the cold air-conditioning practically froze the sweaty clothes that now clung to my body. I proceeded to spend the longest few minutes of my life completely motionless in that frigid, windowless bathroom.

Until I heard a knock on the door.

I said nothing. The door jiggled in its lock as someone tried to pull it open.

There was another knock. Followed by a woman's voice. "Hello? Anyone in there?"

I hesitated a second. Then I replied, "just a minute."

I remained frozen for another moment. I looked at the time on my phone. It had been less than ten minutes since I hung up with Fr. Frank. Could I hold on for another ten minutes? Another fifteen?

The door jiggled again and I decided that I needed to get out. I didn't want some woman having a burrito bathroom emergency to draw a bunch of attention. I unlocked the door and stepped out. An overweight woman with brown stringy hair pushed past me into the bathroom. As I stood there, through the window in the front of the restaurant, I saw Carlisle's blue sedan cruise by.

Then I saw it turn into a parking spot.

Did he see me through the window? Oh, crap. Did he see me? I had no idea. What should I do? I couldn't go out into the main restaurant, illuminated brightly in the dark parking lot like a Mexican fast-food fishbowl. And I couldn't get to an exit without revealing my presence in the fishbowl. I really only had one choice.

I reached out and, praying it wasn't locked, turned the handle of the men's room door. I pushed myself in and closed the door, locking the dead bolt behind me. The men's room was identical to the ladies': a single toilet, a sink, a paper towel dispenser, and a slightly overfull garbage canister.

I didn't know what else to do, so I stood there, trying to be quiet. But I was pretty sure that my racing heartbeat was audible in the restaurant. It thundered in my own ears. Thirty seconds passed. A minute. I eventually heard a muffled toilet flush. I presumed it was the woman in the ladies' room across the hall. There was the faint sound of running water and the electronic whir of the automatic towel dispenser. The dead bolt clicked and I heard a shriek.

"Let go!" the woman yelled.

"I'm a police officer." Carlisle's voice. My body started to tremble. "Who else is in there?"

"No one!"

"Show me."

"Look for yourself!"

"That's the whole bathroom? Damn it!" I heard a loud bang. By the sound I presumed it was Carlisle punching or kicking the ladies' room door. "I'm looking for someone. A fugitive. About this tall. Light brown hair. Thirty years old. She was wearing jeans and a t-shirt. The guy at the counter said she went in here."

"Yeah. She came out when I went in."

"Where did she go?"

"I don't know. She left."

"Where?"

"I have no idea. I was inside."

"Goddamn it!"

I thought I heard footsteps. And some yelling out in the restaurant. But I couldn't make out the precise words. My whole body was trembling. My knees were about to give out. I leaned against the wall and slid down to the floor, trying to make myself as small and quiet as possible. Some indeterminate amount of time passed. A few seconds? A minute? Several minutes? I truly had no idea. My head was buzzing and my limbs were shaking, especially my knees. The initial adrenaline rush of fear had worn off and I was crashing. I didn't think I could run again. This Taco Bell men's room would be my last stand.

I closed my eyes tight and prayed for Carlisle to go away. Get in his car and go away. Search for me somewhere else. *Go away. Please just go away.*

And then, like a kick in the abdomen, the doorknob jiggled. My eyes sprang open. The door remained locked. But then there was a knock. I said nothing. Was it Carlisle? Another customer? I was a woman in the men's room. My voice would give me away. Another knock.

And then my cell phone buzzed in my pocket, indicating an incoming text. I looked down. It was from Fr. Frank.

I'M HERE

Then: IT'S ME KNOCKING.

I stared at the words for a moment, their meaning not really registering. Was it really Fr. Frank? I pulled myself up and stepped over to the door. With a deep breath, and all the courage I could muster, I reached up and turned the dead bolt.

The knob turned and the door opened, revealing Fr. Frank and Ramona. It was all I could do to keep from crying with relief.

"Are you okay?" Fr. Frank asked in a quiet voice. I managed a nod.

Ramona handed me an oversized sweatshirt. "Here. Put this on," she said. I did as instructed, slipping the pale blue sweatshirt over my t-shirt. She then handed me a Tampa Bay Rays baseball cap and a pair of plastic sunglasses. "Now these," she said. "Tuck your hair up under the hat." I complied. "Let's go."

"He was here," I said, grabbing Ramona's arm, not moving from the small alcove that led to the restrooms.

"The cop?"

I nodded.

"He seems to be gone now," said Fr. Frank.

I peered around the corner of the alcove. The restaurant was empty.

"Who was it?" Ramona asked.

"Detective Walter Carlisle. Do you know him?"

"No. What is he driving?"

"I don't know. A cop sedan. A Chevy Malibu, I think. He was just here. I heard him through the door."

"Okay," Ramona said. "We didn't see a car like that. But we need to be careful. Come on."

Fr. Frank put a reassuring arm around my shoulders and guided me out into the restaurant. We walked quickly through the brightly lit dining area and out the front door. I kept my head down, my gaze on my feet, and let myself be led.

A moment later I was in the back seat of Fr. Frank's silver Ford Fusion. Ramona was in the front passenger seat. Fr. Frank started the engine and pulled out of the parking lot.

I buried my face in my hands, unable to hold back the tears any longer.

* * *

We drove in silence to Ramona's house. The roads were mostly empty this late at night.

Was it even possible that when I woke up this morning I was in Chicago? It felt like I had lived an entire lifetime in one day. My mind turned to Tyler and the chicken nuggets we shared for dinner. My God, what had I gotten myself into?

Ramona lived in one side of a downtown duplex. Fr. Frank parked in her driveway and they led me inside. The décor was inexpensive but nice and surprisingly sparse. Robotically, I shuffled to the couch and slumped down, my knees giving out in my exhaustion and post-adrenaline crash. I was too tired to even cry anymore.

"Where is Tyler?" Fr. Frank asked and I was alert again.

"With my brother."

He nodded.

Then Ramona said, "Do you think that's safe? Maybe they should go somewhere else tonight?"

"Yeah. Yeah, probably." I pulled out my cell phone from my pocket, but Ramona held up her hand.

"No. Don't use that. In fact, turn it off. They can track your location. The phone's GPS can ping the nearest cell tower, even if you're not using it. Use mine." She handed me her cell phone. I hadn't even thought of the risk associated with using my cell phone, or even simply having it powered on. I had a sudden appreciation for Ramona's street smarts.

"Thank you," I said. "For everything. Both of you. If you hadn't come for me, I don't know what . . ." My voice caught but I kept from crying.

"No need to thank us," Fr. Frank said.

"It's just . . . I didn't know who else I could—"

"Sandy. It's okay," Ramona said, placing a gentle hand on my arm. "We're glad to help. Now call your brother."

"Right." I nodded. "Right." I dialed Billy's number. With an unrecognized number calling, I wondered if Billy would even answer. But, in his line of business, he couldn't afford to screen too many calls. He picked up after three rings. We exchanged greetings.

"It's pretty damn late, Sandy. Nobody calls this late for a good reason."

I immediately jumped to the purpose of the call. "Listen, I know you're not gonna like this, but you and Tyler need to get out and go stay somewhere else tonight."

"Why?" His voice was wary, maybe concerned, with a touch of dread.

"It's bad, Billy. Real bad. You two need to get out and go somewhere safe. Someplace where the cops wouldn't think to look for you."

"Cops? Why am I avoiding the cops, Sis?"

"I saw something tonight. Something awful. I saw one of those detectives, Carlisle, shoot his partner in the back of the head. He killed her, Billy. And then he came after me."

"Jesus, Sandy. Are you okay? Where are you now?"

"Yes. I'm okay. I got some help and I'm hiding out. I'm not going home. I don't want to say much more about where I am. For your sake."

Billy seemed to understand. "Okay . . . I guess. Damn, you're right. This is really bad. For God's sake, be careful."

"You too. I don't know which cops we can trust. I don't know who might be working with Carlisle. And even if they aren't working with him, he can still sic dozens of uniformed officers on us. And they'll bring us to him. Just stay out of sight. Don't talk to any cop until you hear from me again."

"Look, I'm tight with a couple of cops from both OPD and Orange County. Guys I trust. I could make a few calls, bring you in to talk to Internal Affairs and Homicide. They could protect you."

It was a tempting offer, but I needed time to process before I made any decisions. The events of the evening were so fresh and so raw, I needed at least a few minutes to calm down and consider my options. While this seemed like the most reasonable, my mind was far from rational and clear.

"Maybe. But not yet. I just need . . . I need a few minutes to think. I'll tell you when to make the call."

"Sandy..."

"Please, Billy. I'm safe where I am. I just need to know that you and Tyler are too before I do anything else."

"Okay." A weary sigh sounded through the receiver. "But I'm not gonna wait too long."

Something else occurred to me. "Maybe you should keep Tyler out of school tomorrow. Call him in sick. They already know how to get to him there."

"Yeah. Good idea. I'll take care of it."

"And if you go to a hotel or something, don't use a credit card. Wherever you go, use cash. Only use your cell when you have to make a call, and don't make a call anywhere near where you are actually staying. Keep the phone off so the GPS doesn't ping nearby cell towers and give away your location. The cops are probably already coming for you so they can get to me. Stay off the grid."

"Got it." He paused for a beat. "You know what, Sandy?"

"What?"

"You really sounded like a detective there. You might just be cut out for this business after all."

I couldn't keep a wry smile from twisting my lips. "Maybe I'm due for a raise."

"You just keep your ass safe."

"You too. And, Billy—protect my boy."

"I will. You know I would die for him."

"I know. I love you, Bro."

And with that, I hung up. I put the phone down and Ramona was standing above me, holding out a glass of ice water. I took it.

"You did good, Sandy. Real good." She then handed me a pill. "Ambien. You need to get some sleep. We'll figure everything out in the morning."

I took the pill and swallowed it with a gulp of water.

"You can sleep in the guest room." She pointed at a door in an alcove off the kitchen.

I nodded and carried the water with me into a small bedroom. There was a scuffed dresser, a twin bed, and small writing desk. A fat purple hairbrush was on top of the dresser.

I washed up in the bathroom, where Ramona had thoughtfully placed on the counter an unopened toothbrush from some hotel front desk. I took off my jeans and my bra and put my t-shirt back on. I slipped into the twin bed. Suddenly comfortable, with the Ambien starting to kick in, I closed my eyes. Before I slid into complete blackness, a name popped unbidden into my head. I knew who I needed to call. The same person who was there six years ago, the last time I was in this kind of trouble. The only one I knew I could trust.

Garrity.

CHAPTER 21

WHEN I EMERGED FROM THE BEDROOM the next morning, rubbing the sleep from my eyes, I found Ramona at the kitchen table, drinking coffee with a woman I didn't know. The woman was in her mid-thirties with brown hair pulled back into a ponytail. Tanned complexion. Perhaps Latina. She wore funky glasses in red frames, and she considered me thoughtfully over the lip of her coffee mug as she sipped.

"Good morning," Ramona said. She was wearing a blue terry-cloth bathrobe.

"Morning," I replied. I was rested but disoriented. I had never taken an Ambien before. I was also in a strange house, and, let's face it, my life was pretty much upside down at the moment. I presumed that being disoriented could be forgiven. "What time is it?"

"Ten thirty," Ramona replied. "A little after."

"Jeez." It was rare for me to sleep this late. It was rare for any parent of a six-year-old to sleep this late.

"You want a cup of coffee?" Ramona asked.

"Yeah. Please. Cream and sugar, if you have it. Can I borrow your phone again? I need to call Billy. My brother. I need to check on him and my son."

"No need," Ramona said as she poured me a cup from a carafe. "He still had my number stored from last night. He called early this morning and said they were fine. He drove out to Cocoa and found someplace on the beach. He didn't tell me where. He said they were going to hang out there a few days."

"Okay. Good. That's a relief."

"But he also said that he wasn't going to wait long before he called his friends at the department." She stirred some milk and sugar into the mug and handed it to me.

"Yeah." As I sipped, I eyed the brown-haired woman, who continued to consider me from the kitchen table.

Ramona noticed the nonverbal exchange. "Sandy, this is my friend Heather."

"Hi," I said. Heather nodded, but didn't say anything. "What about Fr. Frank?" I asked.

"He left last night. He stuck around for a while. Didn't want to leave you. He's a good man."

"He is."

"I told him we would keep him in the loop and let him know how he could help. He's very concerned about you."

"Well, that makes two of us."

Heather downed the last of her coffee and stood. She put a hand on Ramona's shoulder. "I'm going to take a shower and get ready for work." Ramona patted her hand before Heather disappeared into the master bedroom. Ramona observed me watching Heather exit the room.

"You have a question about something?"

"Nope." I sipped my coffee. Then, "So . . . is Heather a . . . live-in friend?"

"Sometimes. It's complicated. But we have more important things to talk about than my love life. We need to figure out your next move."

"Yeah, I've been thinking about that. I have a friend. A P.I., ex-cop. I think he can help me figure out what to do."

"His name?"

"Mike Garrity. You know him?"

Ramona pursed her lips and shook her head. "Do you trust him?"

"I do."

"Then what's his number?"

*   *   *

Surprisingly, I didn't have to do a lot of explaining to convince Garrity to get in his truck and drive to Ramona's duplex. Maybe it was our shared history. Or his experience as a cop. He had a well-developed B.S. meter, and he knew that I was in legitimate trouble.

By the time I had showered and called Tyler's school to tell them he would be out for a few days, Garrity was pulling into the duplex driveway. The only clothes I had were those on my back, and they were the same ones I had put on yesterday morning in Chicago. It felt like a lifetime ago. They had been soaked in sweat during my escape in MetroWest. So, while I showered, Ramona had kindly thrown them all in the washer. Unfortunately, Ramona was shorter and heavier than me, so I couldn't wear anything of hers. Heather was closer to my size, but she was a bit taller. So, by the time Garrity crossed the threshold, he found me wearing a pair of baggy jeans that covered my feet and an oversized t-shirt.

"How are you doing, Sandra?" Garrity asked, once he and Ramona had been introduced.

"Been better, to be honest."

"Yeah. And speaking of honesty, maybe it's time we got the whole story."

I sighed. "Okay. But we're gonna need some more coffee."

"I'll start another pot," Ramona said.

We gathered around the kitchen table, mugs in hand. I cupped my mug with both hands and sipped it, steeling myself for the tale. I shared the whole sordid narrative, from my first meeting with Collette at the food court, to the visit to the morgue, to the trip to Chicago, the conversation with Dan Bishop, Laura's assault, the message on Tyler's homework, and Benders' murder. Everything. It took me over thirty minutes to lay it all out.

Garrity and Ramona said little. Garrity occasionally jotted notes on a small pad in a battered leather portfolio. He asked a couple of clarifying questions, mostly about the timeline or why I made a certain decision. I started to realize how much I do based on intuition.

"I'm sorry, Sandra," Garrity said. "Truly. You've been through a lot."

I responded with a grateful smile and a sip of now cold coffee.

"About Detective Benders," Ramona asked. "Do you think Carlisle just left her lying in the grass when he chased after you? That doesn't seem to make a lot of sense. Surely someone heard the shot and called the police. Carlisle couldn't risk having a patrol car find her on the lawn while he was chasing you."

"I—I don't know. I kinda freaked and then ran. I wasn't really watching him closely. And, like I said, I thought I saw someone else in the shadows. They were kind of big—maybe Ivan, the big blond. He could have taken care of the body, hosed off the lawn, while Carlisle went after me." Then something occurred to me. "When Carlisle raised the gun, I got a quick look at it. It was dark, but I could see it silhouetted against the side of the house. It looked odd. The barrel was too long. I think it might have had a . . . y'know, a silencer. Sorry, a *suppressor*. Billy always corrects me. The shot was loud—I definitely heard it—but not as loud as it should have been."

"What about Collette?" Garrity asked. "Have you heard from her yet?"

"I don't know. My phone is off."

"Keep it off," Garrity instructed. "We'll have to turn it on and check later when we're near a different cell tower. The truth is that the cops will need a warrant to track your cell location. I actually doubt Carlisle will have gotten one, especially this soon. He would have to tie you to some probable crime and convince a judge. And I don't see how he connects you to Benders' murder without implicating himself. But better safe than sorry at this point, until we can figure your next move."

"We still need to warn Collette," I said. "I tried texting her when I got back from Chicago yesterday but she didn't respond. If Carlisle is working with Ivan, and Ivan is working with Omar, then who knows what Carlisle will do to Collette to try to get to me."

"We'll get word to her," Garrity said. "This is quite the party you've crashed, Sandra. Corrupt cops, Russian pimps, and international sex trafficking."

"Oh my . . ." I said wearily, like Dorothy in Oz. Except in my Oz I couldn't just throw a bucket of water on the bad guy and solve all my problems. "Listen, I realize that I can't stay in my house for the time being, but I really need to get some clothes and other stuff if I'm going to hide out somewhere for a while." The *other stuff* I was referring to was the 9mm Ruger subcompact currently stuffed in my purse in my living room. I hadn't taken the purse with me when I left with Benders and Carlisle last night.

"You can stay here," Ramona said. "For as long as you need."

"Thanks. Will that be okay with Heather?"

"We're cool. She's used to girls hiding out here from psycho pimps."

Garrity grimaced. "I don't know if you should go home. Omar knows where you live. So does Carlisle. They're probably watching the house right now. It's what I would do. I would also send someone—maybe Omar's sidekick—"

"R.J.," I spat as if the name were poisonous.

"—Yeah, R.J. I would send someone like him to the hospital to stake out Laura's room." Garrity paused and looked briefly out the window. "You must have gotten too close. I'm sure that Carlisle didn't want to take out Benders last night. That was messy and dangerous for him. A desperation move. You mentioned that she said something about a task force. I've been a part of those types of task forces in the past. If he hadn't put her down last night, she would have brought you to the task force and you would have completely compromised his side hustle. And implicated him. I hate to say this out loud, but you seem to already know it. Carlisle's only play at this point is to find you and eliminate you. That's what would have happened last night if you hadn't run."

I said nothing. It felt like I had lost all the saliva in my mouth.

"But here's the good news," Garrity continued. "Now you have us in your corner."

Ramona put a hand on my arm. "And we're not gonna let anything happen to you," she said. I put my hand over hers.

"So . . ." I said, trying to suppress the overwhelming gratitude I was feeling. I didn't know what I would do if I had to go through this alone. "What *is* my next move?"

A short buzz sounded from the next room. The dryer was finished. "Well," said Ramona. "First, we put your clean clothes back on you."

"Then," said Garrity. "I call the FBI."

*   *   *

It felt good to get my now clean clothes back on. I didn't like wearing someone else's ill-fitting clothes. Wearing them, I felt more exposed, more on the defensive. Wearing my own clothes that fit me properly and held me in the right places made me feel more confident.

When I went in to dress, Ramona went down the street to the drugstore and bought me a cheap burner phone. With it, I called the hospital and talked to Laura, checking on how she was feeling—better, but not ready to be released—and letting her know that I might not be able to see her for a few days. I didn't tell her why, but she knew something was up. Before we hung up, she admonished me in her raspy voice to be careful.

Next, I called Billy. He wouldn't tell me where he and Tyler were except at the beach. I assured him I was okay. It was only when I told him that I had called Garrity and he was bringing in the FBI that Billy relaxed and stopped threatening to call his contacts on the job.

While I was talking to Laura and Billy, Garrity made a few calls of his own in the living room. I didn't hear everything he said, but I caught the gist. Some agents would be making their way over for a chat. Good. When he concluded his call, Garrity came back into the kitchen.

"The FBI is sending someone over," he said. "We're supposed to wait here."

"I can't," I said. Garrity narrowed his eyes. "At least not yet. I need to check my phone to see if Collette has gotten back to me. And I can't call her. I didn't memorize her number—it's stored in my phone. And to get it, I need to turn my phone on—which means I need to be near a cell tower nowhere near here."

"I don't know, Sandra . . ."

"One of you will have to drive me. If we go now, we can be back before the Feds get here."

Garrity exchanged a look with Ramona. "Fine. I'll do it," he said.

We got into Garrity's aging, green F-150 and pulled out of the duplex driveway. "Go north on Summerlin," I said.

"Why?"

"So we can get halfway between Ramona's house and my house. I'll check the phone, turn it back off, and then we can continue to my house."

"Your house? Sandra, I told you, that's not a good idea. They're probably watching it."

"I know, but I need to at least roll by. I need to know that everything is okay—that Omar or Carlisle hasn't burned it to the ground."

"I don't like it," he said. But when we reached Summerlin Avenue, he turned north. After a few blocks, I pressed my iPhone on. There were no texts or voicemails from Collette, or anyone, for that matter. I had no idea whether that was a good sign or a bad one. It was unusual to have no activity, but not unheard of. Billy was my main online correspondent, and he and I were currently radio silent except through the burner phone. I input Collette's number into the burner phone and powered mine off again.

"Do you remember where I live?" I asked Garrity.

"I remember." A few minutes later we approached my house, and I was immensely relieved to see it still standing and not a charred shell. "There's a hat in the glove box," Garrity said. "Put it on and stay low." I did as instructed. It was a well-worn Miami Dolphins baseball cap.

I didn't see any unfamiliar cars on the street or in neighbors' driveways. It looked like a typical, quiet, sunlit workday on my street. I felt myself exhale deeply. I hadn't even been conscious of holding my breath.

"Okay," Garrity said. "You feel better?"

"I do." I paused. "But when you get to the end of the street, circle back."

"Sandra—"

"Are you carrying?"

"Excuse me?"

"Are you armed?"

"Yes. Why?"

"Because I'm getting out and going in my house. I am getting the 9-millimeter Ruger Billy gave me, plus maybe some clothes. After what I went through last night, I am not going to be caught without that gun again. You can either come with me or not. But if you do, I'll feel better if you're carrying." I looked at him with my most determined face, hoping I didn't merely come across as constipated. There was a long moment before—

"Fine," he said. "Fine. It's a mistake, but I'll come with you. However, we're not going in the front door." He circled around the block, and we parked on the street in front of my backyard neighbors. We slipped out of the truck and walked quickly along the side of my neighbor's house toward my backyard. I kept the Dolphins cap on. Garrity pulled a pistol from a holster hidden under the back of his shirt. Somewhere several blocks away, a lawn mower droned.

We emerged around my neighbor's short Ligustrum hedge and crossed my small backyard in a few quick paces, moving around Tyler's plastic, turtle-shaped sandbox. We stepped up under the roof overhang of my back patio. The house was silent and dark. Garrity placed a finger to his lips to signal quiet. I nodded. He reached out and gripped the handle of the sliding glass door. But the door remained shut.

"Locked," Garrity whispered.

"We have to go around front," I whispered back. I tilted my head and, before Garrity could argue, started moving along the back of my house, staying close to the wall. I slipped along the side and tried to stay in the shadows cast in the fairly narrow space between my neighbor's house and my little Craftsman bungalow. I paused when I reached the excessively large garbage and recycling bins that the City of Orlando made me use. I peered out into the front yard, scanned the street left and right, but saw nothing unusual. It was almost eerily motionless. No cars moving. No people. Not even one of our usual squirrels. The only sound was the dim whirring of the distant lawn mower.

I locked eyes with Garrity. We exchanged a quick nod, then stepped around the house and into the front yard. In another moment we were up the three steps to my porch and standing on either side of the front door. Garrity continued to scan the street nervously. I reached out a hand and turned the knob.

"It's unlocked," I whispered.

"Do you normally leave it unlocked?" he replied quietly.

"No. Not when I'm out. But the cops and crime scene techs were still here when I left with Carlisle and Benders last night. Maybe they left it unlocked."

"I don't like it, Sandra—"

I pushed the door open and before I could step in, Garrity was over the threshold, gun drawn, sweeping the room with it. I followed behind him and shut the door. The house was dark. I reached for the foyer light, but Garrity put a hand on my arm and shook his head.

"Get what you need," he said quietly. "Make it fast. I'll do a quick search."

I nodded. I checked the kitchen table and found my purse. Inside was the drawstring bag and the Ruger EC9 in its holster, along with the two boxes of ammo. I put the gun in one hand and the purse in the other and quickstepped down the hall to my bedroom. As soon as I got inside I pulled a duffle bag from my closet shelf and started throwing clothes into it. Jeans, socks, panties, bras, t-shirts, even a couple of random blouses. I shoved a pair of slip-on moccasins along the side. Did I need my makeup? Toiletries? Should I grab my toothbrush? I decided to skip all that. I could buy anything I needed at a Walgreens.

I mashed everything down into the duffle, put the purse over my shoulder, and picked up the gun. I heard Garrity moving in the hallway behind me.

"I'm done," I said and zipped the bag closed. But then I realized that the sound was coming from the doorway to my master bath to my left and not to the hallway behind me. I heard a sliding footstep. Breathing.

I whipped around and saw a darkened figured in the bright opening, the light from the bathroom windows silhouetting someone who was clearly not Garrity. I suddenly realized that Garrity had been right. I should not have come back to my house.

I raised the gun with both hands and pointed. My hands visibly shook.

"Don't move," I ordered. I tried to sound forceful but could hear the quaver in my voice.

"Sandy," the figure said. "I was hoping you'd show up."

CHAPTER 22

"Collette?" I said.

"Hi, girl," Collette said, bracing her hand on the bathroom doorjamb. "I hope you don't mind me crashing. Your door was open and I really had no place else to go."

I lowered the gun and stepped toward her. I had to calm my breathing and my heartbeat, which was thundering from the adrenaline now coursing through my body. As I got closer, my eyes adjusted and I got a better look at her. Her raven hair was caked in blood. Her face was swollen and bruised. One eye was closed in a purple mass and half her lips were slick red and the size of breakfast sausages.

"My God," I said. "What happened?"

I heard Garrity appear in the doorway behind me. I turned and saw him lower his own pistol, the concern registering on his face. I turned back to Collette.

"Omar," she whispered. "Omar happened." Then her knees gave out and she slid along the doorframe to the tile floor. I grabbed her the best I could to keep her from hitting too hard. By now Garrity was beside me, helping to cradle her.

"She has to go to the hospital," I said. Garrity nodded. Collette's head lolled to one side as she lay slumped in the bathroom doorway, looking like she was about to lose consciousness.

"I'll carry her," Garrity said and slid an arm under her knees.

Collette's bloodied hand reached up and gripped the front of my shirt in a fist. She tilted her battered face to me. "Omar asked about you," she said, her voice hoarse. "He wanted to know where you were. I've never seen him like that. I told him I didn't know. I swear. I didn't know." Her swollen face was clearly anguished. She swallowed a choked sob.

I lifted my hand and gently pried her fingers off my shirt. They left a bloody smudge on the fabric. "It's okay, Collette. Shh. It's okay. We have to get you to a doctor."

"As soon as he left, I ran. He took my phone in case you called. I knew I had to warn you. One of the other girls got me a cab and gave me some cash. All I could think of was to come here." Her breathing was ragged, desperate. She was unsuccessfully fighting back tears. "He's going to kill you, Sandy."

"I know." Working together, Garrity and I were able to get her to her feet.

"I'll carry her," Garrity offered again.

"No," said Collette. "I can walk. I got here, didn't I?"

"Okay, hon," I said, trying to mirror her own language to reassure her. "Let's get out of here."

At that moment, outside the house, we heard the rumble of a tweaked muscle car muffler approach and then suddenly stop. Garrity and I exchanged a look.

"I'll check it out," Garrity said.

"It's R.J.," Collette said. "I know it. He has a Dodge Challenger. It sounds just like that."

"We'll go out the back," I said.

"Go," Garrity ordered. "I'll catch up. If you get to the truck before me, get in and start the engine." He pulled his keys from his pocket and handed them to me.

"Right," I said. I grabbed the duffle and threw the strap across my chest like a messenger bag. I put the Ruger in my right hand and helped brace Collette with my left. I turned right out of my bedroom, heading toward the back patio. Garrity turned left toward the front door.

I moved as quickly as I could, but Collette was in bad shape. She had a hard time putting weight on her left leg, and I wasn't overly confident that she would remain conscious. I did my best to support her weight while also propelling her toward the patio sliding door. It was going to be a long journey across the backyard, through the rear neighbor's yard, and to the truck on the street a block away.

I unlocked the door and slid it open. I maneuvered Collette over the metal door runner and the small step down onto the concrete. I wanted to run but there was no way she would be able to do that. So, I quickstepped her as much as she could handle across the patio. Just as we reached the grass and stepped out from under the shadow of the patio roof and into the bright midday sunlight, I heard a single gunshot behind me from in the house.

I stopped and looked behind me but didn't see any movement inside. Should I go back? Did Garrity need help? He told me to start the truck. But he didn't say what to do about gunshots. We kept moving. Then there were two more gunshots in quick succession, followed by several more.

"Come on, Collette," I urged. But she knew. She heard them, too. Garrity was in a shoot-out in my house and here I was running away. By now we were across my yard and through the Ligustrum hedge. We limped along the side of the neighbor's house. "There's the truck." It was parked where we left it on the street.

I fumbled with the keys but got the truck unlocked and helped Collette into the back seat of the crew cab. I threw my duffle in the truck's bed and ran around to the driver's side. I yanked open the door and fired up the engine.

Leaving the truck running and the driver's door open, I jumped back out, raised the 9mm Ruger, and charged back alongside the neighbor's house toward my home. However, before I reached the hedge I saw Garrity emerge from the open sliding glass door, running hard.

"Get in the truck!" he yelled.

Just as I was turning, I saw a figure move in the darkened opened doorway. R.J. stepped out onto the patio in a t-shirt and baggy jeans. He was holding a pistol in one hand and pointing it at Garrity's back.

I held the Ruger in both hands, arms extended, just like I had been trained. There was far too much distance between us to expect any kind of accuracy, especially for the little subcompact. But nevertheless, I put the sights on R.J. and pulled the trigger. I kept pulling the trigger until I saw R.J. jerk sideways and duck. Did I hit him? I had no idea. I might have clipped his right shoulder. Or not. He didn't fall, but I didn't stick around.

I turned and bolted, reaching the truck and jumping into the driver's seat. Garrity was right behind me. He leapt into the front passenger seat.

"Go!" he barked, slamming the passenger door closed.

I threw the transmission into drive and floored it. The response from the six-cylinder truck was a lot more robust than that of my four-cylinder Honda Accord. We were all thrown back against our seats, and I fishtailed us into the middle of the road. I was afraid I might careen us directly into one of the homes on the other side of the street or perhaps into one of the stately old live oaks that overhung the sidewalks. But I regained control of the vehicle and managed to put us back on the right side of the road.

I reached the end of the block, rolled through the stop sign, and turned left, away from my house. I pushed the gas pedal down and accelerated down the street. I was going way too fast for the posted limit in this residential neighborhood, but strict speed limit compliance wasn't exactly on the top of my list right now. I had to stretch a bit to reach the pedals. Garrity was taller than me and I didn't have time to adjust the seat, wheel, and mirrors. I risked a quick glance in the rearview mirror. It was clear. I exhaled a sigh of relief. Then—

"Shit," I said.

In the mirror I saw the orange muscle car skid out from the street in front of my house into the road I was now on. Collette and Garrity both turned and looked.

"That's him," Collette said. But I didn't need her confirmation. I was already increasing my speed.

"Make a right at the intersection," Garrity said. "We need to get on a bigger road, with traffic and obstacles. We can't outrun his car."

As I approached the intersection, I slowed down, but not quite enough. I squealed the tires and swung too wide, swerving out into oncoming traffic. A metallic blue minivan jammed on its brakes, and I just barely missed it. I jerked the wheel right and got back onto the correct side of the road. We were back on Summerlin Avenue. That could take me to the much larger Colonial Drive. I just couldn't afford to get stuck at a light.

I looked again in the mirror and saw that the orange Challenger was still tailing us and, when not being slowed down by my turns, was gaining. I leaned hard on the horn, veering around a white Kia sedan, standing on the brakes to avoid a red Camry, and then mashing the accelerator again to grab an open spot in the lane next to me. Collette, Garrity, and I were jerked back and forth, side to side, with my reckless driving. I bounced around in Garrity's driver's seat, having not had a chance to buckle myself in before I left my neighborhood.

As if reading my thoughts, Garrity climbed up on his seat and reached across me, grabbing the seat belt, and yanking it across my body, snapping it into place. He quickly reset himself in his own seat and did the same.

"Where do I go?" I asked, eyes darting to the mirror. R.J. was still back there.

"Not sure," Garrity said. He scanned the traffic ahead, trying to determine if there was a path. "Stay away from Ramona's."

"Collette needs a doctor," I said. I changed lanes again, accelerating through a yellow light. The red light would slow R.J. down. I hoped.

I heard the roar of the muscle car followed by the screech of tires. A quick glance in the rearview told me that R.J. had ignored the red light and powered through the intersection. Several cars squealed their tires as they avoided him, coming to rest at awkward angles under the traffic light. The roar of R.J.'s engine intensified as he accelerated toward us. There was now open road between him and us and he was closing fast.

I pushed the accelerator harder, stretching my leg and just reaching it with my toes. I was not even close to as tall as Garrity. The angle of my body pushed me up too close to the steering wheel, making it difficult to turn. This whole situation just completely sucked.

And it was about to get worse.

"Collette—get down!" Garrity barked. Collette immediately lay prone across the back bench of his truck cab. I heard a loud crack. Another. Gunfire.

Another glance in the mirror showed R.J. driving toward us with his left arm extended out the driver's window, a pistol in his hand pointed in our direction. Another shot. None of his wild shots had connected with our truck. Yet.

By now the Dodge was directly behind us. He swerved to come up alongside us.

"Get in the left lane," Garrity said. "Keep him on your right." Garrity rolled the passenger window down and pulled out his 9mm Glock.

I jerked the wheel to the left, forcing R.J. across the double yellow line and into the oncoming lane. He quickly recovered, braked, and veered back across the lane behind us. In the passenger-side mirror I saw him inching up alongside us. He was pointing his gun.

Another loud pop as R.J. fired. A dime-sized hole appeared in the middle of the passenger side of the truck's windshield. R.J.'s bullet had come up through the open passenger window and out through the glass of the windshield, leaving behind a small hole in the center of a web of white cracks.

My instinct was to turn the truck left, away from where the bullets were coming from. But there was now a line of cars streaming in the opposite direction in the lane to my left. We were trapped in this lane, pinned between oncoming traffic on one side and R.J. shooting on the other.

"On my signal," Garrity said. "Brake hard. Okay?"

I nodded.

"Ready? Now!"

I put both feet on the brake pedal and stood on it. We decelerated quickly. I felt Collette brace her arms against the back of my seat to keep from rolling onto the floor. As the truck rapidly slowed, we caught R.J. off guard. I saw the orange Dodge pass us on the right as R.J.'s face registered what was happening. As the car passed, Garrity leaned out the window and got off a half dozen or so rounds from his Glock.

One of the bullets must have hit the Charger's left rear tire because it exploded, sending a salad of black rubber and wire into the street, shredding under the direct weight of the car's wheel rim. I didn't know if R.J. had been hit or not, but his car was now incapacitated, which was good enough for the moment. The Dodge skidded off the road, bouncing over the curb onto the sidewalk, and smashing the front grille into a concrete bus bench in front of an Asian market in the middle of Orlando's Vietnamese district. I saw R.J.'s slumped form behind the deflating airbag.

I pressed the accelerator and put us back in the right lane. "Did you hit him?" I asked.

"Don't know. I think so. Maybe through the door." Garrity glanced around. "We need to get off the main road again."

"Way ahead of you," I replied.

I made the first right, which took us down past the executive airport, passing the single engine Cessnas parked out by the fence. I drove under the 408 expressway and into a residential neighborhood. The shade of the tall oaks made it feel almost like driving through a wide tunnel.

"Collette," I said. "Are you okay?" Five seconds passed with no response. "Collette?" I asked with more urgency.

"I'm awake," she replied. Her voice was weak, fading.

"I'm taking her to the hospital," I said, as much to myself as to Garrity. First Laura. Now Collette. Two women—friends—beaten severely because of me within the past two days. My guilt was only surpassed by the bile-inducing rage I felt toward Omar, R.J., Carlisle, Ivan, and all the rest. I was going to take them down. All of them.

There were likely dozens of witnesses to the chase and shoot-out on Colonial Drive. Surely cops had to be on their way. But, so far, I could hear no sirens. I was doubling back through the shaded residential blocks around downtown, heading for one of the many hospitals in the area. I really didn't care which one at this point. I just cared that it was close.

I made a left and then a right, working my way closer to South Orange Avenue and the Orlando Health complex. My racing heartbeat was just starting to settle.

"What happened?" I asked. "Back in the house?"

"He pried open your front door with a crowbar," Garrity said. "It'll need to be replaced. Sorry. I assume he was looking for you or maybe something he could use to find you. He didn't seem to know we were there. Or Collette. He didn't say anything. He just went straight for the kitchen. When he did I made a break for the back door. But he heard me, and that's when we exchanged shots. You know the rest."

"I'm sorry, Mike. We shouldn't have gone there."

"It's okay. If we hadn't, Collette would probably be dead now."

If Collette heard that, she didn't say anything. I hoped she was still conscious, lying across the back seat. I glanced in the rearview mirror to steal a look at her, to check that she was okay. Not that there was much I could tell from my vantage, but I looked anyway. And that's when I saw them.

"Shit . . ." I said, eyes in the mirror.

The flashing lights atop a police car were directly behind me.

CHAPTER 23

GARRITY TURNED QUICKLY and saw what I saw.

"Do you think it's about the chase—and the shooting?" I asked quickly, slowing the car and looking for a suitable place to pull over.

"I don't know," he said.

"Even if not, I can't give them my license, right? Carlisle might have put me in the system or something?" I was asking, unsure how police procedures really worked.

"Maybe. He would have to make up some reason. And risk someone who isn't involved taking you in and having you start talking. Stop up there. Next to that mailbox." He shoved his handgun into the glove compartment and turned to Collette. "Collette, I need you to get down on the floor. I'm going to cover you with this blanket." He reached behind the passenger seat and pulled up a ratty old blanket covered in stains and mulch. "Come on, Collette. Hurry."

She eased herself down off the seat as I pulled slowly up against the curb next to the mailbox Garrity had pointed out. As far as I could tell, none of what Collette and Garrity were doing was visible to the cop behind us through the tinted back window of the truck cab.

Collette was a trooper. She didn't cry out or moan or say a word, although I could only imagine the amount of pain she was in. Reaching back, trying to not be conspicuous to the cop pulling up behind us, Garrity started drawing the blanket over to cover her when something occurred to me.

"Wait—" I said. "Your license. Collette, do you have your driver's license?"

She reached under herself and produced a small credit card sleeve from the back pocket of her jeans. Smart girl. Always have ID, credits cards, and emergency cash, just in case. In fact, I might have been the one to first teach her that so many years ago. Garrity took the sleeve of cards and covered her in the blanket.

"I know what you're thinking, Sandra. And it's a very bad idea."

But I was already shoving my much lighter hair up under the Miami Dolphins baseball cap. I reached up and pressed the compartment at the top of the windshield between the sun visors that held sunglasses and found a pair of Garrity's mirrored aviators. I plucked them out and put them on. Garrity was sorting through the contents of the credit card sleeve and located Collette's license. I reached over and pinched it away. I scanned it quickly. My name was now Collette Green. With her jet black hair and more angular features, I really didn't look anything like her, except that we were both Caucasian women. I prayed that the hat and sunglasses were enough. I then rolled down the window. In the side mirror could see the cop exiting his car.

"Collette," I said. "Don't make a sound."

Garrity found his registration in the truck's center console and pulled out his own wallet. I then suddenly became aware of the bloody stain on the front of my shirt. And the bullet hole in the right center of the windshield. And the 9mm Ruger pistol wedged openly between my thighs on the seat.

The cop had already reached the truck, passing the rear crew cab door. It was too late to do anything with the gun, to shove it under the driver's seat. The cop would see me reach down. The movement would be more than suspicious. At a minimum it would put his antenna up and draw his attention to the floor of the vehicle—where Collette was currently hiding. Worse, it could spook him and lead to some very unpleasant results all around. The only thing I could do was gently lift my left thigh and use my right hand to shove the gun under my leg. Fortunately, it was a subcompact. But I'm not a big gal. I had no idea if my leg was actually concealing the entire pistol. I kept my head up to avoid drawing the cop's attention anywhere else. I could feel the hard steel of the slide and sights pressing into the back of my thigh.

The cop stepped into view in the open window. It was good that my eyes were concealed behind the mirrored aviators because I blinked them in surprise. The police officer was a woman in her mid-thirties, brown hair pulled back. Her figure had been hard to discern under the bulky Kevlar vest and viewed in the tiny side mirror. The name tag on her navy blue OPD uniform read GUTIERREZ.

"Ma'am," she said. "License and registration, please."

"Of course," I said, unconsciously lapsing into a slight southern accent, as if this lady cop had any idea how Collette Green sounded. *Idiot.* I handed her my license. Garrity handed me his registration and license. "I'm actually driving my friend's truck. Here's his information."

She took it and glanced briefly at my license—Collette's license—and then at Garrity's documents. She spent a few seconds longer examining his than mine. The gun was pressing uncomfortably into my leg. It felt like it was expanding, like it was lifting my leg, growing so large that it would become visible and expose my secret, like a 9mm version of the heartbeat from that Edgar Allan Poe story.

"I'll be right back," the cop said.

"Uh," I replied cleverly. "Can you tell me what this is all about?"

"Just stay in your vehicle, please. I'll be right back." She kept our documents and walked back to her squad car, where she sat in the driver's seat.

"I don't like it," I said. "What's she doing?"

"Probably checking our licenses for outstanding warrants or anything else that might be a problem. You better hope that Collette has a clean record."

In my haste, that hadn't even occurred to me. I reached under my leg and pulled the Ruger out. I then quickly stowed it under the driver's seat.

"Jesus, Sandra," Garrity said. "You want to get us killed?"

"I'd rather not, to be honest." I looked back at Officer Gutierrez sitting in her car. I watched her for what seemed like five minutes, although the passage of time was hard to track. "I don't like it, Mike. It's taking too long. Maybe I should take off."

"Bad idea. Terrible idea."

"What if she's working with Carlisle?"

"Then we're both in a lot of trouble. But it's really unlikely. You have any rounds left in your magazine?"

"No. You?"

"A few. The odds are that she's not working with Carlisle. He would have to keep his circle small."

"We're about to find out," I said. The cop had exited her car and was walking slowly back toward us. Was her hand resting on the butt of her pistol? I couldn't tell. I gripped the steering wheel with both hands, involuntarily squeezing. Garrity placed his palm on the dash, near the latch to the glove box where his Glock was hidden.

She appeared in the open window and leaned down slightly. There was a long, anxious pause while she considered us. Then she handed me the two licenses and registration.

"Your left brake light is out," she said.

"Oh," I said, genuinely surprised. I glanced at Garrity. "Oh. We'll have to get that fixed." Inexplicably, I was still persisting with the fake southern accent.

"Yeah," Garrity said, taking his documents from me.

The cop leaned down and rested her arm on the edge of the open window. She addressed Garrity. "You probably don't remember me. I worked a few of your crime scenes as a rookie when you were in Homicide. I'm Maria Gutierrez. Now Sergeant Gutierrez."

Now it was Garrity's turn to blink in surprise. "No, I'm sorry. I don't remember."

"It's okay," she said. "It was a long time ago. The detectives weren't always nice to the patrol officers. But you were." She stood up. "Get that taillight fixed as soon as possible, okay? Or next time I'll have to give you a citation."

"I will, Sergeant," Garrity said. "Thanks."

She patted the car door and stood up straight again. She then looked directly at me. "Nice dye job. Good color on you." She offered us a nod and strolled back to her squad car.

* * *

When we brought Collette into the hospital, they admitted her right away. She would need X-rays and other tests to determine the true extent of her injuries, both external and internal. It was clear that she had been the victim of a beating. There was no plausible "she tripped" excuse for her condition. The hospital staff would certainly have to call the cops.

Although Carlisle's circle of confidants would have to be small, I had no way of knowing who would be in that circle—and if they were monitoring the hospitals to watch for Collette's arrival. Her beating could have been a lure to draw me out of hiding and get her some help. They—Carlisle, Omar, Ivan—could be on their way here now, tipped off by whatever dirty officer was waiting to respond.

Was I being paranoid? Could Carlisle really have accomplices on the force? It seemed unlikely. But I never expected to see him shoot Benders in the back of the head, either. After that, any terrible thing now seemed possible.

I had no idea if Collette had health insurance. Thankfully, the hospital admitted her anyway. When the admissions staff asked my name, I gave the alias I had used in my most recent cheater sting—Karen Johnson. Garrity made up an equally lame name. Once I knew that Collette was going to be taken care of, that she would receive the medical attention she needed, Garrity and I slipped away before the police showed up to start asking questions about the cause of her injuries.

I couldn't make up some elaborate lie about an abusive boyfriend. I'm not that good a liar and my brain was starting to check out after all that had happened to me in the last couple of days. And I certainly couldn't tell the truth about Omar—not without shooting off a giant metaphorical flare for Carlisle to locate me. No, the only thing to do was to slink away into the lengthening afternoon shadows. I had now left two different women lying alone in two different hospitals within one day of each other, each beaten by the same culprits because of me. The circumstances did not make me feel very good about myself.

As we stepped out of the emergency room waiting area and into the parking lot, Garrity's phone dinged with a text message. He checked it and excused himself. He walked a few paces away under a broad-leafed palm and placed a call. I took out the burner phone and did the same.

Billy answered on the third ring. All was well with him and Tyler. They were still somewhere along the coast. They had been to the beach. Tyler had seen a live crab on the sand. They saw a cruise ship passing by near the shore, on its way out of Port Canaveral. Tyler was happy. Until that moment, I hadn't realized how much tension I had been storing in my body. It had been by any measure a stressful morning. But hearing that Tyler was not only safe but happy allowed me to relax, to reflexively let some of that pent-up tension drain away, like finally exhaling a long-held breath. Garrity approached just as I hung up with Billy.

"You hungry?" he asked.

"Actually, I am." His question prompted the realization that I was in fact famished, having not eaten since earlier in the morning at Ramona's duplex.

"Come on," he said. "I know a place."

As we drove, I reloaded the Ruger's magazine, racking one round into the chamber, releasing the mag and topping it off, just as Billy had shown me. We ended up a few blocks away at a small pizza parlor on Orange Avenue across the street from the Pulse nightclub. As Garrity parked the truck, I looked through the window at the nightclub's empty parking lot and couldn't help but think about the forty-nine people who had been mercilessly gunned down several years ago, along with more than fifty injured. I didn't personally know any of the victims, but their memories hung palpably over the building, even in the bright sunlight. I felt uncomfortably self-conscious carrying a gun within sight of the place.

Garrity held the door for me and we entered the restaurant. It took a moment for my eyes to adjust to the darkened dining room. When they did, Garrity led me to a small table near the back where an East Indian man sat with his back to the wall. He was lean, but in shape, wearing a light blue dress shirt and navy tie. He was clean shaven with close-cropped black hair, perhaps in his early forties, maybe younger. He was sipping a cola as we approached. He put the glass down and stood.

"Sandra," Garrity said. "This is Sam Kumar. Sam's an old friend."

Sam extended his hand and I shook it. I was confused. "Uh, hi . . ." I said.

Sam offered a warm smile. "Thanks for coming."

I looked over at Garrity for an explanation. *Who is this guy? Why are we here?*

"Sandra," Garrity said. "You need to talk to Sam and tell him everything."

"Oh?" I replied. "And why's that?"

"Because Sam is with the FBI."

CHAPTER 24

Special Agent Sam Kumar had a warm smile that I wouldn't have expected from a federal agent. His dark eyes seemed intelligent and kind. But none of that meant I was particularly eager to talk to him. However, I trusted Garrity and I knew I wasn't going to get out of this mess without help.

So, for the second time today, I went through the whole story. I interspersed my tale with bites from an unexpectedly good chicken parm sub. Kumar listened patiently, asking a few questions. He was especially interested in Ivan—his description, mannerisms, accent. He filled several pages of a yellow legal pad with notes. I slurped the last of my Diet Coke.

"Do you have the house address?" Kumar asked. "The one where Detective Benders was shot."

"Yeah. Waterview Street. 1622 Waterview Street."

Kumar jotted that down. "I'll have someone check it out. Although I expect that everyone who had been in that house is now long gone, we'll make sure." He excused himself to make a call. I turned to Garrity.

"Thanks," I said. He patted my forearm a bit awkwardly, like an embarrassed big brother. Something had occurred to me while I was talking. "I can't leave my house open like we left it. It is downtown, after all."

"Okay. We'll take care of it."

I got a drink refill from the waitress and Kumar returned. He sat.

"All right, Ms. Corrigan," he said. "We're going to send an agent by to check the house on Waterview Street. If possible, we might be able to find some physical evidence related to Detective Benders." I shuddered involuntarily. *Physical evidence* must be some sort of FBI euphemism for human brains. He continued. "I think we are well within our jurisdiction to step in. Potential crimes include international human trafficking, prostitution, racketeering, assault, police corruption, and probably more. Your testimony will be critical, Ms. Corrigan. We'll put these guys away for a long, long time." I nodded slowly, hoping he was right.

Garrity leaned forward. "What about protective custody? She and her family need to be kept safe. Hell, we were in a shoot-out just a couple of hours ago."

Kumar nodded. "I understand. I'll see what I can do. But it's not a guarantee. This will have to go a couple of levels up for approval." He turned to me. "I don't think a hotel is the best idea. You'll have to use a credit card, and let's keep you off the grid as much as we can for the time being. Do you have somewhere you can stay for a few days, maybe longer? Somewhere safe besides your house?"

"Yeah," I said. "Ramona offered. That's where I stayed last night."

"Okay, good. I'm not sure how long it will take to get things arranged and in motion." Kumar's phone chirped and he answered. I could only hear his side of the conversation, and that didn't reveal much. He asked a few one-syllable questions. When? Where? He hung up and looked at me. "Your friend R.J. was unconscious when the EMTs arrived at his accident scene. He was taken to the trauma center at ORMC. There was also a 9-millimeter bullet in his left hip." He eyed Garrity meaningfully. "The bullet was non-life threatening. Orlando PD is on site and will question him when he wakes up. I don't know any other injuries at this point."

"The ballistics of that bullet will match my Glock," Garrity said.

"I'll do what I can to help," Kumar said. "But get a lawyer anyway. A good one."

We finished our lunch and Kumar and I exchanged numbers. I gave him both my real number and the burner phone number. I also gave him Ramona's number. Although I knew where Ramona lived and could get to the house, I actually didn't know the address. Fortunately, Garrity had it and shared it with both of us. Kumar promised to check in often and made me do the same.

After we left the pizza joint, Garrity and I found a Lowe's hardware store and he bought a hasp clasp and a padlock. We returned to my house and parked a few blocks away. After fifteen or more minutes of watching, we didn't see any movement in or near it. It seemed deserted. We exited the truck and Garrity grabbed a small toolbox from the pickup bed. We approached the house cautiously.

It was just as quiet as when we were here this morning. However, the late afternoon sun cast an entirely different set of shadows on the property, making it seem almost as if the house had rotated and become something unfamiliar and strange.

As we stepped up on the porch, I saw where the doorframe had splintered from R.J.'s crowbar. The door hung slightly open, exposing the darkened interior to anyone who might want to enter.

"I'm going to lock the back door," I said. Garrity nodded and opened the packaging on the hasp we had just purchased. I slipped inside. Unlike this morning, I went ahead and flipped the switch to turn on the lights in the living room and dining area. An end table was overturned and a ceramic bowl was shattered on the hardwood floors. Laura's *People* magazines and Tyler's picture books were strewn across both rooms. These were the vestiges of Garrity's earlier gun battle with R.J.

I looked at the walls. It took a moment, but I found several bullet holes around the front door. Garrity's shots. As I made my way down the hall, I saw the holes made by R.J.'s gun where he had shot at Garrity. I went to the rear of the home and pulled the sliding glass door shut, clicking the lock. I passed the hall bathroom and saw Laura's blood dried brown on the tile floor. It seemed like a hundred years ago that I had found her lying there. I reminded myself to call her at the hospital and check on her. All of this would have to be cleaned and repaired another day. I intended to erase all of this evil from the sanctuary of my home. It had no place anywhere near Tyler.

I made a general survey of the interior and, not finding anything else visibly amiss, I returned to the front door. Garrity was finishing the installation of the hasp. It would keep the front door shut and secured until I could get it properly repaired. He placed the padlock on it and gave me the keys. I pried one of the two provided keys off their small metal ring and handed it to him.

"Just in case," I said. He nodded and pocketed it.

"Come on," he said. "Let's get you back to Ramona's." He turned to step off the porch.

I hesitated. "Mike—" I said. He stopped and gave me a wary look. "I appreciate everything you've done for me. In fact, I'll never be able to repay you—"

"Sandra—"

"But I'm okay. Really. You've got the FBI looking out for me now. Agent Kumar is right. You need a lawyer. You probably have the cops looking for you right now. And if Carlisle is involved, that means you're not safe, even if you get picked up. You need to take care of yourself right now."

"I'll be fine."

"I know. But so will I. My car is here. I'm going to take it to Ramona's. No one will know to look for me there. I'll even back it into the driveway so the tag isn't visible. It'll be okay."

"I don't know . . ."

"It's okay. I promise. Please. I won't be able to handle it if something happens to you, too."

He paused for a long time, considering. Finally, he sighed wearily. "All right. But you need to check in with me, too. All right?"

"Pinky swear." I smiled. Impulsively, I reached out and hugged him. It surprised him even more than I surprised myself, and he awkwardly half-returned the hug. As I held him perhaps just a moment too long, I was overwhelmed with a surge of emotion. Relief. Gratitude. Respect. Tears welled up behind my clenched eyelids. I let go and stepped back, quickly wiping the tears from my cheeks. He had the good manners not to comment.

We descended the porch stairs and he made his way down the street to his truck while I walked around to the carport that sheltered my Honda Accord. He retrieved my duffle from his truck bed and brought it back to me. We nodded our final good-byes and Garrity pulled away in the pickup.

I unlocked my Accord and slipped in. Sitting in it felt both comfortable and unfamiliar at the same time. So much had happened since I had last sat in the car that it seemed like greeting an old friend I hadn't seen in a long time.

I slipped the key in the ignition and turned. As I did, it occurred to me that Carlisle or Omar or Ivan—or whoever—had complete access to my car since I had returned from Chicago. They knew where I lived. They had been in my home. They were certainly not above killing people. Was it too much to assume that they had the capability to wire my car to explode?

All of this flashed through my mind in the millisecond after I had begun turning the ignition. I tried to stop my hand but it was too late. The engine turned over and came to life.

I held my breath. I was more than a little relieved to not immediately erupt into a million little pieces, destroying the quiet middle-class ambience of my neighborhood. I finally exhaled. Apparently I was not going to go boom.

Was I becoming paranoid? Had I seen too many movies? No. I was just responding as anyone would who had been through what I had the last couple of days. It surely wasn't going too far to assume the absolute worst from these monsters.

What about a GPS tracker? Was that possible? I had no idea. I left the Accord running and got out. I crawled around the perimeter of the car feeling up under the wheel wells, along the underside of the bumper, the trunk, the grille, everywhere I could think. I didn't see or feel anything out of the ordinary. But the truth was I really didn't know what I was looking for and a real professional would probably be able to conceal whatever they wanted from my detection.

Screw it. I got back in the car, used a wet wipe from the glove box to clean the grime from my hands, and backed down the driveway. Before I reached the street, something else suddenly occurred to me. I stopped and closed my eyes, trying to slow down my racing thoughts and work through it logically.

Ramona. I needed to get back to Ramona's place. That's where Garrity and Agent Kumar thought I should hole up. But . . . was it really safe? Why was my Spidey sense telling me it might not be safe? Could the bad guys find me there? How?

Brenda. Ramona was the one who had put me in touch in with Brenda the night when Omar and R.J. chased me through the apartments and homes behind OBT, where R.J. was introduced to that especially unfriendly Rottweiler. Omar had seen us together, talking about Naomi. He could lean on Brenda to learn how she had been connected to me. He would easily do that. And Brenda would surely give up Ramona.

But why hadn't Omar done that before now? Why not right after that night? He'd been after me since I pepper sprayed him in the apartment. Because he didn't need Brenda to find out where I was. He already knew where I lived. But now that Carlisle had killed Benders and I was on the run, he would be much more likely to be desperate to find me and do desperate things. And R.J. coming to my house confirmed that they knew—or suspected—that I would not be staying at my house. Omar may be morally corrupt, but he wasn't stupid. He would make the connection between Brenda and Ramona sooner or later.

I called Ramona. She answered on the second ring.

"Where the hell have you been?" she asked. "You've been gone all day. I thought you were dead."

"Yeah. I'm really sorry about that." I gave her a very abbreviated version of the day's events, from the shoot-out at my house, to the car chase on Colonial Drive, to the hospital, and then Special Agent Kumar.

"You should have never gone back home," she scolded. "Jesus, Sandy. You're lucky you aren't dead."

"I know. But Collette probably has some serious internal injuries. I think she would have died if we hadn't shown up and gotten her to the hospital. Not to mention what R.J. would have done to her when he found her." I took a deep fortifying breath, preparing for the really hard part of this conversation. "Listen, Ramona. It might not be safe for you to be home. You or Heather."

"Oh? And why's that?"

I explained my theory—how Omar could use Brenda to find her. He had already savagely beaten Collette in an attempt to find me, and Collette was a high-priced A place escort. He would be even more merciless to a B place Trail streetwalker like Brenda.

"Do you have someplace else to go?" I asked. "To hide out for a while?"

She thought for a moment. "I guess. We could go to Heather's place for a while. It isn't very big but we could make room for you on the couch." She gave me the address, which I quickly jotted down on the back of a gas receipt I found crumpled in my cup holder.

"Thanks," I said. "But I can't go there now. Not yet. I . . . I need to do something else first."

There was a pause in the conversation. "What are you talking about, Sandy?"

"I just . . . I can't let anyone else get hurt because of me. How many more girls are going to get beaten or killed?" I thought about Marta, the teenaged Guatemalan girl Collette and I took to Burger King. She was a child, barely even old enough to drive. I thought about the girls I met in the apartment when I first started searching for Naomi—Melissa, Jordan, even Tonya. Then I thought about poor Naomi, terrified and abused, far from home. Now dead.

"Sandy," Ramona said. "This ain't on you. This is bigger than you. You need to sit this out and take care of you."

"No . . . That's what I said six years ago. Back then I did make the choice to take care of me. At the expense of everyone else. I just wanted out. I had *killed* someone. I was pregnant. I could have given up Omar then, but I didn't. I was afraid. So I said nothing. And because of me Omar and Ivan and whoever else kept using girls, hurting them, dragging them from their homes as literal slaves." I paused to collect myself. The emotions were surging up uncontrollably. I realized that I was crying. "I have to warn them. I have to help them get out, if I can, before they get hurt like Collette. Or Laura. Or"—I was briefly unable to continue as the tears overwhelmed me—"or Naomi." How many other Naomis are there because of me?"

"Sandy." Ramona's voice was softer now. "Honey, listen to me. This is on them, not you. You were a victim six years ago. Your only job was to get out. Period."

"No . . . I know what I could have done. I was selfish. I was a coward. And now girls are dead."

"Sandy, I don't know what you plan to do, but you're in no state of mind to do anything right now. Just meet me at Heather's. We'll figure it out."

"It'll be too late. The FBI is working on it, but by the time they can do anything, the girls will already be moved, beaten, or dead. The whole operation will have moved. As long as I'm alive and on the run, they're all at risk. And because of Carlisle, I can't even call the cops."

"I'm gonna call Garrity."

"No. He's done enough. He's already in serious trouble because of me." I swallowed another sob. "No. This . . . This is on me. This is my chance. To do what I should have done a long time ago."

"This is a bad idea."

"I'm only going after the girls. That's it. I'll leave Omar and Ivan and Carlisle for the Feds. Just promise me you'll get out. Go to Heather's. I'll call you. I'm going to need your help with the girls, to get them into Anchor House or somewhere else safe."

"Sandy—"

"I'll talk to you soon." With that I hung up. I knew that Ramona would keep trying to change my mind. But I also knew that my mind was already made up. I found a McDonald's napkin shoved in the door pocket and blew my nose. I took a few deep breaths and collected myself. Then I backed the car out of the driveway and pointed it in the direction of the A place apartment.

CHAPTER 25

IT WAS DUSK AS I PULLED INTO the A place apartment complex. I drove around the parking lot three times searching for the Mercedes. I didn't see it. I now knew what R.J. drove but his smashed orange Challenger was currently at a city impound lot somewhere. Back in the day, Omar had a black Lexus but I had no idea what he was currently driving. I found an open spot and backed in. I clipped the Ruger's holster to the back of my jeans and got out.

The exterior floodlights were just coming on as I made my way around the apartment complex pool area. I looked up at the second-floor apartment where the girls were. A light was on behind the curtain that led to the balcony. I slipped behind the trunk of a palm tree and stayed in the shadows. I watched for a few minutes but saw no movement behind the curtain. I pulled out my cell phone and found the A place number Collette had given me, the one Melissa had answered the day we went to the morgue. I pressed CALL.

I listened to the electronic ringing on the other end. I was too far away to hear anything from inside the apartment. I let it ring ten times before ending the call. Now what?

Finally, I stepped out from behind the palm and walked quickly to the exterior stairs. I stayed in the shadows as much as possible and quickstepped up to the second floor. I found the apartment door and approached. Adrenaline made my head buzz and my heart was practically beating out of my chest. Almost anyone could be on the other side of this door. Or no one. I inhaled deeply and held it, trying to calm down. I slowly exhaled. Then I removed the Ruger from the holster and knocked on the door.

I stepped back, trying to set myself up for a quick dive behind the wall if necessary. There was no answer. *Damn*. I moved back to the door and knocked again. I waited, holding my breath. I thought I heard something on the other side. A rustling maybe.

"Hello?" I said.

There was a pause before a quiet female voice responded. "What do you want?"

"Open the door. You need to come with me. You're not safe."

"He wants to kill you."

"I know. Please. Open the door."

I heard a chain slide and a dead bolt turn. The door opened revealing Jordan, the blonde I met my first time in the apartment. *Sunshine*. She was wearing jeans and a tank top, her hair loose.

"Jordan. You have to come with me. You're not safe." I was speaking urgently. Maybe I came on too strong. Maybe it was the bloodstain still on my shirt. Or maybe it was the 9mm in my hand, but Jordan backed away, easing into the apartment. Instinctively I followed, shutting the door behind me.

There was one other girl there, standing in the living room, someone I had not met before. She was wearing an oversized pink t-shirt, along with shorts and flip-flops. She was short, perhaps

5' 2", with light brown hair pulled back into a ponytail. She looked like she should be studying for a trig test instead of in this awful place.

"Jordan, we have to go. Both of you. I can help you. But we have to go now."

"Is that her?" the brunette asked. Jordan nodded.

I turned to the brunette. "I'm Sandy. I'm a friend. I'm here to help, but you have to come with me now." She stared nervously at me. "What's your name?"

She hesitated, cut her eyes at Jordan, and finally answered. "Heidi."

"Okay. Good. Heidi. You're not safe either. I'm sorry. But let me help you." Neither one of them moved. "Please . . ." I pleaded. "Do you know what he did to Collette?" Jordan nodded, terrified. "I found her. I got her to the hospital. She was hurt bad, but she's going to be okay. I don't want that to happen to anyone else." They both stood there, staring wide-eyed at me. It was like talking to two frightened deer, immobilized by headlights, trying to convince them to get out of the road. "Where's Omar?"

Mentioning Omar woke something up inside Jordan. She blinked at me. "He took them."

"He took them? Took who?"

"The others. He's coming back for me and Heidi. We're the last ones."

"Where did he take them?"

This time Heidi responded. "The B place. He's looking for you. He messed up Collette bad, but she wouldn't say anything. He knows you took Missy to the morgue. He said he would kill her unless she told him where you were."

"Where is Missy now?" I asked.

"The B place, I think," Heidi said. "He took her with the rest. He's coming back for us. He said we couldn't live here anymore."

"I've never seen him like this before," Jordan said.

I nodded. "He's scared. A cop has been killed. I witnessed it. That's why they're after me. R.J. is in the hospital. You need to come with me now before something happens to you. I have a place you can go. It's safe. It's for former prostitutes. It's designed to help you get out of the life and move on to something better. They helped me once upon a time." Jordan and Heidi exchanged a look. They were hesitating.

"Okay," Jordan finally said. "Okay . . ."

"Good," I said. "Don't pack anything. They can give you clothes. Whatever you need. Let's just go."

"Jordan," Heidi said, her face betraying both doubt and fear.

"I'm going," Jordan said. "You can do what you want." She stepped toward me and I turned to lead her out of the apartment. On the other side of the door, we heard voices. Male voices raised in an angry tone.

"Shit," Jordan hissed. "He's back."

I looked around quickly. "Where can I hide?" Jordan just stared, petrified. I moved my eyes to Heidi, who slowly shook her head as if to say, *It's no use. You're cooked.* Well, screw that. I wasn't going to just stand here and let Omar kill me. I turned toward the front door and raised the Ruger. As I did, my gaze fell across the curtain covering the sliding glass door that led to the small balcony. Without thinking, I threw myself across the room and yanked the sliding door open. I caught a break—it wasn't locked.

I pushed myself out the opening, leaving the gauzy curtain in place. I twisted around and pulled the door back along its runner.

I wasn't able to get the door completely closed before I heard the front door open and the raised male voices become immediately louder. I stopped pulling the door, leaving about an inch and a half gap. I prayed that the opening wouldn't attract attention. I backed up against the balcony wall as far from the door opening as I could get, although it probably wasn't more than six feet. I squeezed up against the wall and the railing and slid down, resting on my backside, bringing my knees tight to my chest, trying my best to disappear.

When I was inside the apartment, I couldn't really see the balcony. With the darkness outside and the light in the living room reflecting back against the semi-transparent curtain, I didn't think I would be seen, unless of course someone specifically looked out here or turned on the balcony light. But it didn't appear to be a well-used space. There was literally no furniture. I scanned through the railing at the nearby trees for signs of a breeze that might rustle the curtain and give me away. The branches and fronds seemed motionless for the moment.

From my curled-up vantage point, I had a remarkably good view of the interior of the apartment. The light from the inside allowed enough illumination to pass through the curtain fabric to allow me to distinguish one body from the next, even without the details. The gap left between the sliding glass door and the frame allowed sound to carry surprisingly well. I could both generally see and hear what was going on inside.

Into the apartment stepped Omar, Carlisle, and Ivan. They appeared to be in mid-argument.

"I don't care," Omar said. "How many times do I have to tell you? Don't tell me how to run my goddamn business. You done enough already."

"What does that mean?" Carlisle said.

"You know what it means."

"I'm just saying—" Carlisle said.

"Well stop sayin," Omar said. He turned to Jordan and Heidi, who had not moved. "Yo, I told you bitches to be ready. We're leaving."

"We're ready," Jordan said. She gestured at the couch where I saw two duffle bag-shaped blobs through the curtain. I had not noticed them before.

"Then let's go," he said.

"They *know*, Omar," Carlisle said. "I'm telling you. They know where she is. They're covering for her."

"What do you want me to do?" Omar said, wheeling on Carlisle. "You think I should beat 'em all? Knock out some teeth? The johns will love that. Pay extra for less teeth. Shit . . . Black eyes take time to heal. And time costs me money. Time costs *him* money." He pointed at Ivan.

"No—I'm just saying that they know something," Carlisle said. "Some of them do. She took that one with her to the morgue, for God's sake. What's her name."

"Nasty," Omar said.

"Melissa," Jordan said.

Omar turned slowly and gave her a withering look. The apartment got very quiet and very still. It felt like a wave going out and holding, collecting itself to crash back harder than before. "Did I ask you her name, bitch?" Omar said quietly, slowly. It wasn't really a question. It was a test. Jordan didn't respond.

"Omar—" Carlisle said, drawing Omar's attention back.

"Goddamn, will you shut up?!" Omar barked at Carlisle. "Fine. Fine. Okay." Omar took two strides toward Jordan, which put him right in her face. He was a couple of inches taller than her. "All right, *Sunshine*, where is she?"

Jordan hesitated. "Who?"

"Who?!" Omar looked at Carlisle and Ivan. Then he turned back to Jordan. "Who?" He suddenly slapped her hard across the cheek, knocking her sideways. To her credit, unlike me, she stayed on her feet. "Diamond. That's who. Sandy Corrigan. Where is she?"

Jordan stood there, rubbing her face. She said nothing.

Omar reached around to his back and produced a chrome semiautomatic pistol from under his t-shirt. He waved it menacingly under Jordan's chin. He typically carried a .45 ACP back when I was in the apartment. I assumed this was his latest model.

"Where. Is. Sandy. Corrigan?" he asked. Even through the curtain, I could see his eyes. They were wide. Challenging. Dangerous.

Jordan looked over at Heidi. Then back to Omar. She opened her mouth but didn't say anything. She only shook her head.

Omar turned his gaze toward Heidi. He pointed the gun at her face. "What about you, Foxy? You know where she is?"

I tightened my grip on the Ruger. Heidi didn't know me. She had no reason to cover for me. Would she be willing to risk a beating, a pistol whipping, maybe being shot, for a stranger? I didn't know if I would. So why would she do that for me? She didn't even have to say anything to give me away. All she had to do was look over at the balcony. That would be enough. Omar would be out here in a split second and would immediately be depositing multiple .45 caliber rounds into my person. My only hope was to shoot first, maybe catch him with one of my 9mm bullets, and drive him back into the apartment.

From my crouched position I turned my head from the apartment and looked out through the balcony railing. It was a long drop to the ground from this second-floor perch. I could probably do it but I was certainly looking at two broken ankles. And once I hit the ground, then what? Maybe someone would be down there and could help. But I didn't see anyone. I turned back to the apartment.

If Heidi remained silent and elected not to give away my hiding spot, I definitely couldn't sit out here like a coward and let her take a beating—or worse—for me. I would have to do something. But what? Charge into the apartment with my seven-shot subcompact? I might hit one or two of them, but probably not the third before he could react. And the 9mm with range ammo might not even stop the ones I hit—at least not right away. They could still overpower me.

"So?" Omar said, still holding the gun to Heidi's head. "Where is she?"

Heidi took a half step backwards, away from the pistol and toward the partially opened sliding door. Omar followed her, closing the space, keeping the weapon just a few inches from her face.

"Where you going, Foxy?" he said. "I asked you a question. The detective thinks you know where Sandy Corrigan is. So, give it up. Where is she?"

Heidi took another backward step toward the balcony door. So did Omar. Her eyes fixed on the gun, she raised her left hand, the one closest to the door. It was shaking but I could see her forming her fingers, preparing to point.

"We don't know where she is," Jordan said. Heidi froze.

"I didn't ask you, bitch," Omar said. "I asked her." He pressed the muzzle of the gun against Heidi's forehead. I saw her shoulders hunch up as she tensed in fear. "Where. Is. She?"

Heidi didn't respond. I carefully put my hand on the railing, preparing to pull myself up and charge into the living room. The palm of my right hand holding the Ruger subcompact was sweating.

The world seemed trapped in amber for a few long seconds, frozen. I held my breath and felt my heartbeat literally rocking me with each adrenaline-fueled pump.

Omar aggressively shoved Heidi's forehead with the gun, pushing her off balance.

"See?" he said, turning back to Carlisle. "I told you. She don't know." That shove had to have been painful and would certainly leave a bruise on Heidi's forehead. She stood back up, holding her left hand to her head, rubbing the point of impact. "Now shut your mouth," he said, gesturing at Carlisle with the pistol.

"Don't point that at me," Carlisle said.

"Don't tell me what to do," Omar responded, now deliberately pointing the gun.

"That's enough," Ivan said, holding up a massive hand. His accent was thick, Russian or Eastern European. "Put it down."

Omar hesitated but did as instructed. He slipped the gun back under his shirt at the small of his back. "Get your shit," he said to the two girls. "Let's go."

Jordan and Heidi went to the couch and picked up their bags. As she retrieved her duffle, I saw Jordan look pointedly at the balcony. At me. She couldn't see me, but she knew I was there. Watching. Even through the curtain, her expression was clear. Fear. Concern. Sadness. Resignation. She had taken a brutal slap for me. A gun had been pressed against Heidi's forehead. Neither one of them had given me up. I owed these girls a debt. I would not abandon them.

The two women stepped through the three men toward the front door. Then they were gone, moving out of my view from the balcony.

"You go on ahead," Ivan said, nodding at Omar. "I want to speak with the detective." Omar hesitated. "It's okay," Ivan continued. "We'll meet you there." Omar paused for a beat, then nodded and followed the girls out of the apartment.

Carlisle turned to Ivan and held his palms up in a half shrug. "So?" he said. "What?" Ivan didn't say anything right away. He put his arms behind his back, like a soldier assuming an "at ease" position.

"Do you know why we pay you, Detective?" Ivan finally said.

"What?" Carlisle shook his head. "Jesus. We don't have time for this."

"We have paid you a significant amount of money over the past two and a half years."

"Look, I know—"

I glanced back out through the balcony railing and saw Omar leading Jordan and Heidi out from the stairwell and toward the parking lot. I kept listening to the conversation inside the apartment while I watched Omar and the two women below me.

"Your job," Ivan interrupted, "was to keep the cops away from us. To point them in other places. To make sure that we remained invisible to the task force."

"Yeah. And that's exactly what I did."

Omar appeared to still be driving a black Lexus, although a much newer model now. I saw his car clearly under one of the pole lamps that illuminated the apartment parking lot. He put Jordan and Heidi into the back seat and then climbed into the driver's seat. In another moment he had backed out and was pulling away. Crap. I was going to lose him.

I turned my gaze back to the conversation inside the apartment. The two men faced each other. I could see them both, although Carlisle's position made it harder to see his face. My view of Ivan was unobstructed. His hands were still behind his back.

"Really," Ivan said. "That is what you did? Does it seem like the cops are being kept away? Omar is having to shuttle girls across town and get rid of this apartment. It is a waste of good money. The girls cannot go on dates. Our revenue is stopped. And, even worse, you brought your partner to the house. The *house*."

"What was I supposed to do? Corrigan said she knew where it was. I had to have her take us there. I needed to know if she had really found it. Benders was going to report it to the task force the next morning."

"And you thought it was a good idea to *shoot* her in the front yard?"

Carlisle's palms went up again. "Look, I didn't know what else to do. It's not like I had a lot of time to think about it. Everything happened so fast. Once we were at the house and I knew that Corrigan had the right place, Benders was going to act on that info. I couldn't let her leave. So I put her down. I had no choice. That's what you pay me for. To protect you and the operation."

"I do not feel particularly protected at the moment. We are no longer invisible. We had to abandon the house. Do you understand the impact of that?"

"Yeah. I understand. It was unfortunate, but it couldn't be helped."

"It will be some time before we are operational again. Your services have become even more expensive for us." He paused. "And now that Omar's associate is in the hospital, the police will turn up the heat."

"Let me handle the police."

"If you can. This seems to have gotten bigger than your ability to handle." Ivan paused. "And what about R.J. and his big mouth? Can you handle him?"

"R.J. is an idiot. He's a hothead. He makes bad decisions."

"So do you, Detective."

"Hey, wait a minute. R.J.'s involvement is on Omar. Not me. He trusted the guy. *I* mitigated the risks I took. I eliminated Benders *before* she could make trouble. I used a suppressor when I put her down. I even had *you* take care of the body."

"Yes, I took care of the body. So you could pursue Sandy Corrigan and silence her. Which you failed to do."

"We'll find her."

"No, Detective. I will find her. And I will kill her." He said it so coldly, so dispassionately, as if it were already a foregone conclusion. My mouth went suddenly dry.

"What are you saying?" Carlisle said, an edge creeping into his voice.

"I am saying that our business arrangement is over. We have other assets within the police department. Your services are no longer worth what we are paying."

"Hold on. You can't cut me off. You need me. I'm still on the inside."

"I doubt for long."

"You son of a bitch. How dare you? I'm gonna talk to Katia. Does she know what you're doing here?"

"Of course she does."

Carlisle opened his mouth to respond but stopped himself. It seemed as if that wasn't quite the answer he expected. "Look," he said. "You need me. You have no idea what I'm doing, what I *have been* doing for you. For the operation. No idea. Believe me, things would be a lot worse now if it wasn't for me. I'll talk to Katia."

"Katia has instructed me to clean up this mess. Your mess. To get rid of the loose ends. Sandy Corrigan. R.J. And you."

"Wait. Just a sec—"

Ivan sprang forward. He was quick for a man his size, much quicker than I would have expected, like a puma suddenly pouncing on prey. There was now a knife visible in his hand and he buried it deep in Carlisle's abdomen. I saw the grimace of intensity on Ivan's face as he dragged the blade sideways across Carlisle's gut, slicing him open. In three more swift strokes he pulled the knife out and plunged it back in, perforating Carlisle from stomach to clavicle. Then he pushed Carlisle to the ground. He kneeled over him, removed the detective's service pistol from his belt, and wiped the blood from the knife blade on Carlisle's shirt. Then he stood, surveyed his victim for about five seconds, presumably to ensure that he had done enough to accomplish his task, and then went into the kitchen. He used a paper towel to wipe down Carlisle's gun and placed it on the kitchen counter. Then he disappeared out of view toward the apartment entrance. The whole savage encounter took less than ninety seconds.

I stared in shock, unsure what to do. Should I jump up and try to stop Ivan? My hesitation answered that question for me. I heard the front door close. I waited a moment and through the railing I saw Ivan emerge from the stairwell below me. He walked calmly through the pool deck chairs toward the parking lot. In the distance I saw his black Mercedes parked a few spots down from where Omar's Lexus had been.

CHAPTER 26

I LEAPT UP FROM MY HIDING SPOT on the balcony and almost fell over. My knees were stiff from being bent and pressed against my chest. I jerked the sliding door open and rushed inside to Carlisle. He was on his back in a growing pool of blood that seeped out from under him into the carpet. His abdomen was split open and I could see pale gelatinous bits of fat and intestines oozing out of the bloody gash. I forced my gaze away from the carnage of his gut to his face.

"Detective," I said. "Can you hear me?"

His eyes were staring straight up at the ceiling, but at my voice, he shifted them toward me. He blinked. He tried to say something but all that emerged from his lips were a few bloody bubbles. His torso was a crimson mess. I saw blood pumping out onto his shirt from one of the stab wounds in his chest. I had a sudden and unbidden flashback to six years ago. That night. My night. There were bloody bubbles on his lips, too. And blood pumping out of his neck.

"Carlisle!" I shouted. He only blinked at me in response. "I'm gonna call for help." I stood and pulled the burner phone from my jeans pocket. I quickly dialed 911.

"911. What is your emergency?"

"There's a police officer down. Detective Carlisle from OPD has been stabbed." I relayed the address and apartment number. "It's bad. He needs an ambulance."

"Are you in danger?"

"No. It's over." I looked down at Carlisle. He was no longer looking at me. He was staring straight up at the ceiling. The light seemed to be leaving his eyes as I watched. The pumping blood soaking his shirt was slowing. If he wasn't dead yet, he would be any moment. He was beyond saving.

"We have units en route," the operator said. "Please stay on the line."

"I . . . I'm sorry. I can't do that." I made my decision. I ended the call. I was going after the girls. I had to find them while I still could—before they disappeared forever back into the darkness of Omar's pit of vice. I dashed out of the apartment and charged down the stairs, taking them two at a time, balancing myself with a hand on the rail to keep from falling on my face. I raced out into the pool area, no longer worried about sticking to the shadows.

My car was near the low gate that led to the pool. I pushed through the opening and was soon behind the wheel. But where was I going? Jordan said Omar had moved everyone to the B place. So that's where I needed to go if I was going to help the girls. But how would I find it? I would use the same method that I was worried Omar would use to find Ramona. Brenda would be the key.

It was a long shot. A one in a thousand chance. But it was all I had. I would go to the Trail and start looking. I would ask every stiletto-heeled streetwalker and grocery cart-pushing homeless guy I could find. Someone had to know where she was. Brenda, if she was still alive, would be out there somewhere, doing Omar's bidding. And once I found Brenda, I then had to convince her to betray Omar and reveal where the B place was. There was definitely no guarantee she would be willing to do that. I had no incentive to offer. Her life was ruled by addiction and fear. But I had to try.

I backed the car out and turned it toward the apartment complex exit. As I did, I was shocked to realize that I was directly behind Ivan's black Mercedes, which was still sitting in the same parking spot I noticed earlier. Instead of exiting the complex, I continued past the car and watched it in my rearview mirror.

Ivan was sitting in the driver's seat, holding a cell phone to his ear. He didn't seem to notice either me or my incredibly mundane Honda Accord as I passed behind him. I rolled to an open spot farther down the row and pulled in. I turned off the ignition and slumped low in my seat, keeping just enough of my head visible so I could see the Mercedes through the car windows next to me.

I sat motionless like that for a minute or two, not daring to move or hardly breathe. I felt like I was back on that balcony, inches away from being discovered. In the distance, I heard sirens approaching. A lot of them.

Ivan must have heard them, too. I saw him put the phone down and start his car. I did the same. He wheeled out of his spot and accelerated out of the complex. I followed, trying not to be obvious, but doing my best to keep up with his high-performance German engine. As we drove away, we were passed in the opposite direction by three police cars going at least eighty, lights flashing, sirens wailing. They were quickly followed by an ambulance, two more sheriff's deputy cars, and a paramedic rig.

Ivan was probably wondering how they had been called so quickly. He had to know that Carlisle would never have been able to call for himself. I had to be especially careful. Ivan would be paranoid, watching his tail, wondering who had found Carlisle. Who had called?

The only reason I was even moderately able to keep up with him was the many traffic lights throughout suburban Central Florida. They periodically stopped him long enough for me to catch up. I tried to keep a car or two between us so that I was not positioned directly behind him. The last thing I needed was for him to spot me.

I considered calling Agent Kumar and telling him about Carlisle, about where I was headed. But I couldn't take my attention from my pursuit for even a second. Ivan drove so aggressively that it took everything I had just to stay close without being spotted. I would call Kumar as soon as I could—as soon as I arrived at where Ivan was going. I assumed our destination would be the B place. I was sure that was where Omar was taking Jordan and Heidi. Ivan had told Omar back in the apartment that he would meet him there.

Ivan stayed on surface roads and made his way in the general direction of Orange Blossom Trail. It made sense that the B place would be near the Trail. Soon we found ourselves on Oak Ridge Road, which runs from the outlet malls by International Drive on one end and crosses OBT on the other end, very close to its seediest section. There were several apartment complexes on Oak Ridge within a block or two of the Trail. One of them was likely where I began my mad dash from Omar and R.J. the night I met Brenda behind the 7-Eleven.

We kept driving east and I was starting to wonder if we would eventually reach OBT and turn. Perhaps the apartment was farther north or south on the Trail. Or on the other side of OBT. I was trying to anticipate which way he might turn so I could get in the appropriate lane when his brake lights suddenly illuminated. I jammed on my own brakes to avoid rear-ending him, sending the Accord into a jarring deceleration, locking my seat belt tight across my chest. He turned right into an apartment complex, something with a "Pine" in the name. I didn't get a good look at the sign and was unable to follow him into the parking lot without completely blowing my cover. I had no choice but to continue driving.

I moved past the apartment entrance, craning my neck to see where the Mercedes went. It pulled around one of the apartment buildings. I looked ahead to see if maybe there was a second entrance to the complex but there wasn't. The next stop was Orange Blossom Trail. I had to make a quick decision. Go through the intersection or turn right? The red light made my decision for me. I couldn't wait for the light to cycle back to green.

I waited for an almost reasonable gap in the cross traffic and turned right, accelerating to keep from being hit from behind. I immediately turned right into a Wendy's restaurant parking lot. I didn't have time to wait for the light at the intersection to change or to drive a few more blocks and try to make a U-turn. It would have been ten minutes—or longer—before I was able to work my way back to the apartment. No, this was my only choice.

I parked in the Wendy's lot and grabbed my iPhone. With Carlisle now out of the picture, I didn't think that anyone would be tracking my movements via GPS, if they ever were tracking them at all. After removing it for the drive, I again clipped the subcompact Ruger 9mm's holster to my jeans and locked the car.

Then I ran along the sidewalk that bordered Oak Ridge Road back toward the apartment complex where Ivan had pulled in.

I pushed through a scraggly hedge of bushes and emerged on the other side in the parking lot of the Pine something apartment complex. The place was bathed in shadow, each parking lot lamp casting a pool of dull yellow illumination in a small radius directly below. There were a few floodlights on the corners of the brown buildings but at least a third of the bulbs seemed to be out. The lights that were positioned for the exterior stairs that led up to the second floor of each two-story building were also yellow and weak. They washed the stairs in a dim amber glow that only made the place look eerie. Clusters of scrub pine trees added to the deep shadows that enveloped everything.

There was no grass or discernible landscaping other than the unkempt hedgerow that ran along the sidewalk. A soft carpet of pine needles covered everything, even most of the parking lot. Surprisingly large black pinecones dotted the ground like acne.

The pine needles absorbed my footfalls and made my approach unnaturally quiet. I saw no movement anywhere in the complex, except for one heavyset African American woman visible in the covered laundry hut across the parking lot. In the fluorescent lights of the small open building, she leaned against a row of washers looking at her phone.

This complex was several rungs below the A place, which had a resort-style pool, palm trees, and clubhouse gym. This place was dark, run-down, and with no visible amenities. As I walked quietly across the pine needles, I scanned the rows of cars, searching for either Ivan's Mercedes or Omar's Lexus. I assumed that they would be relatively easy to spot. I doubted that the typical residents of Pine whatever could afford such luxury transporta-tion. From behind me, I heard the low constant thrum of cars moving up and down Orange Blossom Trail.

I worked around the first building and then the second. There appeared to be at least six separate structures angled around the property. I saw Hyundais and Fords. An Impala. A Camaro. A couple of Toyotas and Nissans. A Kia. There were even a few Accords, with one very much like my own. I even saw an older model BMW. But no Lexus or Mercedes.

I moved through the inky shadows, trying to stay out of the circles of light cast by the parking lot lamps and the floodlights on the eaves of the building corners. And then I saw it. A black late model Lexus. Omar's car. A few spots down the row was the Mercedes. I took out my iPhone and powered it on. I hunched over and moved quickly behind each car, snapping pictures of the license plates with my phone. Then I slipped behind a pine tree and trained my gaze upon the third building. Somewhere in there, in one of those two dozen or so apartments, was the B place.

So, here I was. I had found it. That was amazing enough. But now what? What was my plan? How did I expect to get the girls out with Omar and Ivan in there? I wasn't exactly sure, but I knew that patience would be my ally. I could wait.

I glanced down at the phone. Last night at around this time Carlisle and Benders were interrogating me in my house. Benders had now been dead less than twenty-four hours. It felt like a year.

I punched in the number for Special Agent Kumar. It rang a few times before his voicemail picked up. I left a message. I tried to convey as much information as I could in a brief voicemail—about Carlisle, about the location of the B place, about the fact that I knew I should wait but I just couldn't allow another girl to be hurt because of me. I ended the call. I had no idea if I had just helped or hurt my current situation.

I don't know how long I waited. Long enough that I began looking around for someplace where I could pee—preferably an actual bathroom with a toilet. I didn't see any public restrooms. Why would there be any restrooms when everyone here had their own apartment? Going back to the Wendy's would be too far. I didn't want to stray too far from my lookout spot. I *really* didn't relish the idea of squatting behind one of these pine trees.

Fortunately, I didn't have to wait too much longer.

CHAPTER 27

Omar and Ivan emerged from the shadowed overhang of a first-floor corridor. They did not come down the stairs—at least not any stairwell on this side of the building. That probably meant that the apartment was on the first floor. Maybe.

I could see them talking. Ivan shook his head. Omar nodded. I was too far away to hear anything they said. After a minute or two they each headed for their respective black luxury cars. In another moment, they were pulling past me. I slinked around the pine tree I was hiding behind to avoid being seen. They both turned right on Oak Ridge, heading for the Trail.

I watched the two cars disappear from sight, waited a moment, and took a deep fortifying breath. Then I trotted across the parking lot to Building 3 and into the covered hallway that separated a row of apartment doors on each side. The space was cast in the same dull amber glow as the stairs. The odor of stale cigarette smoke hung invisibly in the air. Used butts were scattered all over the dirty concrete floor like confetti.

I walked slowly up and down the two rows of doors as quietly as I could, listening intently to try to get some clue as to which one led to the apartment I was looking for. I couldn't hear much—mostly the muffled sound of Telemundo coming from a

TV inside somewhere. So now what? Perhaps it was time for some good old-fashioned private detecting.

I approached the first apartment door and knocked. There was no answer. I knocked again. After thirty seconds or so, it opened, revealing a tired-looking woman in her early twenties, Hispanic, holding a chubby, dark-haired baby who was sucking his fingers. The aroma of cooking wafted out—peppers, garlic—something ethnic and delicious. She said nothing but looked at me with plaintive, sunken eyes.

"Sorry," I said. "Wrong apartment." She shut the door without a word. I moved on to the next door in the row. Despite knocking repeatedly, there was no answer. The same with the door after that. The next apartment door was answered by a shirtless white guy in basketball shorts. He had a large tattoo of a crucified Christ on half of his chest.

I came up empty on two more doors. A door on the other side of the hallway opened. A skinny African American guy with a patchy beard stepped out. He lit a cigarette and leaned against the wall. He took a long drag and eyed me briefly, before glancing away.

"Excuse me," I said. He looked over at me warily. I saw his eyes move over the bloodstain on my shirt. "I'm looking for an apartment, one with a bunch of girls living there." His eyebrows went up. "Can you help me out?"

He took another deep drag on the cigarette, its ashes glowing red in the dim light. He exhaled the smoke and with the cigarette perched between his index and middle fingers he used it to indicate an apartment two doors down from where I stood. I pointed to make sure I had the right door. He nodded.

"Thanks," I said. I stepped over to the door. As I was about to knock, I felt the guy watching me from across the hall. I was suddenly self-conscious, anxious about what might lay on the other side of that door. I knocked loudly and waited. After a moment, I heard the dead bolt click and a chain slide.

The door opened to reveal a skinny blonde girl in shorts and a tank top. Her face was dotted with pimples and her hair was unwashed. She looked me up and down. Then she stepped back and held the door open for me.

"Another one," she said. "We can't fit any more of you A place hos."

I stepped across the threshold and closed the door. I walked into the living room and took in the scene. The walls were scuffed and the furniture was worn and frayed. Pots and pans were piled in the sink and fast-food wrappers littered the counters. The placed smelled musty, like a locker room. I detected the spicy sweet aroma of marijuana very faintly, as if it had been smoked a long time ago but was permanently infused into the carpet and the fabric of the furniture.

There were at least six or eight young women spread on the couches, chairs, and floor. Two were in the kitchen. I recognized Jordan and Heidi, who were clearly shocked to see me. Melissa stared at me from her seat on the floor. She leaned against the wall with a wet paper towel against her swollen face. I did not see Marta. Or Brenda. Although most of the girls were strangers, I was pretty sure I could tell the A place girls from the B place ones.

"You . . ." Melissa said.

"Yeah," I said. "Listen, I'm here to help."

"How did you find us?" Jordan asked.

"Long story," I said. "But that isn't important now. Listen, we need to go."

"What are you doing here?" Jordan again.

"That's what I'm trying to tell you. I'm gonna get you out of here. All of you."

"What?" Melissa said.

"Jordan," I said. "You were about to leave with me at the other apartment. Right before Omar came back. Well, it's time. Let's go. Now. All of you."

"What is she talking about?" the blonde who opened the door asked.

"Who is she?" a short brunette with thick hips and thighs asked the room. She looked like a B place resident.

"It's over," I said. "It's over for Omar. They've gone too far." I held up two fingers. "There are two dead cops. The FBI is involved. You all need to get out now before he does something stupid. He beat Collette almost to death." I gestured at Melissa. "Look at you, Missy. Next time he'll probably kill you."

"Yeah, he beat on them because he was looking for *you*," Heidi said.

"I know. And you could have given me up when Omar asked you where I was. But you didn't. Why not?"

Heidi hesitated. "I don't know."

"Who the fuck *is* she?" the brunette asked, pointing at me.

"She's Diamond, that's who." Tonya emerged from the hallway that led to the bedrooms and bathroom. She wore pink booty shorts, a tight t-shirt, and an open robe. Her close-cropped hair was covered with a tight red stocking. She crossed her arms and leaned against the wall.

I turned to her. "Tonya. Please. I'm telling the truth. I'm trying to help. I don't want any more of you hurt. Or killed like Naomi."

I addressed the whole room. "I can help. I can get you all into Anchor House. They can get you off the streets, give you new clothes, a new home, a new life. They can guarantee your safety."

"Omar will freak if he comes back and we're all gone," a different girl said.

I turned to Jordan and Heidi. "Carlisle is dead. Ivan killed him right there in the apartment after you left. He's a cop and they were willing to do that. What—what do you think they'll do to you?"

"Omar won't do shit if we just tell him where you are," Tonya said. "In fact, he'll probably give us a reward. You made a big mistake coming here, Diamond."

I turned and faced Tonya. I heard my heartbeat thudding in my ears. My breathing slowed. I took a step toward her. Through my teeth, I hissed, "My—name—is *Sandy*."

Something about my demeanor cautioned Tonya from responding. Her only reaction was to twist her mouth and make a dismissive sound with her lips.

"Carlisle is dead?" Heidi asked. "But I just saw him a few minutes ago." It wasn't computing for her.

"Ivan stabbed him," I said. "I saw it. He's dead."

"Jesus . . ."

I pulled out my phone and held it up. "I'm gonna call my friend Ramona. She can help you get into Anchor House. All of you. Some of you probably know her. She used to walk the Trail like a lot of you. But she got out. Now she works trying to help girls like you get out."

"I know who she is," the blonde said.

"Me, too," the thick brunette said. I saw another nod or two from a couple of the other girls.

I dialed Ramona on my iPhone. The burner phone just seemed like an unnecessary precaution at this point. She answered on the first ring.

"Sandy. Where are you?"

"The B place."

"What? Girl, are you crazy?"

"Listen. I don't have much time. It's in an apartment complex off Oak Ridge, next to a Wendy's, about a block or two from OBT. The name is Pine . . . Pine something." I looked up and caught the eye of a Latina girl who was staring at me. "What's the name of this place?"

"Pine Landings," she answered, clearly not sure if she should help me.

I repeated the name to Ramona. "Apartment 8 in Building 3. I think. There are maybe a dozen girls here. We need to get them all to Anchor House as soon as possible. Before Omar shows back up."

"A dozen?"

"All of them, Ramona. Tonight."

"Shit. I don't even know if the van can hold that many." She sighed deeply. "Okay . . . Okay . . . Jeez, Sandy. That's a tall order. I—I'll make some calls. See what I can do. Are you all right?"

"At the moment. And no cops. I don't know how deep this goes. Carlisle isn't the only one on the take."

"Damn. Okay . . ."

"See you soon."

"Be careful, hon."

I hung up and faced the girls in the apartment. They were all staring expectantly at me like I was the star of some one-woman freak show and they were waiting for my next trick.

"What do I have to say to convince you all to come with me?" I said. There was a long pause as they continued staring at me.

"Tell me . . ." It was Jordan. She was hesitating, unsure how to form the words. "You could tell me . . . that I never have to get on my knees for another man again."

I nodded at her. "Never."

"Or lay on my back." It was one of the B place girls. She couldn't have been a day over seventeen.

"Or do *anything* Omar tells me to do." It was Melissa. She stared up at me from where she sat on the floor. "Ever." She pulled the bloody paper towel from her face, revealing a purple cheek and an eye so darkened and swollen that it was closed shut.

"Never," I said. I turned and locked eyes with Tonya. Her bravado had melted a bit. She grimaced and shook her head.

"This is all I've ever done," she said. "I don't know how to do anything else. What else is there?"

"Anything you want. Are you kidding? You're smart. And a survivor. Any business would be lucky to have you." I addressed the whole room. "You can all have your lives back. This is your ticket out of here. And it costs you nothing." I felt the room starting to tilt my way. But they were still hesitating. I reached my arm across my body and pulled my sleeve up, showing the large scar on my upper arm. My Diamond Cut. "The only reason I got out was because a john tried to kill me. I should be dead. But I got lucky. I survived. And now I have a job and a life. And"—my voice caught as I fought back the emotion—"and a beautiful son who loves me and calls me 'Mommy.' And I'm here now to help you so you don't end up getting stabbed like me. Or dead like Naomi."

And just as I felt as if I had shifted the mood of the room my way, I heard the front door handle rotate. Time seemed to slow as a sense of dread descended on everyone there. We all turned our heads toward the sound and watched the front door swing open, revealing Omar on the front stoop.

CHAPTER 28

AT FIRST OMAR WAS CONFUSED why so many of the girls were standing around, staring at him. He quickly took in the scene.

"What the fuck are you doing?" he demanded with an unsure, almost nervous smile. No one answered.

I was mixed in with the group and he didn't register my presence. I felt a few of the girls look at me. We all remained frozen for a very long moment while Omar surveyed the room and tried to discern what was going on. I debated my next move. I could rush the sliding doors that led out the back. Unlike the apartment I had just come from, this one was on the first floor. But I was unlikely to get far, especially if the door was locked. I assumed Omar could easily run me down.

Maybe I could charge him and, with the element of surprise, shove him out of the way and escape. But he was bigger and stronger than me. That was suicide. My only play was the 9mm pistol strapped to my waist. The one thing that was clear was that, if he could, Omar would most certainly kill me. I shifted my hand slowly to reach for the holstered Ruger. But the movement caught his eye. His gaze found me, and the recognition spread across his face.

"No shit," he said in amazement. "Diamond. We've been lookin' everywhere for you. And here you are in my crib." I didn't say anything. "I heard you found Spice." He shook his head. "I knew she was dead. I told you to let that be."

"Carlisle's dead," I said. "Ivan is probably gonna do the same to you." If I could sow some doubt, put him off balance mentally, I might find an opening to escape.

He smiled and wagged a finger at me. "I know all about Carlisle. And the next one to die definitely ain't gonna be me."

"The cops are already on their way," I lied. I seriously doubted that Ramona would involve the cops and I had no idea if Agent Kumar had even heard my message. "But it's not too late. Just turn around and go. They'll never find you."

Omar shook his head again. "I ain't afraid of the cops."

I held up a palm to gesture for him to stay back. "Omar," I said. "Stay there. I don't want any trouble."

"Oh, you got plenty of trouble, Diamond."

"Omar—"

He sprang forward and was on me in two violent steps, a strong left hand around my neck, driving me backwards across the room. I didn't get to the 9mm in time. He was too quick. I was unable to react, to even call out. I had no balance. He was larger and stronger than me. I stumbled, but he kept pushing me, holding me up by my throat. I couldn't swallow or scream. I couldn't breathe.

I tripped backwards over the low coffee table and toppled onto the worn couch, onto the lap of one of the girls. I heard her shriek and felt her scramble out from under my back.

Omar shoved me heavily into the couch cushions, leaning his full weight on my windpipe, constricting my breath.

"You bitch," he hissed. "You put R.J. in the hospital. You ruined my business. You *disrespected* me."

"*Oh . . . mar . . .*" I hissed out as a barely audible whisper, pushing just enough air through my larynx to make a rasping croak. It was the sound of a desperate animal caught in a predator's trap. My voice was the sound of pure fear.

While holding my throat with his left hand, he punched me hard in the cheek with his right fist. I felt the impact and knew it was a serious blow, but I didn't register any pain. Adrenaline coursed through my body as the realization of imminent death sent me into a panic. I clawed desperately at his arms. I knew I must have drawn blood with my fingernails, but he only tightened his grip. I pushed at his face, punching and slapping. I tried bucking my body and kneeing him in the back, but I had no leverage on the couch. He was too heavy and too strong. He leaned all his weight on me. The edges of my vision blurred and darkened. I was losing consciousness.

"Why couldn't you just leave it alone?" he seethed at me through gritted teeth. "You ruined my business six years ago and you just did it again." He tightened his grip on my throat. I felt the blood pressure building in my head. "You think you're different. You think you're better 'cause you got out. Well, you're not. You're nothin'."

He leaned even more heavily on my throat. I started to gag, my body shuddering uncontrollably. The blackness at the edges of my vision closed in. I no longer slapped his face. I had lost control of my hands and arms. I flailed them feebly at his torso. In the last second before I completely lost consciousness, I saw Heidi step behind Omar and look at me. She raised up a large metal pot with both hands and swung it hard at the back of Omar's head. It connected with a loud thud.

The blow knocked him sideways. He released his grip on my throat and turned toward Heidi in disbelief. She swung the pot again with two hands like a tennis racket. Omar was too stunned to react, and the bottom edge of the pot connected with his temple, making another audible thunk. He fell over onto the coffee table, limp and unmoving.

I rolled off the couch, coughing and gasping for air. Mucus streamed out of my nose and my eyes watered uncontrollably. But I could breathe again. My vision was clearing.

I pulled myself to my hands and knees, trying to control my involuntary coughing and gagging. I took long, heaving breaths and wiped my face and nose on my shirt. After what felt like thirty seconds or more, I had recovered enough to sit on the couch. The girls stared at me, probably wondering if I was going to die. Until a few seconds ago, I was wondering the same thing. I looked up at Heidi, who still stood over me holding the dirty pot from the sink. The crusted brown residue from some unknown sauce was visible on the pot's lip.

"Damn, girl," Tonya said to Heidi. "What did you do?"

Heidi was also breathing heavily, probably from her own adrenaline. "He—he was going to kill her."

"Thanks . . ." I croaked in a hoarse rasp.

I heard several other girls' voices. *Oh my God. Is he dead? Did you kill him?*

"What now?" asked Jordan.

They all looked at me as if I had an answer. But my mind was far from operating at full capacity. I was just trying to recover both physically and mentally. I feared that my throat might have some kind of permanent damage. The stinging pain from the punch to the cheek was starting to register. But I needed to pull myself together. They needed to hear something, anything. They needed to feel that someone had control.

"Ramona is on her way," I said, still struggling to speak. "She'll get you all out of here."

"This is bad," someone said.

"I can't believe you did that, Heidi," said another.

"Are you okay?" Jordan asked me.

"I . . . I don't know," I said, my voice a wheezy mixture of sandpaper and an air leak. "I think so. I can hardly swallow. But I can breathe."

"Someone get her a glass of water," Jordan ordered. A girl in the kitchen grabbed a plastic cup, filled it from the tap, and brought it to me. I sipped at it. It hurt to swallow. My bruised throat felt like someone had tried to punch their way out from the inside. But despite the painful swallowing, the water helped. A little.

"What if he wakes up?" This time it was the Latina girl. She indicated Omar with a nod.

"We probably can't call the cops," I said. "We should tie him up or something."

"Tie him up? Seriously? With what?"

"Rope," I said. "An electrical cord. Jesus. Whatever. Anything. Think."

The two girls closest to the kitchen started yanking open drawers, searching for something. As they did, a low moan emanated from Omar, who was still sprawled over the coffee table like a tranquilized tiger waking up. We all turned to him. As he stirred,

I looked at Heidi to ready the pot for another swing. But she went wide-eyed and took an involuntary step backwards.

Omar rolled over and pushed himself up into a wobbly stance. His head rolled back and forth as he tried to get his bearings. A moment later his eyes appeared to focus and he scanned his surroundings, reorienting himself to his circumstances.

He spotted me, but I didn't see any immediate recognition in his eyes. He blinked twice, like I seemed familiar but he couldn't quite place me. He did the same to another girl. His gaze then found Heidi holding the pot. He reached a hand up and felt the side of his head. There was no blood visible, but a red welt the size of a golf ball was already forming. Omar made the connection between the pot and what was very likely an excruciating concussion.

"You . . . bitch—" he slurred. Then, in one swift motion that belied his compromised state, Omar swung the chrome .45 up from under his shirt. He steadied the pistol and pointed the muzzle at Heidi.

The loud crack of gunfire suddenly filled the apartment, sending screaming girls diving for the floor and behind the kitchen counter. Omar fell over backwards as I emptied all seven rounds from the Ruger into his chest. I never gave him an opportunity to fire his .45. A half dozen bloody red spots bloomed across his now perforated torso.

He lay on his back, staring up, his eyes eerily similar to Carlisle's earlier in the evening. Tonya strode across the room and put a slippered foot on Omar's right wrist, pinning it to the carpet. Then she reached down and removed the semiautomatic pistol from his hand. She stepped back and stood over him, watching him bleed. I looked around. All the girls in the apartment, both standing and cowering on the floor, just stared at him dispassionately. His eyes moved across the room, from one girl to the other, silently pleading for help—help that would not be given.

"Someone call 911," I rasped and collapsed back on the couch, finally and completely overwhelmed.

CHAPTER 29

THE POLICE ARRIVED BEFORE RAMONA, as did the paramedics and an ambulance. Despite my concerns about the police, and Ivan's comment to Carlisle about having other assets within the department, I couldn't exactly leave Omar lying dead on the floor of the apartment, especially since it had been my gun that had rendered him in that state. Slipping quietly away was not only highly illegal, it was simply bad form.

So we called the cops and we all became embroiled in a very messy and complicated crime scene. At least two of the B place girls ran before the police arrived, maybe more. They disappeared into the asphalt-covered darkness of the Trail.

But I was pleased that all the A place girls who had been there stayed. Heidi, Jordan, Melissa . . . even Tonya. The cops worked the scene, bringing in what seemed like a cast of thousands. This event apparently warranted a much more robust response than what had been deployed to my house a couple of days ago. Uniformed officers, crime scene techs, and, of course, the requisite detectives in wrinkled dress shirts with darkened armpit sweat visible under their rumpled sport coats.

The whole event unfolded around me in a sort of time-lapse progression. I stayed in my seated position on the couch, still holding my now empty glass of water, watching more and more people arrive. I saw girls being separated to give independent statements, coming and going. Occasionally a uniformed officer would approach and ask me something, but I just blinked at them and didn't respond. In my defense, it had been a seriously unprecedented last couple of days. My mind had gone a bit numb.

Finally, a plainclothes detective leaned down into my view. He was perhaps in his late forties, dark hair a bit too long for what I imagined for a cop. Very tan.

"Is this her?" he said to a uniformed officer standing nearby. The uniform nodded. The detective turned back toward me. "Hi, Sandy. I'm Detective Colon. Are you hurt?"

I looked up at him slowly. His eyes were very dark, almost black. I shook my head *no*, but then shrugged, unsure, and pointed at my throat.

"Your throat is injured?" he asked. I nodded. "Okay. I can see the redness and bruising starting to form. And what about your cheek? Does that hurt?" I nodded a feeble *yes*. "I see blood on your shirt. Is that yours?"

I looked down at my shirt. Collette's blood had dried almost brown by now. Was that just a few hours ago? Was that possible? It felt like last year. I shook my head.

"Okay," Colon continued. "We've already collected your gun. I am going to also take that holster I see on your waist there." He reached around my hip and gently pulled the holster out. He handed it to a nearby tech who slid it into a clear plastic evidence bag. "Sandy, we need to get some photos and collect evidence. Have you washed your hands since you fired the weapon?" I shook my head. "Okay, good." The tech swooped in and swabbed my hands with some sort of cotton ball and dropped that into another evidence bag. "According to the rest of the ladies here, the guy on the floor attacked you, you defended yourself, and when he pulled a gun, you shot him. Is that right?"

"Don't answer that," came a woman's voice from the apartment entrance. "Don't say anything." Ramona strode across the room like it was her own home. I was so glad to see her, tears welled up in my eyes.

"*Ra . . . moan . . . ah . . .*" I managed in my hoarse voice and reached for her.

"I know, baby," she said. "Everything is gonna be all right."

The uniformed officer stepped in front of her to keep her from touching me. "You were supposed to stay outside the crime scene tape."

Ramona gave him the death stare. "Puh-leeze. You really *don't* wanna get in my way."

"Who are you?" Colon asked.

"Ramona Landry from Anchor House. I'm here for the girls. And Sandy."

"Well, I'm sorry, Ms. Landry, but this is a crime scene. Everyone here is a witness. They're all coming downtown to be interviewed and give statements. Sandy needs to be processed and checked by a medic. She appears to have been through a trauma."

"You're damned right she has," Ramona said. "I'm coming with her. I know the drill. This ain't the first girl I've escorted through an assault process. I'm her advocate."

Colon exchanged a look with another, slightly younger detective. Finally, he shrugged and nodded. The technician put plastic bags over my hands. Ramona pulled my elbows to help me stand, and I sleepwalked my way out of the apartment, leaning against her.

Omar's body had not yet been removed. He was lying motionless on his back in the middle of the living room floor, open eyes staring lifelessly up at the ceiling. I hesitated as we approached.

"Don't you look, honey," Ramona said. "Ain't nothin' worth seeing there."

"What . . . about . . . the girls?" I asked.

Ramona patted my back. "As soon as they're done downtown, we'll take care of 'em. I got the whole team on the way. Even Father Frank."

The uniformed officer led us out to an unmarked sedan. The parking lot of the apartment complex was cordoned off with yellow police tape. A large group of apartment neighbors stood among the half dozen or so police cars, CSI and medical examiner vans, and TV news trucks. Bright news camera lights unnaturally illuminated the dark complex. I caught sight of the skinny Black guy who had pointed me toward the apartment. We locked eyes. His face was expressionless.

Ramona helped me into the back of the sedan. I put my head on her shoulder. She patted my leg reassuringly. I laid my bagged hands on my lap and looked at them. They seemed like someone else's hands. I felt like someone else at the moment. Or, more precisely, I felt like my former self. My self from six years ago, the last time I had killed someone.

"You know . . . what?" I said quietly.

"What's that?" Ramona replied.

"I could . . . really go for . . . one of those milkshakes right now . . ."

She smiled. "Amen, sister. I tell you what. When this is all over, I'm taking you to Beebee's for shakes. My treat."

I just nodded and closed my eyes. I felt the sedan door close and the engine rev to life. In a moment we were moving. I didn't know where we were, and at this point, I really didn't care.

*   *   *

They took me to some sort of crisis center clinic and then led me into an examination room. The overhead fluorescents made the space seem unnatural and antiseptic. A couple of generic chairs and a hospital bed did not enhance the ambience.

Once the clear plastic bags had been removed from my hands, a young female medical technician gently scraped whatever skin and blood I had clawed out of Omar's arms from under my fingernails. She used tweezers to remove a short dark hair from my shoulder. Everything they found went into small glass vials. Then she used a sticky lint roller over my shirt and pants and put the tape into an evidence bag. Another young woman came in with a camera. They photographed both the bruising on my neck and my swollen cheek.

Ramona stayed with me the whole time. She didn't say much but her presence helped. Just having her in the room offered me some comfort. Once the technician had completed her work and left, a red-haired woman in scrubs entered. She wasn't much older than me, and her hair and complexion were straight out of *Riverdance*. She introduced herself as a physician's assistant. Her name was Ashley. She spoke gently and reassuringly, but she seemed very tired.

"We need to examine you to make sure you're okay," she said.

She checked my neck bruises and my tender cheekbone. I got a good look at each of her many freckles as she leaned in close.

She shined a light into my pupils, had me balance on each foot, and hold my arms out. She had me strip down to bra and panties and checked me over from head to foot.

"I think you're going to be all right," she finally said. "We'll want an X-ray of your throat and probably an MRI, too. Maybe a CT. But we can do that in a follow-up appointment. I don't think there's any permanent damage. Your voice will start coming back pretty quickly." She made some notes on her tablet computer. "You can take a shower if you want. We need to collect your clothes as evidence. Once you're done, you'll need to go to the police station. They'll want a statement." When she saw the exhausted look on my face she added, "I know. I'm sorry."

As they took away my clothes, it occurred to me that I had no idea where my iPhone was. Or the burner phone. They were probably in evidence bags somewhere getting swabbed and dusted.

Ashley brought me some generic navy blue sweatpants and a sweatshirt, along with some unopened cotton underwear. I decided that a shower was exactly what I needed. I stripped down, pulled the curtain in the tiny stall, and turned the handle all the way to the left. I made the water as hot as I could stand it, maybe borderline dangerous, and let it course all over me. I stood soaking in it for several minutes, long enough for Ramona to call in and make sure that I was all right. I assured her that I was.

I used some provided hospital-grade shampoo and bar soap to clean myself, rinsing off in the scalding water. It hurt but it felt good, almost purifying. When I was done, I put on the clothes they had provided and, although they were a little large, it felt rejuvenating to be clean and in a fresh set of clothes. Despite the late hour and the unrelenting events of the past few days—my trip to Chicago had only been three days ago—I was surprisingly refreshed.

"How you doing?" Ramona asked.

"I'm okay," I replied. "I'm good. Time to give my statement, I suppose." The PA had been right. My voice was starting to improve.

"You have a lawyer?"

"Yeah. We work with a lot of lawyers in the agency. Whenever he needs something, there's a guy Billy always calls."

"Give me his name, and I'll call him when they take you in. Don't say nothin' without a lawyer in the room."

I gave Ramona the lawyer's name. I had met him a couple of times and had even done a job or two for him. Process serving mostly. His name was Kent Miller.

The door opened and Ashley the PA entered. "Ready?"

I nodded. She led me out of the room and down the clinic hallway. Two uniformed OPD officers waited for me at the entrance to the facility. Ashley followed me out through the lobby and to the circular driveway out front.

"Take care of yourself, Sandy," she said as the two cops placed me into the back seat of a patrol car. I responded with a feeble, inadequate wave. I wondered at her job. She spent all day, every day—or all night in this case—examining women victims. Rapes. Assaults. Domestic abuse. It certainly wasn't the life I had previously known, but it was a life that left its own brand of scars. As we pulled away, Ramona was already on her cell phone, watching me.

It took only a few minutes to drive from the clinic to the Orlando Police Department headquarters downtown. We parked, and the cops opened the back door for me. They led me through the building and onto an elevator. We ascended a few floors, and they escorted me through a warren of offices and cubicles to a small interrogation room. I sat alone in the tiny space in a worn chair behind a small empty table. Glancing up, I saw a security camera positioned in an upper corner.

I sat in there for a while, more than a few minutes. It was long enough that I wondered if they had forgotten about me. Just as I was contemplating getting up and poking my head out, the door opened. Detective Colon and his younger partner from the apartment entered. He introduced himself again.

"I remember," I said. My voice had improved a bit more, although it was still pretty rough. I now sounded like I had been a smoker for fifty years.

"Good. To be honest, you were a bit out of it back at the apartment. I wasn't sure you were completely with us." He sat in another chair across the table and set down a bottled water for me. His partner remained standing. The younger guy was a little shorter with light brown, close-cropped hair. "This is Detective Anderson," Colon said with a nod at his partner. I nodded back at the guy. "So . . . why don't you tell us what happened?"

"I don't even know where to begin."

"Wherever you like. At the beginning. What were you doing in the apartment?"

"What about the girls?" I asked. "Where are they?"

Colon pursed his lips. "They're fine. They were all interviewed while you were at the clinic."

"I asked where they were."

Colon considered me for a long moment. He sat back in his chair and looked at his partner.

"I'm pretty sure they're all at Anchor House by now," Anderson said. "There were some staff here with a couple of vans. Including some pushy priest."

I exhaled in relief. "Good . . ."

Colon leaned forward. "So, you were about to tell us why you were in the apartment."

"No . . . Actually, I was waiting for my lawyer to arrive."

"Lawyer?" The two detectives exchanged a look. "You haven't been arrested. Or charged with anything."

"Yeah. But I'm pretty sure you already know what happened in that apartment. And you know why I would want a lawyer."

"We're just trying to help, Ms. Corrigan."

Ah, now I had graduated from Sandy to Ms. Corrigan. There was no way in holy hell that I was going to speak to these guys without a lawyer present. First, I shot and killed a guy a couple of hours ago. I probably had a strong case for self-defense, but you never know. Second, Ivan's comment about having other assets in the department gave me the shivers. I had no idea who I could trust. I couldn't say anything without a third party witness and some legal protection. I didn't want to end up like Benders. Or Carlisle. A loose end to tie up.

Colon sat for a moment, considering. Then he nodded to himself and stood. He gave me a hard look. If he was legit, I kind of felt for him. I was just complicating his job and making his night even longer. He and Anderson left without saying a word, leaving me alone in the room.

Over the course of the next thirty minutes, I entertained myself by slowly finishing the bottle of water. It hurt to swallow, but I think it helped my voice. Thanks to Ramona's call, Kent arrived shortly after the bottle was empty. We exchanged quick greetings. He was in a rumpled brown suit over a golf shirt. The suit was probably pulled out of the dirty laundry bag in a rush out of his house. Kent was in his mid-forties with short hair that had prematurely gone almost completely gray. I had never seen him unshaven, but now I noticed that his stubble was the same gray as his hair.

"Jesus, Sandy," he said, pulling a yellow legal pad and a pen from his leather bag. "You look like hell. Are you okay?"

"Yeah. I've been worse."

"The cops are really chomping to get your statement. We only have a few minutes. What have you gotten yourself into?"

It was a good question. I gave Kent the broad strokes of the past few days, just enough for him to understand the basics. I also told him I had reason to believe that there might be other cops in the building who were compromised.

"Shit," he said. "That complicates things . . ." He made a few notes on the pad. He had filled a couple of pages with illegible scratching while I was speaking. He looked up at me. "So what do you want to do? I can try to stall them, maybe give you a day. We could go over your statement carefully, make sure that you're covered for self-defense. But you're still going to have to talk to them."

"No . . . I'll talk to them tonight. I'm ready to lay out the whole story. I'll tell them everything. I'm ready." I turned the empty water bottle in my hand. "But I need two things first."

"Okay. What?"

"First. You need to call Special Agent Kumar of the FBI. Get him down here ASAP. I want him here when I give my statement. He's aware of the situation."

"The FBI? You didn't mention them yet."

"Kent, you won't believe the things I haven't mentioned yet."

"Yeah," he said, taking more notes. "Special Agent Kumar. Got it. I'll find him. And the second thing? What else do you need?"

"I have been sitting in this room for a very long time." I held up the empty water bottle. "I really need to pee."

CHAPTER 30

IT TOOK A LITTLE UNDER AN HOUR for Special Agent Kumar to get to the OPD headquarters and find my interrogation room. I had no idea what time it was. It had to be the early dark hours of the morning, but I couldn't be sure.

Once Kumar arrived, Kent and I briefed him quickly on the events of the evening. As before when I spoke to him, he didn't say much. He also had a yellow legal pad and took copious notes. Finally, we called Colon and Anderson back into the room.

Colon looked at Kent and Kumar. "So, a lawyer *and* the FBI. Should I assume this is going to be a long story?"

"Yeah," I said. "You're gonna want to bring in a few more chairs for everyone. This could take a while."

Anderson and Colon left for a moment and returned with a mismatched set of chairs. Everyone took a seat, jamming the little space without much room left for movement.

"Okay, Sandy," Colon said. "Just so you know, we are recording this statement. Where would you like to begin?"

I took a deep breath. "Well, I assume you both already know that I used to be an escort and that I lived for more than five years in one of Omar's apartments. My online profile name was Diamond." I could tell that everyone in the room except Kent was already aware of my history. Kent's mouth literally dropped open. "I escaped that life in a bloody encounter with a violent john who tried to kill me. But he was the one who died." I did not look at Kent. I did not want to see his reaction.

I then proceeded to recount the entire string of events that started with lunch with Collette at the Florida Mall and ended with me emptying my Ruger into Omar's chest a few hours ago. Discovering Naomi in the morgue. The house on Waterview Street. The trip to Chicago. Dan Bishop's awful story. The threats to Tyler and the attack on Laura.

Colon paused me a few times to ask questions, mostly about times and locations. I answered everything honestly—perhaps too honestly. I didn't care anymore. It was time to get it all out. Colon and Anderson stopped me when I described Carlisle's murder of Detective Benders. They made me go through the details several times.

Agent Kumar leaned forward in his chair. "Earlier today," he said, "Bureau staff at the house on Waterview Street discovered the body of Detective Benders inside a plastic bag in a large garbage bin inside the garage. It appears that she had been shot in the back of the head at close range."

"Why didn't we know about this?" Colon demanded. "We're the homicide detectives."

"Well," Kumar said. "First, I believe that particular street lies just outside of city jurisdiction. It would be a county sheriff matter. Second, the proper personnel within OPD Internal Affairs have already been notified and are involved."

Colon opened his mouth but then elected not to respond. He exchanged an enigmatic look with Anderson and then looked at me. "Go on, Sandy."

I picked up my tale. Carlisle chasing me after Benders had been shot. Hiding in the Taco Bell. Being rescued by Fr. Frank and Ramona. Garrity's involvement. Collette's beating. The shoot-out at my house. The car chase that left R.J. crashed on the side of the road. The only thing that I made sure to omit was Garrity shooting at R.J. on Colonial Blvd. That was his business and it was the least I could do to try to protect him. Agent Kumar didn't mention it either. Good.

I then described hiding on the A place apartment balcony, overhearing the conversations that occurred inside. Omar's threats to Jordan and Heidi. Ivan telling Carlisle that he had become a liability and that they had other assets within the department.

"What did he mean by that?" Colon asked. "*Other assets.*"

I hunched my shoulders. "I assume other dirty cops working for him."

"Shit," Colon said. "How many? Who?"

"I have no idea." I paused, then added, "You?"

"Very funny," Colon said, but he didn't smile. "This is serious. You're telling me that a cop killed another cop to protect his crime boss. And there may be more accomplices in the department. I need everything you know."

"That is everything I know. I am literally telling you *everything* I know."

"Okay. All right. Tell me about Carlisle. Did you see him get killed?"

I paused. I hadn't yet mentioned that Carlisle had been killed. But of course, two homicide detectives would already be aware of a cop who had been murdered hours ago. I described what happened.

"You saw the whole thing from the balcony?"

"I did."

"So, after this Ivan left, what did you do?"

"I came inside, checked Carlisle, and called 911. But it was too late. I knew he was either dead or would soon be."

Anderson tilted his head. "So, you're telling me that you checked on the guy and then called 911, even though he was trying to kill you?"

"Yeah, I guess so."

"Why?"

"At that point he was way past being able to kill anyone. And maybe there was a chance he could be saved if I called for help."

I wrapped up my story, describing the events at the apartment, culminating in Omar attacking me and then brandishing his pistol at Heidi.

Kent touched my arm and asked pointedly, "Did you fear for your life and the lives of the others in the room?"

"What do you think?" I answered, pointing at my swollen cheek and lifting my chin to show the bruises on my throat.

Colon and Anderson sat back in their chairs. Colon rubbed his face and exhaled loudly. I had no idea how long I had been talking. At least an hour. Maybe more. My throat was rough and dry.

"Well, that's some goddamn story," Colon said.

Kent stood. "Look. She has cooperated fully. She's been through a traumatic experience. She needs to go home. I assume that you need to turn this recording into a document that she can sign. That will take time. And we'll want time to review it. So, unless you plan to arrest her or charge her, we're leaving."

I reached out a hand and placed it on Kent's arm. "You can sit back down, Kent." He looked at me, confused. "I don't think the story is quite over yet. I want to talk about what comes next."

Kent sat back down. The four men all looked at me expectantly. I leaned forward and explained what I was thinking.

* * *

It was more than two hours later, alone in the small interrogation room, when I heard a knock on the door. It opened.

"Ms. Corrigan?" It was a young patrol officer. He was in his twenties, fit, with wavy black hair. With his chiseled features and sharp jawline, he was lifeguard cute. "I'm Officer Vaughn. I'll be taking you home. I was told you might want to go pick up your car instead."

"No. Home, please," I said. "Definitely home." I could get my car later. It should still be parked at the Wendy's on OBT. Fortunately, it was a cheap, nondescript Honda Accord. It wouldn't attract any attention sitting there.

He led me out of the building and to a patrol car parked out back. Dawn was just breaking, casting an early morning light over the city skyline. The glass facades of the bank buildings and tall apartments shimmered a brilliant orange. Officer Vaughn opened the back door and helped me into the seat behind the cage.

"Watch your head," he cautioned.

He closed the door and got into the driver's seat. We were soon pulling out of the parking lot and making our way leisurely through the downtown residential streets toward my house. I closed my eyes and leaned back, taking several deep relaxing breaths. I felt the motion of the car under me, the soothing, familiar vibration of the downtown brick streets. After several turns, I felt the car slow and stop. The engine cut off, leaving the interior of the car suddenly very quiet.

I opened my eyes and through the window saw my home sitting peacefully on the other side of the street. I could see the padlock and hasp on the front door that Garrity and I had installed the day before. I had been given my purse back and fortunately had my keys. I had asked for my phone—either my iPhone or the burner, or preferably both—but Colon had kept them to retrieve evidence from them. He said I might get them back in a day or two.

As I sat looking out at my house, I slowly realized that Officer Vaughn had not moved from his seat. Maybe I was supposed to let myself out. I tried the door handle but, like the back seat of all police patrol cars, the door would not open from the inside. I reached up and tapped on the cage that separated the back seat from the front.

"Officer," I said. "You need to let me out. I'm locked in."

He remained unmoving behind the wheel. After a few seconds he glanced at his watch.

"Uh, Officer Vaughn . . ." I said. "That's my house. You need to let me out." I looked around through all the windows. Perhaps we were waiting to make sure there were no threats. I had, after all, been in a shoot-out here less than twenty-four hours ago. "Uh, everything looks okay to me. I think you can let me out now."

He looked again at his watch. A long pause. "Just another minute or two," he finally said, still facing forward.

"Okay . . ." I replied. "What are we waiting for?"

Another long pause. He picked up the radio receiver and pressed the button. "This is Charlie One One Four. I have dropped the witness off at her home. Heading out to Sector E7. Over."

A staticky female voice chirped through the radio speaker. "Acknowledged, Charlie One One Four."

We sat for another second or two. I banged on the cage again, a bit more violently. "Hey!" I said, raising my voice. "What the hell? Let me out." My Spidey sense was definitely starting to tingle. I didn't like this. At all.

Officer Vaughn turned the ignition and the car engine rumbled to life. He put the car in gear and slowly pulled away from the curb, leaving my home to recede behind us.

"Hey!" I repeated. "Where are we going? Hey! That's my house!" I pounded on the cage with the flat of my palm, rattling it loudly. "Hey, asshole! Stop the car. Let me out!"

As he drove he raised a cell phone and pressed the screen. He put the phone to his ear. "It's me . . ." he said. "Yes . . . In the back seat . . . No . . . A few minutes. Long enough for the car GPS to register the location . . . Yes . . . Okay . . . Soon . . . I understand . . . Right . . . Okay." He pressed the screen again and put the phone down.

I pounded again on the cage with both hands. Vaughn drove on as if he couldn't hear me. I laid back on the seat and kicked at the wire mesh with all my strength. All it did was make a huge racket. Vaughn didn't turn his head, didn't even look in the rearview mirror. It was like I didn't even exist.

By now I knew this car wasn't going anywhere good. In a few minutes we had doubled back basically the way we had come from the police headquarters and were again in the business district of downtown. We drove up the on-ramp and merged onto the elevated portion of I-4 heading west.

"Where are we going?" I demanded, knowing he wouldn't answer. "Where are you taking me?"

Unfortunately, his silence told me everything that I already suspected. I was pretty sure I knew where we were going. Or, rather, to whom we were going.

CHAPTER 31

IN THAT SECTION OF I-4, "West" was actually "South." We continued driving for about fifteen minutes, getting off the interstate by Universal Studios. We then worked our way due west, joining the growing traffic of morning commuters, school buses, and lawn crews crowding the surface streets of suburban Orlando.

I had stopped pounding on the cage grate. I tried yelling for about twenty seconds when we got off the highway, but it was useless. No one in a nearby car would think twice to see a hysterical person locked in the back of a police cruiser, especially one with a puffy, bruised face. Plus, my voice was still quite raw and screaming was practically impossible.

So I sat back and surveyed my surroundings. There was no apparent escape from the back seat. I knew the roads we were on. I tried to pay attention to our route. We turned off the busy main roads and into a subdivision in Southwest Orange County. The landscaped sign in front said HERON BAY. Even amidst my current terrifying circumstances, I couldn't help but observe that there were probably plenty of herons in the neighborhood, but we were at least an hour's drive from the nearest bay. Odd how the brain works.

We made several leisurely turns through the curved streets of the neighborhood, passing manicured lawns with tall palms. We weren't that far from the house on Waterview Street. I guessed we were less than ten miles away. Eventually, we slowed, and Vaughn pulled the car into the driveway of an attractive, upper-middle-class ranch home. There was nothing particularly notable about it. Trimmed grass, edged cleanly along the sidewalk and driveway. Two-car garage. A light beige color. I did not see any other cars. However, I would have been willing to bet that inside the garage was an expensive black Mercedes.

As if on cue, the front door opened and out stepped Ivan. He seemed even bigger in the bright daylight, wearing a golf shirt and a pair of jeans. Vaughn opened the driver's door and exited the car. He closed the door and met Ivan where the driveway joined the walkway to the front stoop. They stood talking together for a minute or two. Then Ivan nodded and they approached the car. Vaughn opened the back door on the driver's side.

"Get out," he said.

"Go to hell," I replied.

"Get out or I'll drag you out."

"And I'll kick your teeth in."

The other back door suddenly swung open and Ivan reached in. I tried to pull away but he was too quick. He grabbed a fistful of my hair and yanked me backwards out of the car. It hurt like hell. I resisted for a moment, but he was so strong. I felt like a child being manhandled by an adult. He strode quickly around the front of the car, pulling me stumbling along with him. All I could do was grab his wrist with both hands to lessen the pain on my scalp and keep from falling and being dragged along the concrete.

"You can go," Ivan said to Vaughn in his heavy accent as he passed the car and pulled me along the walkway and into the house.

Ivan dragged me across the threshold and into the foyer, closing the door behind him. He pulled me into a large family room area and deposited me in a folding chair in the middle of the room. I landed roughly in the seat and almost toppled completely over, chair and all. My hair was disheveled and all over my face. My scalp felt like it was burning. As I sat up, I attempted to brush my hair back to clear my vision and assess just how much trouble I was in.

The house itself was nice. The room I was sitting in was carpeted in a thick tan plush, surrounded by a cream-colored tile that ran into the kitchen, which appeared to have granite countertops and an expansive open island. Large sliding glass doors led to a screened patio with a pool.

However, there was almost no real furniture. There were a couple of folding chairs scattered around the living room. The kitchen breakfast area had a folding table and a few more chairs. I saw some groceries still in plastic Publix bags on the counter.

There were exposed wires and a flat TV mount on the main wall of the family room but no TV. All the walls were bare. I saw other wires snaking from wall outlets to the corner of the room where a router and a modem sat. There were at least three or four different laptop computers on the floor, chairs, and kitchen table.

Sitting across from me in one of the family room chairs was an older woman, maybe in her sixties. It was hard to tell her age because her hair was clearly dyed an unnatural black. Her pale skin was loosening around her face and did not match the age she was trying to portray with her hair. She was wearing a long maroon dress, loose-fitting but decent—not a housedress. Her legs were crossed, revealing a pair of sandaled feet. She picked up a burning cigarette from an ashtray on the floor next to her and took a long drag through blood-red lips, surveying me carefully.

"So this is her," she said in an accent that matched Ivan's.

"Yes," Ivan said, still standing. His short blond hair was not as customarily coiffed as I had seen in the past. I also noticed now that he was unshaven, golden whiskers dusting his cheeks and chin.

"I remember you," the woman said, shaking her cigarette at me. "From six years ago. How could I forget the trouble you caused? You remember, don't you, Ivan?"

"No," Ivan said, not taking his eyes from me. "That was before I came."

"Ah," she said. "Yes. Of course. It was Michael back then. Or maybe Gregor." She tapped her cigarette into the ashtray. "Yes, how could I forget Diamond? You know, we have not used the name Diamond again since you."

"Listen," I said, my voice again raspy and hoarse from my brief attempts at screaming in the back of the patrol car. "Whatever you want, just let me go and you can have it."

The woman pursed her lips and nodded. "So is it true that Omar is dead? That you shot him?"

I said nothing.

"It is true," Ivan said, his gaze still boring into me.

"So again you cause trouble," she said. "Again you force us to move. The girls are scattered." She took another long drag on her cigarette and blew the smoke out the side of her mouth. "You are *proklyattya*, you know that? That means curse. You are curse. Diamond curse."

"Just let me go," I pleaded. "I'm no threat to you."

"No threat?" she said and glanced at Ivan, who did not return the look. He still only stared at me. She turned back to me. "But you have already spoken to the police, no? What did you tell them?"

"Nothing."

"Nothing?" She tapped more ashes from her cigarette. "Nothing? You shoot and kill Omar. Spend all night in the police station. But you tell them nothing?"

"That's right. My lawyer told me not to say anything. They might charge me with murder."

The woman considered this and tilted her head side to side as if weighing the truth of my statement. "Maybe," she said. "Maybe that's truth. But you are still *proklyattya*, so I don't believe you. So what do we do now?"

"Just let me go and I won't say anything."

"I am sorry, but I think you lie." She stuck out her bottom lip in exaggerated thought. "Unless . . . Unless you have reason not to say anything. We do know where you live. That means we can find you whenever we want. A good thing to keep in mind. And what else do we know, Ivan?" Ivan said nothing. He seemed to be growing angrier with each passing moment. "Ivan is modest. So I will say. We also know where your son goes to school. Ivan has already been there. Several times. Cute boy. Tyler Corrigan."

At the mention of my son, a sudden pang of emotion gripped my insides so hard that I almost doubled over. I fought to control the quaver in my voice. "Leave him out of it. I'll do whatever you want."

"Good," she said. "That's good. But still I don't trust you, Diamond curse. So now we have to decide what to do with you. You cannot talk to the police again."

"I won't. I promise—"

"Quiet!" she snapped, her faux calm veneer cracking. "Maybe you must die. Ivan can make it so you just simply disappear. Maybe that is what is necessary." She narrowed her eyes at me. "Or, maybe something else." She stood up and stepped over to me. She squeezed my chin in her bony hand and examined my face, turning it from side to side. "You are still very pretty. Not as thin as once, but still pretty." Her breath was stale with the stench of cigarettes. She returned to her chair. "We have a house. Another house. Not here. In Miami. Maybe you go live in that house now."

"What are you talking about?" I asked.

"You have ruined my business twice now." She pointed a finger at me and practically hissed. "You owe me. Maybe you should make back the money you have cost me."

I understood what she was saying now. My mind immediately flashed to the story Marta told about being trafficked from Guatemala and imprisoned in a Texas house as a sex slave. She had been chained to a bed and forced to service a never-ending string of men.

"Wait a minute—" I said.

"It's okay. We have drugs that will make you more . . . compliant. Maybe someday if we feel you have paid us back, we let you go."

I held my hands up in front of me, as if that would do anything. "No—" I said.

The woman tilted her head at me. "You rather die?"

"Enough," Ivan said. "She has ruined too much. She dies." He took an aggressive step toward me.

"Wait!" I barked. But Ivan did not stop. "Wait! Katia! Tell him!" I pointed at the woman. Ivan stopped and stood up straight. He looked over at the woman, clearly confused. She returned his look and then turned to me.

"How do you know that name?" she asked slowly.

"That's your name, right?" I said. "Katia." I pointed at Ivan. "Tell him to back off."

"What did Omar tell you?" she said, squinting at me.

"Not Omar," I said. I pointed at Ivan. "Him." The woman turned her head very deliberately and looked up at Ivan. The whole gesture was clearly a question.

"She lies," said Ivan.

"No," I said. "I heard you. I was there. In the apartment with the girls when you, Omar, and Carlisle showed up. I was on the balcony the whole time and heard every word you said. I heard you and Carlisle talk about Katia. Then I saw you kill him."

Ivan's face reddened. "She cannot go to Miami. She knows too much."

The woman, Katia, nodded, seemingly to herself, her eyes far away. "Yes . . . You are right . . . Kill her."

Just as Ivan tensed to move closer to me, I held up my hand again. "Wait!" I ordered. "There's more. There's more." They both fixed me with their full attention. I continued, "That's not all I heard you say in the apartment. I heard you tell Carlisle that you had 'other assets in the department.' Other cops on your payroll, right? I mean, obviously, based on who brought me here today. So, when I was at the police station last night, I got to thinking. I knew you couldn't leave me out in the world after—what did you say? Yeah, ruining your business. I shot your partner last night. The girls are gone. Plus, knowing what I know, you're right. I *am* a key witness. As long as I'm alive, I remain a threat. So I thought there was a chance that you would do something like this. I thought you might come for me, using one of those *assets in the department*. You probably wouldn't even let me get home. And somehow I convinced the cops and the FBI to believe me. So they got a quick court order for a wire and strapped me up. They've been listening this whole time. A tactical SWAT team has been staged since the moment Officer Vaughn put me in the car. They've been tracking me through GPS and should be smashing through that door any second now." I pointed at the front door. "So my advice is that you should probably start running right now."

Ivan and Katia exchanged a doubtful look, unsure if I was serious or just saying anything that would save my ass.

"You lie," Ivan said. "I will make you suffer."

"Okay," I said. I raised my right leg and reached down. I stretched out the elastic cuff of the blue sweatpants and pulled it up almost to my knee. Taped to the back of my calf was a small square device. "GPS," I explained. Then I sat back and lifted my shirt. Strapped tight across my rib cage under my breasts was a microphone and a small rectangular transmitter. "Microphone," I said. "Say hi."

This time when they looked at each other their expressions betrayed uncertainty and fear. They exchanged a few words in some harsh Eastern Bloc language. Ivan reached behind his back and produced a black semiautomatic pistol. Katia stood and grabbed the nearest laptop on one of the folding chairs.

The front door suddenly exploded open with a police battering ram. Armored tactical officers swarmed into the space, rifles drawn. Through the sliding glass doors I saw several more appear on the patio. I dove for the floor and covered my head, curling up as small as I could, just as I had been instructed at the police station last night. Stay out of any potential crossfire, make myself the smallest target possible.

The officers were loudly shouting commands. "Drop the weapon! Drop the weapon!" I heard Ivan's pistol thud on the carpet. "On the floor! Face down! Now! On the floor!" I felt the movement of heavy bodies all around me. Finally, I felt a hand on my back.

"Sandy, are you all right?" It was Detective Colon. I cautiously uncurled myself. He kneeled over me wearing a Kevlar vest on top of his street clothes, one hand on my back and the other holding his service pistol.

"Yeah," I said. "I'm okay."

He smiled and gave my shoulder a small, reassuring squeeze. "You were right."

"I guess so." I looked over and saw both Ivan and Katia face down on the carpet, arms zip-tied behind their backs.

"You did real good, Sandy," Colon said, and helped me to my feet.

A stocky SWAT officer, close to my height, approached us and removed his helmet. He was older than I thought he would be. "We're clearing the house," he said to Colon. "But it looks like the rest is empty."

"Okay," Colon responded. "Let me know when we can get the techs in here to bag and tag."

The SWAT officer nodded and then considered me. "You, young lady, are a certified badass." He turned and rejoined his fellow tactical officers.

Colon put a gentle arm around my shoulders and led me back out the front door. Standing outside in a blue windbreaker emblazoned with the letters FBI was Special Agent Kumar. He had said last night that he would be in some sort of official observer role. He gave me a supportive thumbs-up when he saw me.

Colon led me over to an unmarked sedan. He reached in the back and produced a bottle of water. I took it gratefully and downed half of it in one continuous gulp.

"You have any vodka?" I asked as I replaced the cap.

Colon laughed. "A little early in the morning for me. But I'll see what I can do. Listen, it's probably going to take a while to process the scene."

I sighed. "I understand."

"But . . . I don't see why you need to be here for it. What do you say? Would you like to go home? For real this time?"

"Oh God. I would like nothing more."

"Okay. Agent Kumar has agreed to drive you."

Kumar appeared at our side. "It would be my honor." He led me over to another nondescript dark blue sedan. I turned and surveyed the scene behind me. Multiple police cars. A SWAT rig. Crime scene tech vans. There were even two ambulances that had been staged with the cops, just in case. I had put all this in motion just a few hours ago inside that tiny interrogation room. Kumar saw me taking it all in. "Sandy? Are you ready?"

"Yeah," I said. "I'm ready. I'm definitely ready to go home."

CHAPTER 32

"I DON'T HAVE A LOT OF TIME," Collette said as she slid into the booth, placing her disposable coffee cup in front of her. She looked good. Her hair was shorter, and she had let it return to its more natural, softer brown color. Her makeup was tasteful, although perhaps still a bit over-applied. There was no sign of the injuries from her beating several months ago.

"That's okay," I said. "Neither do I." We were sitting in a back booth at the Panera Bread near Lake Eola downtown. We had met here once before for coffee, right after she had gotten a job as a receptionist at a nearby commercial real estate office. "How's work?"

"Okay, I guess. I mean, they're all nice and everything. Well, except Marsha, but she doesn't like anyone. Bless her heart. I just still feel like a total fraud."

"I know. But that will go away. It's only been a few weeks. They're gonna love you."

She gave me an unsure smile. "Thanks. The money isn't as good, but I get to keep it all—at least whatever's left after taxes. And I have my nights free."

"It takes time. You'll make some friends. You'll see."

"I guess. I just don't want to get too close. I don't want them to know . . . There's even this one guy—one of the listing agents—who keeps flirting with me. I guess he's kinda cute but . . . you know . . ."

"Believe me, I know . . ."

"The rest of the girls are okay. Even the female agents."

"Even Marsha?" I asked with a smile.

She smiled back. "Marsha's actually a lot like Tonya. All bark, but deep down she's as insecure as the rest of us."

"Oh—that reminds me. Speaking of Tonya, I have some updates." I had gone for one of my regular milkshake sessions with Ramona at Beebee's a couple of days ago, and she had caught me up on the status of some of the girls. "Get this. Tonya is now driving an Amazon delivery truck. Apparently, she loves it. She had zero interest in being in an office."

"I believe that."

"Jordan is taking classes at Valencia. She's studying something medical. Sonography, I think. Heidi left and moved back home to Jacksonville to live with her parents to get her life sorted out and figure out what she wants to do. Another girl named Lindsey—"

"She was in the apartment with me."

"She's waiting tables."

"What about Marta? That poor thing."

"Marta's been placed in foster care. She was almost deported back to Guatemala, but it turns out that it was her father who had sold her to the traffickers, and she had a legitimate case for asylum."

"Thank God. Anyone else?"

I took a breath. "Those are the good news updates. The rest aren't so good. Some of the girls disappeared or went back to drugs. Ramona's seen a couple back on the street."

"And . . . What about Missy?" Collette braced herself.

I shook my head. "Ramona doesn't know. She left Anchor House on her own. She thinks Missy might be back on the Trail." I idly turned my coffee cup in a circle. "And Brenda is dead. An OD a couple of weeks ago."

Collette nodded slowly. We sat in contemplative silence for a moment. She reached across the table and squeezed my hand.

"You did good, honey," she said. "You did right by Naomi."

I squeezed back. "So did you."

It had been a busy couple of months. I had become the genuine star witness in a major racketeering and multiple murder case that stretched from Miami to Texas and into Central America. There were also tendrils that reached the West Coast and Southeast Asia. I had spent a lot of time in and out of depositions, giving statements and answering questions. While Special Agent Kumar was still involved, as was the Orlando Police Department, the whole thing was now being driven by the U.S. Attorney for the Middle District of Florida. Kent remained my lawyer and ensured that I maintained complete immunity. It was the biggest case he had ever been a part of, and it seemed to me that he was kind of just happy to be associated with it. He was working pro bono in exchange for some free P.I. work by me and Billy.

The mysterious Katia turned out to be a Ukrainian madame named Katia Kovalenko. She had long been associated with a small network of pimps such as Omar, but also included others in Miami, Tampa, and Houston. They each had kept a stable of clean girls for high-priced dates arranged through a secure website run by Katia and her small band of confederates. A place girls. Girls like me once upon a time.

Once the cops had the laptops and had pressured a few witnesses that the data led them to, the whole thing broke open. For an operation that had successfully operated in the shadows for so many years, it was remarkable how quickly the whole Jenga tower had tumbled once the right pieces were pulled.

Ivan was Ivan Pavlyuk, Katia's primary muscle, enforcer, and fixer. Although they were both Ukrainian, they were somehow connected loosely back to dark networks in the Russian mob. That part was still unclear to me and might always remain so.

In addition to Officer Blake Vaughn, there was one other patrol cop and a dispatcher who had been on Katia's payroll. Like Carlisle, the cops had been able to misdirect inquiries, lose evidence, and ignore certain reports. They had helped to generally obscure departmental awareness of their prostitution operation. The dispatcher was responsible for warning Ivan and Katia of any imminent action that threatened them or their operation. Carlisle had been the highest-placed cop working for them.

Collette was kind to say what she did about Naomi. But I wasn't so sure about justice for her. Dan Bishop managed to plead down to a minor battery charge for the choke marks on Naomi's neck and was given probation. The charges related to being an accessory to Ivan's actions to hide her body were dropped in exchange for his testimony in the racketeering case. Since Naomi had actually killed herself behind a locked door in the bathtub, he didn't face any charges in her death. He was not sentenced to any time behind bars.

Collette pressed her phone and checked the time. "I'm sorry, hon. I really do need to go. My break's almost over."

"Of course. I need to go, too." It was the end of the first week of second grade for Tyler and there was an all-school Mass in the auditorium. I had no intention of missing it.

Collette and I exited the restaurant and hugged goodbye on the sidewalk out front. She walked quickly away around the lake while I went the opposite direction and crossed Robinson Street. As I walked the two blocks to St. James Cathedral School, my phone chirped. I looked down at the message. It was from Billy.

WHERE ARE YOU?

I replied: GOING TO TYLER'S SCHOOL. I TOLD U

YEAH. WELL DON'T BE LATE BACK. WE HAVE 2 SUMMONS THIS PM

I KNOW

I DON'T WANT TO HAVE TO FIRE YOU

I LUV U 2 BRO

I made my way onto the school property and into the auditorium. Family and other guests were directed to sit in a separate section to one side. I found a seat near the front. Just as I sat down, the students were shepherded in by grade. I craned my neck, looking for Tyler. Eventually I spotted him. He was clustered with two friends, but after a moment, he spotted me. I waved. His eyes lit up and he grinned at me. He waved back before being shuffled into a row and his own seat.

The priest did a good job. He kept his homily short, which suited the attention spans of the kids. After it was over, parents were permitted to stick around to have lunch with their children. I brought a couple of sandwiches and pretzels for us, which we ate at a picnic table with one of Tyler's friends and his grandmother. We washed it all down with apple juice boxes.

Tyler slurped his straw until it made a loud suction noise and collapsed the box. For some reason, that tickled him and he giggled, repeating the action twice more. His friend across the table found it equally hilarious. The grandmother looked at me and rolled her eyes.

"Boys," she said.

When we were done, I walked Tyler back into the main classroom building and hugged him goodbye. He went cheerfully to his new classroom filled with all the possibility and hope of a fresh school year. He was happy. My boy was happy, and that was all that mattered.

I began my walk back through the leafy neighborhood to my house to pick up my car. After all, I wouldn't want to be late to the office. If I was lucky, Laura would have baked a batch of the oatmeal raisin cookies she had been talking about last night. As I walked, my phone rang. The caller ID told me it was Mike Garrity. I answered.

"Detective Garrity. How are you?"

"Detective Corrigan. I am well. Are you busy Friday?"

"Don't know. Depends."

"Looking to pick up some work? I have a case."

"Cheater sting?"

"As a matter of fact, yes. Are you in?"

"Yeah," I said. "Count me in."

As I walked up the front step onto my porch, I could smell the distinct aroma of oatmeal cookies.

AUTHOR'S NOTE

The scourge of human trafficking infects all corners of the globe and every state in the U.S. According to the International Labour Organization, as of 2016, an estimated 40.3 million people were in modern slavery worldwide, including 4.8 million who were being sexually exploited. Women and girls represent 99 percent of victims in the commercial sex industry.

Statistics collected by the National Human Trafficking Hotline revealed that in 2019 the top three states for the highest numbers of reported human trafficking cases were California (1,507), Texas (1,080), and Florida (896). The organization also found that the top five cities for human trafficking, as measured by the number of calls per 100,000 between December 7, 2007, and December 31, 2016, were Washington, D.C. (401), Atlanta (317), Orlando (285), Miami (271), and Las Vegas (237).

There are many worthwhile organizations on the front lines of the war against human trafficking. I encourage you to seek out such organizations and do what you can to support their missions through volunteerism, financial contributions, and promotion. Together we can fight the evil of human trafficking, bring justice to the perpetrators, and bring healing and dignity to the victims.

Below are just a few of the many organizations working daily to combat human trafficking.

National:

- National Human Trafficking Hotline (https://humantraffickinghotline.org)
- Polaris Project (https://polarisproject.org)
- Coalition to Abolish Slavery and Trafficking (https://www.castla.org)
- International Justice Mission (https://www.ijm.org)
- End Slavery Now (https://www.endslaverynow.org)
- Human Trafficking Legal Center (https://www.htlegalcenter.org)
- United States Conference of Catholic Bishops Anti-Trafficking Program (https://www.usccb.org/topics/anti-trafficking-program)
- U.S. Department of State Domestic Trafficking Hotlines (https://www.state.gov/domestic-trafficking-hotlines/)
- Safe Horizon (NY) (https://www.safehorizon.org/anti-trafficking-program/)

Central Florida:

- Catholic Charities of Central Florida Human Trafficking Task Force (https://cflcc.org/human-trafficking-task-force/)
- United Abolitionists (https://www.unitedabolitionists.com)
- Samaritan Village (https://www.samaritanvillage.net)
- Love Missions (https://lovemissions.net)
- Florida Coalition Against Human Trafficking (http://www.stophumantrafficking.org)

- The Lifeboat Project (https://thelifeboatproject.org)
- SAFE Central Florida (https://www.safecentralflorida.com)
- Howard Phillips Center for Children and Families Children's Advocacy Center (http://caccentral.com/cac -human-trafficking/)
- Central Florida Human Trafficking Task Force (https:// www.facebook.com/Central-Florida-Human-Trafficking -Task-Force-144909032192536/)
- Metropolitan Bureau of Investigation (https://www.mbi -police.net/human-trafficking/)